A Crimson Harvest

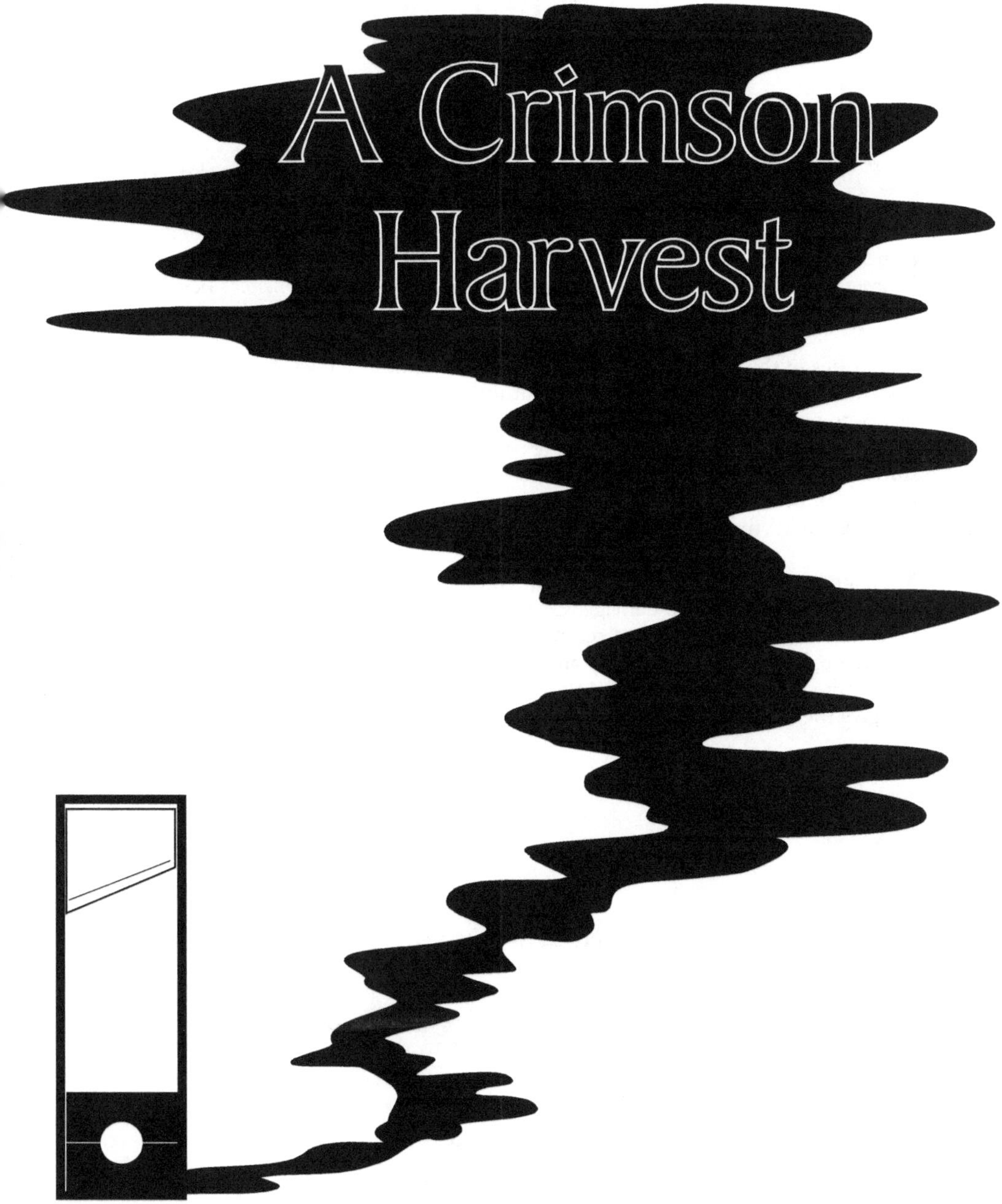

Terror's Terroir
A Silver Creek Press
Tête-Bêche Book
Volume V
featuring:
A Crimson Harvest (from 1909)
A Bout With the Man of Destiny (from 1914)

Terror's Terroir
ISBN: 978-1-945307-20-1

Book compilation and design by Rodney Schroeter.

Cover design generated by Amberlight, www.escapemotions.com

The Silver Creek Press
PO Box 334
Random Lake WI 53075-0334

rschroeter@silentreels.com

Albert Payson Terhune

A Crimson Harvest

SCP Ə⊥Ə⊥-Bêche
Book V

Silver
Creek
Press

2021

CHAPTER I.
In Strange Company.

"AN' that," concluded Shadrach solemnly, as he lighted his long pipe from flint, steel, and tinder-box, "an' that was how I happened to get scalped. I haven't ever told the story before, an' the mem'ries it rouses in me is something scand'lous."

He replaced his broad-leafed hat upon his tousled head, shutting from view the central bald spot which had aroused the sea-captain's curiosity.

Much impressed, though perhaps more mystified, the skipper thanked him in broken English and stumped off toward the forecastle.

"Shad," said I meditatively, "do you know that's the seventh time I've heard you explain your scalping?"

"Well," replied the ex-trapper, shifting rather uneasily on his rope-coil seat, "I s'pose cur'osity must be gratified. An' everybody asks—"

"After you've skillfully led the talk up to the point," I cut in, "and you always end by saying you've never told the story before. As a matter of fact," I added, "that part is true. For you never do tell it twice alike. Once it was a Creek Indian, down in Tennessee, who caught you asleep. And once a war party of Seminoles that—"

"I reckon," began Shadrach in some haste, "I reckon the way them clouds over there seems to be—"

"Another time," I went on remorselessly, "it was a Delaware chief who—"

"We've been blowed three days southward as it is, an'—"

"And another time a grizzly bear, whose paw—"

"Look here, Jack Braith!" roared Shadrach, casting aside his counter-weapons of evasion and menacing me wrathfully with his long pipe stem. "Look here! Whose scalp is it, anyhow? Your'n or mine? That's what *I* want to know. 'Twas *me* that lost it, I reckon. An' if any one's got the right to—"

"Have it your own way," I sighed, giving up the struggle. "It may have been bitten off by a sparrow—for all I care. Only, when we get to France, you'd better hit on some one story to account for it, and stick to that. It'll save trouble."

"France!" he scoffed. "Accordin' to all I've heard, they're doin' so much scalpin' on their own account over there just now that nobody'll have time to bother over how I lost my one little ornery—"

"They don't scalp people over there," I explained for the tenth time. "The guillotine makes rather more thorough work of it. But even that is all over now."

"Then there won't be any sort of fun?" he asked, chagrined.

"Not of the sort you mean. But there'll be something about as exciting for *me*, I think."

"For you? Why not for me, too?"

"Because it's my quarrel. Not yours."

"Quarrel! You never said a word about a quarrel before we started. You claimed you was just goin' over to claim your Great-uncle Shayv-rooze's farm and cash-box and the handle on his name."

"Shad!" I exclaimed in mock horror, "if my highly honored great-uncle, M. le Vicomte de Chevreuse, were alive to hear you refer to his Touraine estate, his fortune and his title as a 'farm, cash-box, and handle,' he'd be more contemptuous than ever at me for preferring to live in America rather than in his beloved France."

"Well," urged Shadrach, "from all I hear, the people in France get as r'iled over the title-and-estate game as I am. 'Twasn't over a year ago I heard about their rippin' their monarchy all to shucks an' sendin' their noble folks screechin' up a tree an' hittin' out on the Ind'pend'ce trail in Uncle Sam's wake."

"By the latest letters, that's all over, though," I told him. "The monarchy is restored and the country going on as of old. That's why I'm on my way there. I'd scarcely be fool enough to go looking for title and estates in a country where wearers of the one are guillotined and owners of the others find their property confiscated 'for the good of the people.' It was only because of those last letters from my great-uncle's lawyer that I decided on the trip."

"But this quarrel? How about it? Who's it with?"

"Upon my soul," I confessed, "I don't know."

"Just goin' to meander around lookin' for trouble?"

"No. I'm afraid trouble is coming to look for me. The De Chevreuse advocate in his letter warned me there was another claimant to the fortune who was resolved, at all cost, to combat my claim. Now, the claimant must be of noble birth. In France his manner of 'combating my claim' will doubtless take the shape of challenging me to a duel."

"A duel? An' you was fool enough not to bring your rifle along? I warned you, time an' again, you'd need it. Think of strikin' a new trail without totin' your rifle! It's like—"

"I sha'n't need it, I think," said I.

"That's so," he admitted. "'Cause mine's always at your service, same as anything else I got. She shoots just a wee trifle high an' to the left, an' you've got to humor her. But, 'cept for that, there ain't a better gun between Nashville an' Pens'cola. I'll—"

"In France," I explained, "they don't use rifles in duels. They prefer *these*," and I touched the small-sword that hung at my side.

"Those!" snorted Shadrach in huge contempt. "Lots of fun there must be in gettin' spitted on a skewer like that! If I was to get in a row an' had no better weepon than one of them steel spits, I'd grab it by the point an' hammer t'other feller over the head with the butt of it."

"That would certainly be a unique improvement on the gentle art of fencing," said I, "but a man who understands how to use a dueling-sword can make it almost as deadly as your beloved rifle. I remember, in France—"

"Oh, *that's* where you learned to use such trinkets? I thought as much. How long did it take you?"

"I fenced for seven years under Cadillac. Even at the end of that time, I could hardly call myself an adept."

"Seven years to learn fool nonsense like that!" groaned Shadrach. "Longer'n it took me to get married an' to find out that women are dangerouser'n cantamounts and to sneak out of my own country to get away from 'em. Did I ever tell you how I happened to get married?"

"Yes," I answered hastily, "as often as you've told me about being scalped. And how you ran away from—"

"No, no, son!" he expostulated, "I didn't run away. She druv me out. An' then she sued me for divorce for leavin' her; an' I lit out'n

America, so the papers couldn't be served on me. It must be a dretful thing to get divorced. Not any of it for me!"

"And *you*—a man whom Washington himself called his pluckiest scout—ran from one little woman!"

"Son, you ain't married. So don't presume to jedge the fears of them that are. It's a—Hallo, there! What's up now, I'd like to know!"

A yell from the lookout, a rush of feet across the deck, and at the same instant the double booming of distant guns. Shadrach and I were at the rail on the moment, straining our eyes across the tumbled mass of gray waters.

May I stop here to explain a little more fully, yet in as few words as I can, the reason of our presence there and then aboard the French brig Solent?

I am Jack Braith, American. At least, so I have ever styled myself, though my grandfather was a Frenchman. He was eldest of the several younger brothers to the Vicomte de Chevreuse, and emigrated to the American Colonies as a lad.

There he married a New Jersey maiden and adopted her name of "Braith," his own being hard for Yankee tongues to master, and Frenchmen being none too popular in the Colonies at that time.

No more was heard of our French relatives until I was a child of six. Then word came that my great-uncle, the *vicomte,* was old, childless, and lonely. He had quarreled with his various other brothers and their children, and his mind had at length turned to our branch of the family.

The upshot of it was that I was sent to visit him "on approval," with a view to becoming his real, as I was his natural, heir. My parents had died in my babyhood.

For the next eleven years I had dwelt in France. It was a loveless, if beneficial, time. My great-uncle wasted no affection on me, nor I on him. Moreover, even as a child it angered me to hear his sneers on America.

Nevertheless, he gave me such education as a young nobleman of the day was supposed to receive. I was taught the various arts and accomplishments, spoke French better than English, could handle a dueling sword, ride, dance, and exchange small-talk with the best of them.

But, oh, it was a lonely, cruel life for a growing boy! Thanks to the *vicomte's* quarrels with his family, I saw none of my several cousins who were scattered through France and Germany, nor was I able to learn much concerning any of them, save Etienne de Chevreuse, a lad of my own age and—to judge from all I had heard—strikingly like me in looks.

He was the grandson of a still younger brother of the *vicomte* than my grandfather, and had already attracted some note as a daredevil, gambler, and swordsman.

Etienne and his wildness the *vicomte* never wearied of denouncing, until, though I had not chanced to meet the unfortunate youth, I began to feel a lively sympathy for him.

It was in 1779, when I was about seventeen, that the crash came. I fell in with some French officers newly returned from America. They told me—what heretofore I had but vaguely understood—the story of my native land's mighty struggle for liberty, and painted in strong colors the glory of that conflict.

It was enough. My boyish blood was fired. The patriotism my great-uncle had spent years in crushing sprang into new life. I announced my intent of going home to fight for my country.

"If you go," roared the *vicomte,* "your name is forever blotted from my will and from my memory. Take your choice—the life of a French noble or of a Yankee rebel."

Next week I sailed.

Armed with a letter of introduction from a friend to the young Marquis de Lafayette, I landed in America after eleven years' absence. I was not likely to starve because of the rank and wealth I had put behind me. For I had inherited a comfortable little New Jersey property and a few slaves from my parents, whose only child I was.

Another month, and I was in the army. Before the Revolutionary War's end I had been so fortunate as to rise to a captaincy and to win praise from no less a personage than the great Washington himself. After which I had settled down to a quiet country gentleman's life, letting memories of France fade gradually from my mind.

It was early in 1793 that a letter from my great-uncle's family advocate sharply recalled those memories. He wrote of the *vicomte's* death, intestate. Thus I, as grandson of his next elder brother, was heir to title and estates.

The letter warned me that other heirs—one especially—were supposed to be preparing to contest most vigorously the heritage of an alien American to such French rank and wealth.

Yet, my rights were clear, and I was minded to claim them. True, garbled tales of the French Revolution had reached our shores—tales that I, with my recollection of the nobles' power and the peasants' crushed condition, could scarce credit.

But later rumors told of an agreement between king and people and a smoothing over of political differences. This, with my knowledge of the France I remembered, I naturally took to mean that old times were restored.

So I secured passage aboard an armed French brig, built and fitted out in New York and manned by a mixed crew. It was the brig's maiden trip. Nor had her officers—who had superintended her building—been home for three years. I could, therefore, learn little of present-day French politics from them. They seemed, in fact, as ignorant as I.

On the day of our sailing I had come face to face, on Water Street, with a man as much out of place there as a bear in the capitol. He was Shadrach Bemis; a lank Tennessee trapper, at whose side I had fought at Cowpens and at Yorktown.

He was one of Washington's own scouts, an Indian fighter of local renown, and a quaint character not easily forgotten.

It was twelve years since we had met. He hailed me with delight as the one familiar figure in a strange, over-populous place. It seemed he was in hiding. Having successfully escaped British and Indians alike, the man was in full retreat before a fair foe. He had recently married a frontier woman who, tiring of him, had threatened a divorce.

Like most backwoodsmen, law had untold terrors for the otherwise fearless Bemis. So he had incontinently fled at threat of the mysterious divorce.

Reaching New York, he was still in fear lest his wife might reach him with legal proceedings, and he had resolved to add the ocean to the stretch of distance between them. Hearing I was bound for France, he eagerly took passage on the same ship—where his long rifle, fringed buckskins and coonskin cap were an endless source of wondering joy to our French companions.

At first our voyage had prospered. Then the new steering-gear had broken in a gale, and we had drifted four days southward on the wings of the hurricane. Hundreds of miles south of our course, when the storm at last died down, we had just repaired the tiller and were on our northward way at the time this story opens.

Shadrach and I joined the crowd at the rails and looked out, across seas as from a stage-box, at an exciting little nautical drama.

Barely two knots to westward lay two vessels. One—by far the smaller—was a French merchant sloop; the other, a brig carrying full gun-ports and floating a British flag.

She was bombarding the smaller vessel, at easy distance, from her starboard-guns. The sloop was making ineffectual retort with a couple of short-range deck-carronades.

It was like a fight between a mastiff and a kitten, so far as fairness went, or chance for the French craft. I took in the situation at a glance.

The brig was doubtless a British privateer, preying on French commerce from the West Indies. My only wonder was that the sloop dared offer fight to so formidable a foe.

The wind was sharp from the south, which had prevented our hearing the firing at first. How long the pitifully unequal fight had waged I could not guess. But already the brig was closing in. The sloop, most of her rigging shot away and smoke curling from her after-ports, was slowly settling by the head. Still she did not strike her little patch of colors, and continued to bark valiantly with her ridiculous little carronades.

Aboard our own ship everything was abuzz with wild activity. Amid a salvo of excited oaths and bellowed orders, we were put about and bore down at full speed to the tardy aid of the Frenchman.

Neither of the antagonists noted our coming until a long-range shot from our bow-gun tore through the privateer's staysail, ripping the canvas clean from its supports. A second shot whizzed across the swarming decks, and her crew beheld us, a bare furlong distant.

So near were we now that we could hear the halloed command from a deck officer's speaking-trumpet, as he ordered all sail crowded on and the helm put down. It was clear he did not mean to fight us.

We were a third larger, for one thing. Besides, privateers are out for plunder, rather than for glory. With them, he who loots and runs away may live to loot another day.

But this particular "running away" was slightly hampered. For the French sloop had sighted us, too. Already her decks were awash. She could float but a few moments longer at most.

On seeing us, her captain hurried a half-dozen persons into the already unslung long-boat. Six sailors then sprang aboard and bent to the oars, sending her flying across the narrow patch of water toward us.

I saw the object of the maneuver. At any instant the sloop might sink. The captain had sent the passengers out of the way, and the long-boat was trying to put enough space between herself and the sloop to avoid the fatal suction of the sinking vessel.

A yell from our helmsman broke in on the glorious excitement of the moment. One of our newly shipped rudder-chains had parted. We were floating, helpless once more—helpless to bear down on the enemy or to maneuver our batteries!

We were for the time simply a floating fort—dangerous to attack, but incapable of pursuit.

CHAPTER II.
Strange Doings in Small Boats.

THE privateer's captain saw our plight almost as soon as did we. Up came his helm, and the brig halted in her flight.

While her port batteries blazed out in a futile duel with ours, two boats were hurriedly put off from the brig. One—a long-boat—headed for the sinking sloop. The second—a gig—sought to cut off the sloop's long-boat before the latter could reach us.

From the direction in which both the gig and the escaping long-boat were coming, our guns could not cover either. Motionless as we were, we could offer no aid, though our captain had belatedly ordered our own long-boat lowered to the water.

Pursuer and pursued must come together before we could send to the rescue. Nearer and nearer the privateer's boat drew to her victim, till hardly fifty yards separated them.

"I ain't much posted on boats," drawled Shadrach, at my side.

His cool, sleepy voice struck on my excited senses like a splash of cold water in a hot face.

"An'" he added, "seein' I'm so ignorant of the pesky things, would you tell me who's the most useful man aboard that British rowboat? Is it that tall feller standin' up in front, or some one else? Which one helps make it go?"

"The one who's guiding it, sits in the stern—the back," I answered, impatient of the interruption. "He is the helmsman, and—"

A thunderous roar close to my ear silenced my words. The helmsman of the privateer's long-boat sprang up, lurched backward and tumbled overboard into the sea.

"Now," went on Bemis, in the same slow drawl, as he began to reload his rifle, "which is next most important?"

It was a wonderful shot. At extremely long range for so old-fashioned a weapon, and fired from a rolling deck at a tossing boat. The tall man who stood in the long-boat's bow turned and assigned another to the vacant tiller. As he did so I saw to my surprise that he was masked.

"That is a ship's officer, possibly the privateer captain himself," I said, noting the masked man's air of authority. "Try him next."

"Anything to oblige," cheerfully assented Shadrach, bringing his rifle up to his shoulder as tenderly as a virtuoso might settle his loved violin under his neck.

A whirl of spray blew about us. *"Click!"* went Bemis's rifle-lock. A drop of salt water had fallen on the priming. With a little grunt the trapper lowered the weapon.

"Had him covered real pretty, too," he sighed. "Right over the heart, an' all allowance made for the ship's roll."

The sloop's boat was within easy view of us now. I could even see the strained look on her helmsman's brown face. Two other occupants of the boat faced us; a thin, pale man with snowy hair and a lad in a sea-cloak and feathered hat.

But for the death of the privateer's helmsman the fugitives must have been much sooner overhauled. As it was, the pursuer was now almost alongside her.

Why the officer in charge did not order his several marines to end the chase by opening fire on the victims I could not imagine. Nor, for many months, did I find out. He seemed bent on capturing the lot of them, alive.

And now our own heavily manned long-boat took part in the proceedings. Thanks to Bemis's shot, she was in time, after all, to be of use.

Bounding forward toward pursuers and pursued, she was within a biscuit-throw of them as the privateer's gig reached the sloop's boat.

The masked officer, as his craft grated past the other, braced himself with one hand on the gunwale. With the other he seized the shoulder of the lad who sat beside the white-haired old man.

With one powerful wrench he lifted the youth from the seat and was about to swing him into his own swiftly passing boat. Truly, an odd enough proceeding and one none of us could understand! That an officer should brave death to pursue a boat merely for the sake of snatching from it one boy seemed laughably incredible. Yet that was apparently the intent.

The whole affair passed in the fraction of a second, almost before the old, white-haired man could spring up with a cry of terror and seize the lad's other shoulder. But, quick as the masked man was, and unexpected as was his action, the boy was quite as agile and as full of resource.

Even as he felt himself lifted from the seat, the youngster whipped out a pistol from beneath his cloak and fired pointblank at his masked assailant. The latter dropped his intended victim's shoulder and reeled back among his own rowers, clapping one hand to the elbow of the other arm, whence blood began to gush.

He lost his balance and collapsed into the bottom of the gig as a bullet from Shadrach's rifle sped through the space his tall body had just been filling.

I heard the masked man call out an order as he fell. The rowers put about and made off for the privateer brig at full speed, even as our long-boat reached the fugitives from the sloop.

My eye strayed to where the sloop herself had been wallowing in the waves. She had vanished. Gone down with colors flying. All left of her was the long-boat with its dozen survivors now coming slowly toward us under the escort of our own boat.

The gig made its way back to the privateer. I saw men carrying the wounded masked man aboard. Immediately, with a parting volley and derisive cheer, the privateer's crew got their vessel under way and showed us a clean pair of heels, while we floated, helpless, and sent an impotent fusillade after them.

Then came the crowning insult. From the departing privateer's mast the British flag dropped. An instant later a French flag was run up in its stead. Pitou, our captain, fairly danced with rage at the sight.

"No privateer at all, but a dirty pirate!" he raged. "Flying British and French flags alternately and robbing both nations. Oh, if I could only get after her and—"

"Sloop's survivors coming aboard, sir," reported an officer.

Pitou straightened himself and hurried to the side to help the refugees over the rail and extend to them a rough but eager welcome.

One after another they toiled up the ladder, passengers and crew alike. Following the majority came the tall, white-haired man.

"An aristocrat of the old school!" was my mental comment as he clambered feebly over the rail, assisted by a couple of sailors.

The old man turned to give a helping hand to the last passenger—the plucky boy whom the masked one had tried to steal and who had shown such presence of mind in the face of sudden peril.

The lad was tight-wrapped in his long sea-cloak. His broad hat was down over his eyes. His hair had escaped from its old-fashioned queue and hung loose and shimmering on his shoulders.

In one hand he bore a heavy portmanteau. The other clung convulsively to the old man.

At sight of the ring of strange, curious faces on our deck, the youth shrank back, and crouched, hesitating, by the rail.

"Brave lad!" cried Pitou, clapping him on the back. "A good shot if ever I saw one!"

"Oh, *don't*," gasped the boy, hysterically. "Don't speak of it! It was *horrible!*"

He sank down upon a chest, covered his face with his hands and broke into passionate sobbing; his whole fragile body convulsed and trembling.

"Come, come!" urged Pitou with rough gentleness. "That's no way to behave! Be a man!"

"I—I can't!" was the wailing reply. "I'm—I'm a *girl!*"

CHAPTER III.
I LOSE SOMETHING NOT WORTH KEEPING.

"I'm a girl!" repeated the weeping figure crouched there upon the chest.

And all at once my contempt was turned to a wondrous unexpected pity for the frail, trembling little creature.

"What's the row?" asked Shadrach, to whom the foregoing French dialogue had been as Greek. "What ails the brat?"

"It isn't a brat," said I in English. "It's a girl."

"A *gal?*"

"So she says."

"Well," he drawled, "I s'pose that ought to settle it. Do all French gals dress like that?"

We had been speaking needlessly loud. Especially by contrast with the hush of embarrassment that had fallen over the rest of the group at the pseudo-boy's announcement.

On Bemis's wondering query I saw the figure on the chest start guiltily and pull the long sea-cloak more tightly about her. I could have kicked both Shadrach and myself for adding to her embarrassment.

"Of course," went on Bemis, unnoting, "if they reely enjoy sech clo'es—"

"Shut up!" I whispered savagely. "She understands English."

"Permit me!"

It was the white-haired man who spoke. He had recovered his breath, and now, with an air of authority, advanced shelteringly in front of the girl. Facing Pitou, he resumed:

"Let me thank you, first of all, captain, for your timely aid. We owe you our lives. Had you arrived earlier—but our debt is none the smaller. I am le Sieur de Périer, Barbados planter, late of France. With my daughter, Mlle. Elise de Périer, I set sail last week in my own sloop, L'Hirondelle, for France on a mission of importance. This morning we were overhauled by the British privateer you saw. I forbade my captain to strike his colors and—"

"But," cried Pitou, "what chance had a little sloop like yours against—"

"It is the creed of my race, sir," reproved De. Périer calmly, "to fight as bravely against hopeless odds as against a weaker foe. It is on such a seemingly hopeless mission I am now bound for Paris. To continue: When we were without hope of rescue I bade my daughter don a suit of the cabin boy's. As a boy she might die fighting. As a woman she would perhaps have been spared and sold as a slave in the West Indies. That will account for her costume, I think.

"If any here," and he bent a stern eye on the curious Bemis, "if any here deems so necessary an action unworthy of a De Périer, I am ready to justify my course and my daughter's behavior in whatsoever method he may prefer."

To which Shadrach, supposing himself addressed, and being sensitive on his ignorance of French, replied gravely:

"I lost it in a knife-fight down in the Everglades. But I kilt the pesky redskin that got it. He won't do any more scalpin', I reckon, unless the—"

I wheeled quickly and walked away, trying in vain to stifle a snort of laughter. Shadrach followed me.

"What's up *now?*" he asked, aggrieved. "I had to answer, didn't I, when the old feller asked me a civil question? Say," he went on, more confidentially, "what was he tryin' to say? Could you make out? I don't see why folks ever made up such a fool language as French, anyhow. I don't b'lieve they understand each other half the time. They just pretend, 'cause they think it's smart. Next time any one tries it on me, I'm goin' to answer 'em in Choctaw or Sioux. I'll bet there ain't a one of 'em that can reel off Indian lingo better'n I can. I'll do that, you can bet."

He was as good as his word. Next morning when le Sieur de Périer met him on deck and said: *"Bonjour, M'sieu l'Americain!"* Bemis answered glibly, in Sioux jargon:

"How, Peha-He-Haska!" (Hello, Man-With-Long-White-Hair!")

It was on the day before we sighted the gray French coast. Elise de Périer and I were pacing the deck.

We had grown to know each other well during our weeks of slow eastward voyaging. Not only through the enforced ship-board informality, which all sea-goers will understand, but because I was the only man on the Solent with whom her father did not discourage association. He judged from my dress and manner that I was of rank not far beneath his own. Also, one of my uncles—my mother's brother—had been New York correspondent for the old man's Barbados plantation. Thus I was not wholly a stranger, to him, as were the rough seafarers who had so kindly offered refuge to the sloop's fugitives.

And I profited thereby in winning leave to tramp the deck occasionally with Elise, under her father's protecting eye.

Age and rheumatism had rendered such exercise out of the question for him. But he always kept us in view from his lounging-chair. For, French girls, for some reason, have not the latitude in such matters that is granted our Yankee maidens.

Yet I had made the most of the daily walks. In fact, I now realized, as they were about to end, that they had meant more to me than all else connected with the voyage. Clad in one of the dainty gowns from that portmanteau of hers, Mlle. de Périer was a far different personage from that weeping, oddly appareled stripling who had cowered so piteously against the rail that day of the fight. By common consent we had never referred to the scene.

To-day we came nearer to it than before.

"You had actually started for France, you and le Sieur de Périer," I was saying, "without having heard that the revolution was at an end? That took courage."

"It was necessity," she answered. "We had received tidings that called us to Paris. It was a mission that could not well be disregarded."

It was not her first veiled mention of her journey's object. But its nature she seemed intent on keeping secret. So I, naturally, could not seek further.

I had long since made a similar resolve of reticence as to my own reasons for going to Paris. Except to Shadrach Bemis, I had confided them to no one. When I should have won my heritage it would be high time to boast.

I was not minded to speak of it beforehand, and then, perhaps, find the whole affair a mistake and be forced to take back my vaunting words.

So Mlle. de Périer and I each had our own secret, and neither sought to fathom the other's. A not over-common trait, perhaps. I sometimes think the reason a man who minds his own business succeeds in life is because he has so little competition.

"You were going to risk your lives in that mob-ridden city for the sake of a principle?" I went on.

"Possibly," she returned. "And for what better thing could a life be risked?"

"From all I hear," said I, "most people of your class in France forgot principles and all else in a rush to reach some other country. Those who stayed had little chance of exploiting principle or anything else. I am thankful, from the bottom of my heart, that the lawless days ended before your arrival."

She looked a trifle surprised at my vehemence. But I thought she seemed embarrassed rather than displeased.

"You are quite certain the 'old order' is restored?" she asked.

"So I gathered from the tidings that reached us," I replied. "The French peasant could hardly hold out long against the men to whom he has cringed for centuries."

"I am not so sure," she protested. "One day or another the real rising must come. When it does, we of the old nobility must pay a terrible price for what we and our ancestors made the peasant suffer."

"That is strange doctrine, *mademoiselle,* for a member of the *noblesse,*" I remarked. "Does your father agree with such ideas?"

"My father still lives in the Golden Age. Time has stopped for him. He has never fully believed there could be a revolution. But, then, he was just as much amazed, I hear, when you Americans revolted. Is it so strange that he should feel as he does? His point of view is no more odd in its way than that of your 'savage' friend, Mr. Bemis."

"You still find pleasure in practising your English on old Shadrach?" I laughed.

"He is a never-ending delight," she retorted. "And we are getting to be great friends, he and I. It was only yesterday that he told me a great secret. I felt quite honored."

"A secret?" I echoed in wonder.

"Yes. The history of that queer bald patch of his. It seems he was set upon one day in New York by pirates who took him by surprise, and—but oh!" she broke off, in contrition. "It was a secret. I forgot."

Another version of the lost scalp! But I held my peace.

"He tells me you are a renowned soldier," she went on—"that you fought in—"

"Bemis is a silly old braggart!" I interrupted crossly. "The only time when my fighting might have been of service to you, I stood idly at the rail here and watched you. It was the hardest thing I ever had to do. Had I known you then I think I should have risked swimming out for a chance at that masked fellow."

Yes, it was a silly speech. I know that. But I think she liked it.

"Tell me," I went on, "if it isn't an impertinence to ask it—is there any one who would have had an object in kidnaping you?"

"Why, no," she answered, puzzled.

"Because," I resumed, "that is the only way I can explain the masked officer's action. Both boats were going at full speed. He tried to snatch you out of your own into his as the two passed each other. What sense would there have been in his capturing a mere boy? Either he acted insanely and risked his life by doing it, or else he recognized you and had some tremendously strong reason for wanting to carry you off."

"I—I never thought of that," she murmured, half to herself, the perplexity in her fair face deepening. "But—why, it's impossible! No one would have any such reason. At least—" She paused for the remotest space, then repeated quickly: "No one!"

"Perhaps not," I admitted, still unconvinced. "Nevertheless, it was a queer freak for a pirate captain to—"

"He was not a pirate captain," she contradicted—"not a pirate at all."

"Not a pirate? But—"

"A pirate or any other man who followed the sea would be tanned. His hands would be rough and brown. That man's hands were as white as a woman's and as well formed as—as yours."

I looked up quickly, suspecting a joke. But she had not even intended a compliment. For, noting my glance, she went on:

"The typical hands of an aristocrat. Such shape is the result of many centuries' heredity—the result of having other people do all one's manual work."

"My father," said I, "was a gentleman farmer in New Jersey. My grandfather was a pioneer in the new land. Both worked hard. The theory does not hold good."

"No one but a man of old French blood has such hands," she insisted; "and no one not of French ancestry could speak French as you speak it. But to return to the 'pirate'—"

"The pirate who was not a pirate?" I suggested, more impressed with her ideas of the mysterious man than I cared to show. "That certainly complicates the matter. What would such a man as you describe be doing in apparent authority aboard a privateer or pirate craft, cruising in the southern seas—unless, perhaps, he is a refugee aristocrat of France who has turned to piracy for a living?"

"If he had turned to such a means of livelihood he would be tanned," she asserted; "yet his hands were white. That means the constant wearing of gloves—not usual among pirates, I should think. And, from the glimpse I had of his forehead where the mask ended, that was white, too."

"But what sort of a freak could have led him to—" I began.

"Then, too," she broke in, more excitedly, "he had not the figure of a sailor. He was tall, and slenderly though strongly built, and had the carriage of a gentleman. Tell me, do pirates usually go masked? No one else in his boat was."

"I never heard of such a case," said I. "I would like to get at the bottom of the mystery. It means much to me."

"But why?" she asked.

"If this man, or any other, is pursuing you or seeks your harm, I want to stand between you and him. I want," I added, carried on by hot impulse—"I want the *right* to protect you. Do you understand me, Elise?"

Now, it was a fearsome thing in those days for a man to address a daughter of the *noblesse* by her Christian name. And I knew it quite well. Also, a suitor should have spoken to her father, not to herself. This also I knew.

Why did I then doubly transgress? I suppose because by heart and nature I am American, not French. I say that in boast, not excuse.

She made no answer, and I looked in vain for some sign from her averted face. To a French girl, reared in the ultra-sheltered fashion that she had been, my words must have seemed a million times more glaringly unconventional than American women can understand.

Small wonder her head was turned away and that the tiny portion of her cheek still visible to me should have flushed so deep a rose color! My only marvel was that she did not leave me on the instant and go straight to her father for protection.

Yet she did not. And I took her staying as a good omen.

Nevertheless, her first start of frightened surprise brought me to my senses—not only as to the proper treatment of a sheltered French girl confided by her father to my escort, but also to a realization of my own position.

While I was fairly well-to-do, according to our rural New Jersey standards, still I was a mere gentleman farmer of no wealth or station. As such I knew myself no fit match for the daughter of a French noble who owned vast Barbados plantations and had the bearing and traditions of a great family name. This, too, was the view M. de Périer was certain to take.

Yet I, who had never till this hour realized that I loved the girl, had plunged—American fashion—into something very like a proposal of marriage. I had smashed Gallic convention, and—had she chosen to take my words so—had committed a mortal offense.

Then a hope cut across my chagrin. Was I not on my way to Paris to claim the splendid fortune and title of the Vicomte de Chevreuse? With that affair satisfactorily settled, I should be in a position to beg the hand of any woman alive.

So when I spoke again it was less ardently, but with a thrill that must have robbed my words of their formal primness.

"*Mademoiselle*," I began, "I ask your pardon for speaking as though you were an American lass of my own station. What I said I had no right, as matters now stand, to say. The next month or so will make or mar my fortune. In the latter case you shall see me no more. In the former, I shall seek out your father and beg of him what I now dare not ask. When that time comes—"

I paused. She had turned toward me again. And in her flushed face so much was written! But what the emotion stamped there might be I had not the courage to guess.

Perhaps it might be anger, or contempt, or impatience, or pity, that softened those big gray eyes to a wondrous light and set the lovely face aglow.

Perhaps—but I, who had faced Cornwallis's regiments without fear, lacked the daring to read her face as I wished to. I could not stand a rebuff—and what else had I a right to expect? I know so idiotically little of women.

Her lips parted. Before she could speak, Shadrach Bemis had joined us.

"Maybe you folks think it's fun for a white man to herd all by himself on a ship," quoth he. "Old Pitou speaks what he thinks is English, but he can't get any one else to believe it. An' all the rest jabber French at me. Lord! Why can't folks learn to speak some civilized language when they first begin to talk? An' you two—the only folks I can chin with—you two walk up and down together, chatterin' French like the worst of 'em. So I couldn't stand it no more by an' by, and I makes bold to jine right in with you. D'you mind?"

"Not at all," said Elise in her pretty, accented English, quite herself again, while I was still confused and angry at the interruption. "Come and walk with us, M. Bemis. So you're lonely on shipboard?"

"Well, I wouldn't hardly say that, miss," he replied. "Only sometimes I can't help thinkin' of what I heard a feller read once in a book. Somethin' about a man on shipboard bein' like a man in jail, with the extry danger of gittin' drowned. I heard Andy Jackson say, down in Nashville once, that—"

"Elise!"

It was M. de Périer's querulous voice. He had risen from his chair, and was signaling his daughter to come to him. Refusing our escort, she ran lightly across the deck to where the old man awaited her.

"Jest as I knew he would!" chuckled Shadrach.

"What do you mean?" I asked crossly.

"Why, the old wool-head don't like his darter talkin' to the likes of me," explained Bemis, with cheerful irreverence for M. de Périer's snowy locks. "I don't talk his lingo, but I notice he always kinder shooes her off when he sees me with her. Thinks I ain't quite in the high-nob class, I reckon, an' not proper company for his gal. So I jined you two on the chance he'd call her off."

"Why did you do such a wretched thing as that?" I asked with more indignation than the case perhaps called for. "What business was it of yours to—"

"I wanted to speak to you alone an in a hurry," he replied colossally, unmoved by my wrath. "There's trouble."

"Mutiny?" I queried in quick alarm.

"No. Worse, I'm thinkin'."

"Speak out then, can't you?"

"Son," Shadrach went on with a gentle severity, "you're a good boy in your way, but you have a nasty habit of tryin' to hurry people that want to take their own time. I jest nacher'ly hate to be hurried. One of these days you'll hustle me too hard, an' then I'll do to you like I done to a Britisher that thought he could chase me down at Norfolk jest 'cause he had a musket with him an' I hadn't. I ran away from him, reel obligin'. It's always good policy to run away from a loaded gun. But he made me run too fast for sech hot weather. So by an' by I got peevish an turned all of a sudden on him. An' what do you s'pose happened then?"

"He probably scalped you," I suggested maliciously. "If not, he must have been the only one, according to your stories, who—"

"That'll do," cut in Bemis in cold dignity. "When it comes to jeerin' at a feller man's phys'cal infirmities, it's time to draw the line. D'you want to hear my views or don't you?"

"I'm sorry, old man," I said, stretching out my hand. "Go ahead, won't you, please?"

Quite mollified, Bemis shifted his quid of tobacco and, sitting down beside me, began:

"In the fust place, we passed a westbound bark from France about two o'clock this mornin'. Did you know that?"

"No. I was asleep. Did—?"

"None of us other passengers did, I reckon. But she 'spoke' us, an' we hove to while they sent across a boat for a confab. She'd just left France three days ago. She had news. Lots of it."

"How did you find out all this?"

"When I told Miss What's-Her-Name just now that no one spoke English here, I told a kind of white lie. D'you know Peer?"

"Pierre, the cockswain?"

"Yep. Him an' me struck up an acquaintance t'other day when I licked him for laughin' at my bald spot. That trouncin' sort of endeared me to Peer, I reckon. For ever since then he hangs around me, tryin' to make friends. He speaks pretty fair English. Worked on a Britisher packet a couple of years once. He don't get more'n one word in two so bad I can't understand him."

"And it was he who told you about the French bark?"

"Half an hour ago. It seems the law-shark that wrote to you was puttin' money on the wrong card."

"What do you mean?"

"A while ago there was some sort of pow-wow between old King Looey an' his lovin' people, an' they came near agreein' not to chase him around no more. That must 'a' been when your friend wrote to you. Since then, Peer says, there's been terrible ructions in Paris. Them same lovin' people took Looey an' cut his head off."

"The king guillotined?" I gasped. "They dared—"

"Measly sort of trick to play on him, wa'n't it?" agreed Bemis. "But that's what the bark folks told Cap'n Pitou last night. King's dead, queen's in jail; an' merry hallelujah's runnin' riot all over the place. This rev'lootion is actin' up pretty petulant. They've cut off all the 'ristocrats' heads they could find an' now they've begun on each other, with a stray batch of nobility thrown in now an' then for good measure. Paris is about as safe just now, from all Peer tells me, as a caveful of rattlesnakes."

I sat dumbly listening to his recital. If what he said was true—and it was hardly to be doubted—my air-castles were about to tumble about my ears.

This was scarcely a propitious time to go to Paris and demand an inherited title of nobility. My own head would not be over-safe, my chances of success barely one in a thousand. I must await quieter days.

Then came the thought of Elise de Périer. She—with no stronger escort than her feeble old father—was venturing into that lion's den.

I was about to carry her the tidings I had just heard and counsel her father to take passage back to Barbados on the next outgoing ship.

Whatever their mission in Paris might be, they must not venture there now.

But, on the moment, I remembered what she had told me. She and her father had sailed for France in the belief that the revolution was still rife. Both had said that such knowledge could not deter them; that their mission was a matter of principle which must come before thoughts of life itself.

No, they would go on, whatever I might tell them. And I—I would go, too. Where Elise Périer led I would follow, were it to the foot of the guillotine itself.

Nor should I prove myself less courageous than she. Since my one hope of winning her lay in my establishing claim to the De Chevreuse title and estates, I would take that chance, even if death should cog the dice against me.

"Shadrach," I said, after a short silence, "I must go on. I'm going to play the game down to the very last card. But when we reach Calais *you* can get passage back. You can—"

"Son," interrupted Bemis, "if I go on I run into a rev'lootion. If I go back I run into a d'vorce. I've lived through one rev'lootion an' maybe I can live through another. But a d'vorce is something I ain't up to tacklin'. I'm goin' on with you!"

CHAPTER IV.
THE TERROR.

WE had been in Paris nearly a fortnight. I had taken rooms for Shadrach and myself on an upper floor of a quiet little hotel in the Rue St. Honoré. On my advice, M. de Périer had engaged a suite in the same hostelry for Elise and himself.

I had gone at once to the office of the Chevreuse advocate, only to find he was absent in Touraine. As he was expected back within a few weeks and as his present whereabouts were somewhat in doubt, I had resolved to await him in Paris rather than waste time on a wild goose chase through southern France.

I was in almost a daze during my first week in the French capital.

The gay, sordid, magnificent, misery-checkered Paris of my boyhood days was gone. The formal courtesy, the contrasting splendor and raggedness of dress, the Old-World charm—all were fled.

In their place, surging streets; a mob no longer servile, but supreme; strange placards everywhere; on nearly all faces a look of ferocity or of panic fear. No man was *"Monsieur."* To use that term was to incur suspicion of aristocratic leanings. Every one was "Citizen," from duke to pickpocket.

And this was Paris! To me it seemed like some stately marquise masquerading as an insane, drunken rag-picker. The king was dead. The "Terror" was king. To Shadrach the whole affair was charmingly entertaining. He would wander for hours, alone, through the maze of the dangerous underworld; always returning safe and elated. Thanks to his woodsman's instinct, he already knew his way about Paris almost as well as I.

The volatile mob, too, had learned to know him. His lank, gigantic, buck-skinned, coon-capped figure, his rifle, hunting knife, and rough, fearless bearing all delighted them. He was hailed admiringly wherever he went as *"Le Grand Sauvage."* He was looked on as the typical American—the race France in those days loved and was loved by.

To-day Bemis and I were standing on the hotel balcony, outside the grand salon, some twenty feet above the street. From wall to wall the thoroughfare was choked with the rabble. A spectacle was on view. For, along the center of the roadway rattled the tumbrels, laden with victims on their way to the near-by "Place de la Guillotine" (later mockingly renamed "Place de la Concorde").

A file of soldiers, in blue coats, white trousers, and tricolor cockade hats, would force a way through the mob for the rumbling, creaky carts with their loads of the condemned. And as each fresh party of victims rolled past, the crowd would break forth anew into that terrible hymn of theirs. Truly, I exaggerated little when I compared them to wild beasts at feeding time!

"You were wrong in one thing, son," Shadrach remarked. "You said we was puttin' our heads in the lion's mouth by comin' here. Now, I'll grant you these folks seem some peevish toward their own feller countrymen. But they act reel cordial to me when I go out. I guess you got scared for nothin'!"

"I hope so," I answered. "They're no more dangerous to us than a tiger to a fawn he has not yet discovered. But I wish I could persuade M. de Périer to get away."

"You wouldn't have any int'rest, I s'pose," observed Bemis, "in his darter's bein' safer. Only the old man you think of, hey?"

He dug his elbow into my ribs and chuckled in a peculiarly irritating way.

"There, there!" he laughed, noting my annoyance. "Don't you care, I ain't blind an' I can see as fur through a stun wall as the best of 'em. She's a fine, sweet-spoken gal. Have you popped yet?"

"What?"

"Have you asked her to be Mrs. Jack Braith? If you ain't you've been wastin' a whole lot of time."

"I'll trouble you to leave my private matters alone," I said stiffly. "It is not good form to speak of a woman in that—"

"Never mind all that," he broke in, "an' don't take offense where none's meant. Nobody asked you to jine forces with me if you didn't like my 'form.' Our 'form' *ain't* alike. That's a fact. You wear fight pants and brass button coat and two weskits an' a fob and a sword an' a glass an' a neckcloth that'd choke most folks. An' you comb that long, yaller hair of your'n. You're what they call a macaroni or a fop, I guess.

"I dress as nater' meant folks should. But I was a good enough man to save you from bein' rode down an' sabered at Cowpens, an' I reckon I'm good enough to talk to you like I want to now."

I laughed. One couldn't stay angry at Shadrach.

"That's all right," he said, his sulks gone. "An' now, tell me why you don't marry her."

"For one thing," I replied, "because I'm not in her station. For another, I'm not rich. For a third, there's no reason to think she would accept me. Those are the only obstacles I can think of just now."

"This business of station and cash is beyond me," answered Shadrach, "but I haven't spent my life studying trails and the sign language without recognizin' a gal in love when I see one. An' if Miss Elise ain't pretty near ready to drop into the basket when you shake the tree, then I—"

A rustle of skirts from the room behind checked him, and Elise de Périer stepped out on the balcony. She looked very fresh and lovely in her white muslin dress.

I set a chair for her at the rear of the little space where, sheltered by the iron trellis, she could look out, unseen from the street below.

"I am waiting for my father," said she. "He has ordered a cab, and sent me down here to let him know when it arrives. But no carriage could make its way through such a crowd to the door of the hotel."

"The crowd will thin out soon," I told her. "The last of the carts will be passing in a minute or two. Then the street will be passable again. In the meantime, Shadrach and I—"

I checked myself and glanced about. Bemis had vanished. I now recalled that he had done the same thing several times lately when he, Elise, and I had been left together alone. I understood, at last, his kindly motive.

"I don't know," said Elise, "why I look at sights like that in the street down there. Heaven knows, it is not from morbid curiosity. I feel as if each of those poor, bound creatures in the tumbrels might be a personal friend of my own. It's horrible! *Horrible!*"

She shuddered as she spoke. A louder shout than usual from the crowd made her glance involuntarily downward.

My gaze was riveted to her face. I saw it suddenly blanch and the big eyes distend in some quick emotion—whether of dread or of mere astonishment I could not determine. For, almost at once, she regained control of her features.

I shifted my glance at once to the crowd, to find what face or other sight could have thus shocked her. But in that sea of red caps, waving arms, and flushed, distorted countenances, I could single out none that seemed especially different from the rest.

"Something startled you!" I hazarded. "What was it?"

"It was—" She paused, laughed in a forced, mirthless fashion, and added: "Nothing!"

"Won't you tell me?" I begged.

"It's absurd," she said shyly; "but all at once I *felt* some one was looking at me intently. I glanced up. There was only one little patch of space—where that iron ornament has been broken off the balcony rail—from which I could be seen from the street. So I looked through it."

"Well?"

"It commanded a view of at least a dozen men and women on the opposite walk. One of them was just turning away as I saw him. So his face was invisible to me. But—"

"But *what?*" I asked, as she stopped again.

"My nerves must be a little shaken by all the tumult and tragedy about us, I think," she said, hesitating. "Perhaps that was why—just for an instant—his pose and figure brought back all in a flash a vision of that masked man of the privateer ship. It's silly, of course. And it *couldn't* be the same man. And he no doubt looked at me just from idle curiosity."

She spoke fast, excusing her weakness as might a child. It went to my heart to see her so distressed. I rose and leaned far over the balcony, scanning the street.

"He's gone!" she hastened to say. "He moved away at once."

"You shall not be annoyed by him or by any one else!" I declared. "It is unsafe for you to go abroad in a hired cab with no other escort than M. de Périer. When you go out to-day, won't you let Shadrach or myself come along? We will not intrude, nor—"

"You are very good," she replied, now quite mistress of herself again, "but we are in no danger. What object could any one have in harming us? I am ashamed that my nerves were so shaken just now. I'm not *really* a coward—honestly, I'm not."

I remembered her shot at the masked man, her serene calm in this city of horrors, and I answered:

"You are the bravest girl I ever knew. Just the same, I should feel easier if you would let me keep near you whenever you stir from the house. Is it too much to ask if your mission in Paris will be accomplished soon?"

"I can't tell," she answered. "We have made no progress thus far. But today we hope—"

Now I had understood why she had vetoed my suggestion to accompany her. And a vague curiosity as to their mission's nature assailed me.

Whatever it might be, she and her father were risking life for it. And I, who loved her, was not allowed even to share her peril.

We had turned away from the street and were looking at each other now.

"And your own errand here?" she queried.

"No progress, nor strong chance of it," I told her gloomily enough, adding: "It means everything to me."

"I am sorry," she said softly.

"It means love, happiness—a future of sunlight," I went on. "Without it my life is not worth the living."

I saw she remembered our talk on shipboard, for again her cheek was dyed a deeper red.

"Now that you know all it means to me, *mademoiselle*," I continued, "do you wish me good fortune in it?"

I hung breathless on the answer that would tell me whether or not she returned my love. She, too, knew what her answer must mean. But her eyes met mine bravely. Then, drowning her first word, came the deafening roar of the crowd's awful song again.

The last cart was passing. The throng, falling in behind, followed it, singing, to the place of execution. Their din echoed and reechoed between the narrow walls, obliterating the girl's soft-breathed answer.

I drew closer and repeated my question. My heart hammered wildly, and my throat felt curiously tight.

I was a novice at this game of love. I am told some can play it as coolly as tennis. I was not one of these.

But my question was scarce half-voiced when an attendant appeared in the doorway of the balcony.

"Citizeness," he reported, in the queer phraseology of the day, "your father, Citizen Périer, bids me say he is waiting for you in the *fiacre*, on the street in front of the hotel."

With a little exclamation, Elise was on her feet.

"How thoughtless of me!" she cried. "I hope I have not kept him waiting long. I certainly understood that it was here on the balcony he was to meet me."

With a hasty *au revoir*, she snatched up her traveling-cloak and was gone. I, looking down into the street once more, saw a cab drawn up before the hotel. I had not noted its approach. On the box sat a frowzy, unshaven driver. A *commissionnaire* held the door of the vehicle partly open, awaiting its second passenger's arrival.

A moment later Elise darted out of the hotel, crossed the narrow pavement, and hastily approached the cab. The *commissionnaire*, with a scant curtsy—for which, in the olden days, he would have been flogged—caught her elbow as she drew near, half-lifted, half-supported her into the dark depths of the hack, and slammed its door behind her with decided haste.

The driver, before the door was fairly shut, set off at a rickety gallop. I had scarce time to note what even then struck me as an odd fact: that the *fiacre's* curtains were drawn down.

Still, on second thought, I did not marvel at this. It was not a period when pretty girls of rank, accompanied by weak old men, drove in public behind raised curtains.

Even as I turned away, the cab was out of sight. So was the *commissionnaire.* I started to reenter the salon. At the very doorway I collided with a man. It was M. de Périer.

"Pardon, *m'sieur,*" he said, stepping back, "I came in search of my daughter. She was to meet me out there on the balcony. I have been over-long, for the latch of my room door became somehow broken, and I could not get out. So—what is the matter?" he broke off, noting my stare of horror.

"Elise—Mlle. de Périer!" I croaked, hoarse with dread. "She — she has gone!"

"Gone?" he echoed querulously. "Where?"

"Heaven knows!" groaned I. "She is kidnaped—stolen! She was taken away in a *fiacre!*"

CHAPTER V.
On the Paris Trail.

"GONE!"

M. de Périer repeated the word once more, dully. His old face seemed to shrivel, his lean body to hover on collapse.

Pityingly, yet with excitement I could not wholly suppress, I laid a hand on his shoulder, and spoke very calmly and simply as to a stupid child.

"M. de Périer," said I, "Mlle. Elise was told just now that you awaited her in the *fiacre.* I saw her run out to the vehicle. A *commissi-*

onnaire helped her roughly into it and the driver galloped off. He was out of sight inside of a minute. Perhaps you can explain this?"

But he only shook his head feebly. All at once his legs gave way and he slid half senseless into a chair.

And there I left him. Clearly, no clue, no help of any sort could be wrung from the senile wreck of a man. The first great shock had crushed him. If Elise were to be found it must be I, not her father, who should undertake the well-nigh hopeless task.

By this time I was out of the hotel, hatless, and running full speed in the direction whence Elise's cab had vanished. My mind was in sickening turmoil. I could not make head nor tail of the business.

In the very last year of the enlightened eighteenth century, it was well-nigh incredible that a girl should be thus kidnaped in broad daylight. Yet I could make nothing else of it.

Elise had certainly been told her father was in the cab. As she approached the rickety old vehicle, *some one* (whom in the gloom of its interior she must have mistaken for M. de Périer) had been awaiting her there. Otherwise, on learning she had been tricked, she would have sprung out again and raised some alarm.

And at what this thought called up I ground my teeth in helpless fury as I ran. I could picture the rough hand that had checked her cry of surprise, the rude arm that had prevented her from leaping out to safety. And again I recalled those ominously closed curtains.

The plot had been well and simply devised and cleverly carried out. The cabman on the box, the *commissionaire* who had hustled her into the carriage—yes, even, no doubt, the hotel attendant who brought her the false message—all were in the scheme. And how many more, I did not know.

I marveled at this. For, in those days, the guillotine stood unpleasantly ready for malefactors as well as for political victims.

Who could have framed the plot—and why? What object could any one—

I thought suddenly of the masked man on the privateer and of Elise's fancy that she had seen him again that day in the crowd. But this conjecture only plunged me the deeper into confused uncertainty. Meantime, at every second, the dainty, sheltered maiden I loved was being borne farther and farther away from me—and whither and to what?

Meantime I had been rushing along the half-deserted Rue St. Honoré, following the line taken by the cab. Now I came to the corner where it had turned into the wider boulevard. There my clue failed. The cab had turned to the right. But into which of the several branching streets?

The proverbial needle in the haystack was as a lodestar compared with my present quest. Yet I did not pause. I dashed at full speed around the corner to the right, whither the *fiacre* had gone as it left the Rue St. Honoré.

So fast and so blindly was I running that I collided violently with three men who were coming up the boulevard from the opposite direction. Before I could check myself I had struck full against the man nearest the curb and had sent him flying into the muddy gutter.

He was a large, stout fellow, clad gaily in the uniform of a colonel of the National Guard. Rain had fallen that day and the streets of Paris were one vast, sticky puddle. Into this same puddle rolled the gaudily clad colonel, collecting more clinging mud than could any professional scavenger in double the time.

But with a nimbleness remarkable in so huge a man, he was on his feet and, with an oath, had whipped out his sword before I could stammer forth an apology and hasten on in my fruitless quest.

With a howl of rage the bespattered colonel rushed at me. I had barely scope to flash my own weapon from the scabbard and guard his first fiery thrust when he was upon me.

There was no time to argue, to explain. The officer was mad with chagrin and bent on wreaking vengeance upon the cause of his misfortune. Indeed, I had need of all my skill as a fencer to save myself from his lightning attack.

But we had scarce engaged again after his initial lunge when one of the two others hurled himself between us, beating down our swords with his walking stick.

"*Sacré bleu,* Carré!" cried the peacemaker, half angry, half laughing. "Look who it is you are trying to kill!"

"What do I care?" roared the colonel, scarlet with fury, as he struggled to pass the other to get at me. "He ruined my uniform. He—"

"But look who it is!" insisted the first speaker.

The colonel blinked at me out of his red, near-sighted eyes. Then, his anger changing to sullen resignation, he saluted and sheathed his sword.

Utterly at a loss to understand this swift change of affairs, I mutely followed his example.

"You were likely to fall into trouble, my good Carré," went on the peacemaker. "Next time be more careful how you draw sword in the public streets. There is a wider, sharper blade than yours over yonder," jerking his thumb toward the Place de la Guillotine, "and it has a way of punishing those who attack the republic's officials. Besides, he apologized. I heard him."

"It is of no moment whether he apologized or not," observed the third of the trio, speaking for the first time and in a high-pitched, dry, precise voice, "you are at fault, Citizen Carré, for allowing your temper to blind you. As is he for running the streets in this drunken state. As a lover of all that is highest in man I feel shame for you both."

I had thought the prim words and falsetto utterance would have raised a laugh. But, instead, both the others listened with marked respect.

Wondering, I glanced at the speaker sidewise through the tangle of hair that had fallen over my eyes during the wild run.

I saw a man, perhaps thirty-five years old, thin, of a greenish, jaundiced, parchment-like complexion, and with the big luminous eyes of a mystic. He was dressed in the very extreme of fashion and wore his hair in a powdered queue. But for the strong, harsh face I should have taken him for a Paris dandy of the most ridiculous type.

"I—I ask pardon, Citizen Robespierre," faltered the colonel, fidgeting like a guilty schoolboy.

Muttering something apologetic under my breath I bowed low and hurried on, leaving the trio so hastily that they had no chance to call me back.

What did it all mean? That they mistook me in the early twilight for some acquaintance of their own I had gathered from the talk. My face, flushed from running and half covered by my long fair hair, that had become disarranged in my flight, had probably resembled that of some official of the republic.

And to this same tumbled aspect I doubtless owed the rebuke for drunkenness wherewith Robespierre had favored me.

It had given me more than a slight thrill, through all my worry and mad haste, to come thus face to face with the great Maximilien Robespierre. He was the most talked-of man in France even then, and was already mounting fast to the zenith of his brief, meteoric career.

It was but recently he had been elected to the famous—or infamous—committee of public safety, that dread body which swayed the nation and turned loose the Terror, like some fearful beast, on its enemies.

Dapper, eccentric, half mystic, half demagogue, wholly incorruptible in an age of corruption and boundlessly popular with the mob, Robespierre had just begun to stamp his name in crimson letters on history's face. Glad enough I was that I had met him as a supposed friend, not as victim-foe.

My delay had robbed me of the last frail chance of tracking Elise. Though I ran from street to street for an hour, like some coursing dog—seeking, inquiring, bribing—even consulting the police bureau, I could find no sign of her nor of the cab that had carried her off.

Footsore, ill with the horror and despair of it all, I retraced my steps at last toward our hotel. I fell to cursing myself for my idiotic, aimless hurry. Had I waited to summon Shadrach Bemis before setting off on that wild-goose chase, his half-miraculous instinct for picking up a trail might perhaps have availed something.

I dimly remembered seeing him lolling on a sofa in the salon as M. de Périer had accosted me. But now I sought him in vain. From top to bottom I searched the hotel, inquiring of servant after servant. Yet with no success.

M. de Périer, so I learned, had recovered from his swoon and had hurried to the prefect of police, to set the law in motion in his daughter's behalf—a thing I myself had done during my useless hunt an hour earlier.

But of Bemis nothing had been seen. And my worry changed to petty anger against the gaunt old trapper. As the moments went by, my wrath grew the hotter and more unreasoning.

There is nothing so trying as forced inaction in time of heart-stress. And Bemis, as well as any other, served as scapegoat for my temper.

As I tramped up and down the hotel foyer, the trapper strolled unconcernedly in through the great doorway, mopping the perspiration from bald forehead and grinning benignly on every one.

I ran up to him.

"Mlle. de Périer has been kidnaped!" I exclaimed.

"Do tell!" he replied calmly. "Got any terbacker? I lost my pouch an'—"

"You idiot!" I blazed out, gripping his arm. "Mlle. de Périer is gone. She—"

"So you said, son," he returned; "an' you needn't holler it at me, nor yet pinch my arm off like you was a measly grizzly. I've been out—"

"Out gaping at the executions and enjoying the crowd's delight at your clownish self, I suppose," I snarled. "While I needed your help to—"

"Son," he said sadly, "you act more an' more peevish the older you get. Honest, it almost riles me to hear you talk so paltry. Be ca'm, can't you? I—"

I turned away in furious despair. Everywhere I was balked. Not a soul could I rely on for help.

And out there, somewhere in the dark, murderous night, my beautiful love was held captive! Oh, the anguish of it all!

I had little hope from the police prefect. If, as I surmised, those who had taken Elise away were powerful in the government, the suborned police would give scant aid toward her recovery.

And I, who would have died for her, was powerless. Worse than powerless. A weak old man and an ignorant, vainglorious backwoodsman were my only allies.

Nevertheless, I had the grace to feel shame for my boyish outburst. I dug my nails into the flesh of my palms and fought for self-mastery. I gained control of myself by a mighty effort and walked out to the street to recommence my hopeless search.

But Bemis caught up with me on the threshold.

"Now, if you're more like a grown man again an' less like a frettin' brat," said he gently, "I'll go on with what I was tellin' you. I've been out. On the trail. The Paris trail. Lookin' for this Miss Elise of your'n."

"Looking for her?" I shouted, wild again. "Did you find any trace of—"

"Why, son," he answered, hurt in his self-esteem, "what a fool question! Any *trace,* eh? Why, I *found* her!"

CHAPTER VI.
A New Mystery.

FOR a moment I could scarcely believe I had heard aright. I stood staring doubtingly into Shadrach's lean, stolid face. Bemis went on as quietly as though describing a deer-chase:

"When I heard what you said to the old man, I knowed there wasn't any use wastin' time in slappin' my forehead an' askin', 'Can sech things be?' So I lights out."

"Well?" I demanded eagerly, as he ceased to speak.

"Why, then," he resumed, "I found her."

"But *how,* man? And where? And where is she now? Is she safe? Is—"

"Son, I've only got one mouth," remonstrated Shadrach, "an' it's built so I can answer only one question at a time. Where'll I begin in that long string of—"

"Is she safe?"

"Sure. If she wasn't I wouldn't be here."

"You brought her back with you?"

"No. Couldn't."

"But where is she, then?"

"I dunno."

"But," I cried, at a loss, my heart again sinking, "you said—"

"I said I'd found her, and she seems all right fer the time. That's the best I could do. So I came back to you for further orders."

"But if you don't know where she is—"

"I don't know the name of the place, but—"

"On what street? Is it in Paris? Where—"

"I dunno. But I can lead you there easy enough. Come on, if you're in such a thunderin' hurry."

He set forth at a swift pace, I at his heels. Passing through the Rue St. Honoré, he turned to the right at the point where I had collided with the National Guard colonel. He followed the boulevard for a hundred yards, made a detour, doubled, crossed the lower end of the Place de la Guillotine, and so came at last to the Pont Neuf, which he proceeded to cross.

"You took a roundabout way to the bridge," I commented, coming alongside him as we crossed above the river.

"So did her cab," he answered; "I follered it."

Reaching the Boulevard St. Germain, he crossed it obliquely, and we entered the network of mean streets known as the Latin Quarter.

"Tell me how you found her?" I asked as we strode along.

"She went in a cab, I gathered from what she told you when she came out on that balcony. An' she was waitin' for her father. When the old man showed up after she'd gone, an' I got a look at your face, I saw what was wrong. So I follered."

"But how? In a city like Paris—"

"In a city like Paris," he mimicked, "it's ten times as easy as in the Everglades. The carts had just passed through. While they was goin', there was no chance for a cab. The cab came just after they went. So it was the first cab in the street after the carts. An' it stopped at the hotel door. An' the streets was all mud from the rain. Why, son, a Cherokee baby could 'a' follered that trail."

"Bait after it turned into the crowded boulevard—"

"By that time I'd studied the wheel-marks enough to know its tracks in a thousand. Loose left-hand hind-tire. Made a blur mark as it shook, in goin' fast. Cracked right-hand hind-tire. Crack as plain in the mud as a piece of printin'. I could 'a' follered it in th' dark. It was too easy to brag about."

And, to his woodsman instinct, it must indeed have been so. The deep mud, of course, had helped; but, none the less, I still look on Shadrach's trailing feat as remarkable.

"Follered it more'n three miles," he continued. "Streets got wider. Fewer houses. I came out on a big house in grounds. Just in time to see the cab rattle off from the gate, a hundred yards ahead."

"Was she still in it?"

"No one aboard but the driver."

"You could see inside?"

"No. But the springs was up straight. If there'd been even a hundred pounds' weight in the wagon, them rickety old springs would 'a' been bent."

"What sort of looking house—"

"Had a cross an' a statoo over the gate. Convent. I've seen lots of 'em here. That's how I knowed she was safe. So I came back for you."

A *convent!* Why should kidnapers take her to such a place? The whole thing grew more and more puzzling. And I plodded along by Shadrach's side, musing hopelessly over the tangle.

At last we came out into the suburbs, and there loomed up before us the black bulk of a building, standing back in its own grounds, which were enshrouded in thick shrubbery.

"Thar it is," announced Bemis in gentle triumph.

And now I saw where we were. For I recognized the old Convent of Our Lady of Montmartre. I knew its history. I had also heard of the use to which the republic had put it since the fall of the monarchy.

It was now not only the abode of pions nuns, but a sort of semi-prison for women of rank or importance suspected of political misdeeds. Not for flagrant cases calling for the guillotine, but a place of detention—subject to the will of the revolution's chiefs—for witnesses, suspects of the milder kind, and others deemed best incarcerated for minor causes.

Here it was that Elise de Périer was lodged. But by whom and for what cause? She might as well have been in the Conciergerie or La Force, thought I, for all the chance I had of rescuing her. Yet I had not come thus far only to turn back without at least an attempt to set her free.

So, without actual plan, I hurried on to the gate, Bemis beside me, and tugged at the great bell-handle. A jangling peal woke the stillness of the courtyard. A moment later a lay sister, accompanied by a little boy, shuffled across the inner yard and thrust open the wicket loop-hole.

"I wish to see the abbess at once!" I said with what authority I could muster.

It was the day of much sudden authority, and disobedience to such was not always prudent. Yet the lay sister demurred while deliberating the matter over in her mind.

"What is your business with the Mother Abbess?" she quavered doubtingly, after a slight pause.

"It is for *her* ear alone!" I replied haughtily. "And it brooks no delay. Admit me at once."

By the light of the gate-lamp the woman eyed me closely. But my dress, which by this time was once more in order, seemed to assure her I was a person of consequence. She seemed, in fact, almost to recognize me. So, after another mumbling pause, she unbarred the portal and let me in.

"Wait here for me," I whispered to Bemis. "If I'm not out in a half-hour, go back to M. de Périer and report. The *maitre d'hotel* will interpret for you."

"If you ain't back in that time, I'll come in an' find out what ails you," he retorted grimly.

I followed the woman and boy across the wide yard, up the steps, and into a dim-lit reception-room off the main hall. There the lay sister left me to my own sad reflections.

From somewhere in the distant recesses of the building came the muffled chanting of nuns in chapel. Then this died away, and I was alone in a silence as deep and cold as that of the cheerless tomb.

What I intended to do, I did not know. Force was out of the question. I had hazy ideas of an appeal to the abbess's heart, and, if that should fail, by adroit questioning I could learn something which might lead to a clue concerning the mystery.

None could have realized better than I how unlikely was success. Yet, it was my one chance. And to feel that I was even in the same house with Elise filled me with a certain illogical, if not animating, elation.

Presently light steps echoed down the corridor. I rose to my feet and stood, waiting.

Through the gloom a woman came toward me. She was tall and stately, pale of face, and of a calm dignity. This much I could discern through the dim light. But the one small lamp that hung in the reception-room was high above our heads, and left our faces in shadow.

The abbess entered and paused. I bowed in silence, uncertain how best to open the interview. But it was she who spoke first.

And, of all the words on earth, those she uttered were the last I should have expected to hear. Commonplace as they were, they left me both dumfounded and amazed.

WHAT the abbess said that so annoyed me was merely this:

"Citizen Braith."

How did she know my name?

I peered forward through the half-light to scan her pallid face. Indistinctly as I could see it, I was none the less sure I had never before looked upon her.

"Citizen Braith," she repeated, as I did not speak, "you wished to speak with me?"

"Yes," I made shift to reply, pulling myself together, and blurting out my message awkwardly enough. "I wished to see you about Mlle. de Périer."

She inclined her head, but with no surprise.

"Mlle de Périer is here?" I went on.

"Certainly, Citizeness Périer is here," she answered, apparently astonished at my question.

"Mother," I pleaded, awkward in my hopeless eagerness, "I have come for her. Won't you let me take her away? I beg it of you. Her old father—"

"Let you take her away?" echoed the abbess.

"Yes. Back to her father. Mother, I do not ask why she—"

"But, citizen," she interrupted, "it is not necessary to entreat. Your order is sufficient. As you well know, the citizeness has been detained here only subject to your wishes. Now that you are ready to remove her, there can be no obstacle to her departure. I hardly expected you so soon. But—"

I did not hear the rest of the sentence. The room seemed to whirl around me.

Was I dreaming? Here I had come, prepared to beg, threaten, intrigue. Yet I had hoped little of my quest. And at my first word I found the door of my wishes flung wide open.

Surely, of all the day's many tangles, this was the most mystifying.

My first thought was that in the gloom the abbess had mistaken me for another. But no. She had called me by name, had said Elise was at the convent awaiting only my word of release. Mad and impossible as it all seemed, I was not idiot enough to spoil my advantage by prying into its reason.

"I thank you, mother," I said, as coolly as I could. "And if I may trouble you to have Mlle. de Périer ready at once, I will have a carriage sent for to take her away."

The abbess bowed, and was about to quit the room when I interposed:

"One moment. May I ask that you do not let her know it is I who arranged her release?"

"But—"

"Let her think it is the police, or any one you will," I insisted. "But I do not wish my name to appear. The carriage, if I can find one at this hour, will be awaiting her in the courtyard in ten minutes. Will you see that she is ready by that time?"

Coming upon the little boy, on the steps, I handed him a gold coin and bade him hurry off to the nearest mews for two *fiacres*, and have them sent to the convent with all speed. Then I joined Bemis at the gate.

To the old trapper I told the story. At its end he muttered confusedly:

"This ain't a joke, is it?"

"I don't know," said I. "My only fear is that I may wake up before we get to Mlle. de Périer's home."

"But what are the *two* carriages for?" he queried, as the cabs rumbled up to the gate.

"I want her love," I replied; "not her gratitude. If she knows I have saved her from this place she may think she owes me something. You and I will get into this second cab. The abbess will put her in the first. I will give directions beforehand to both drivers. One to go straight to our hotel with her; the other—the one you and I take—to follow close to guard her.

"She need never know. I don't care to pose as a rescuer, especially after such a tame rescue as this; nor to have her feel indebted to me. She must care for me for *myself.* Not for what I've done for her."

Which proved to be the most insane plan of my life, and one that was to lead us all far closer to death than most men are brought before their last hour.

CHAPTER VII.
DISMAY.

IT was late next morning when I awoke. And long I lay drowsily wondering why I felt so at peace with the world. Then I remembered. Elise was safe!

True to my plan, Bemis and I had not made known our presence. Elise had entered the cab in the convent courtyard, and had been driven straight to the hotel, we following in the second vehicle.

I had seen her alight and hurry into the hotel, and had noted in that brief glimpse the stricken, harassed look on her sweet face. Small wonder, after all she had been through.

I had not broken in upon her meeting with her father. She would be weary. It was no time to intrude. So I waited.

And now at dawn I awoke. Across the room Shadrach was snoring mightily. In the street outside I heard the rolling of carts. A shrill newsboy's voice cut the air with words whose frequency of utterance had well-nigh robbed them of their gruesome meaning:

"List of the Condemned! List of the Condemned!"

For thus it was that the news-sheets of the time made known to the public the results of each previous day's trials. And people read with bated breath.

None could say how soon his or her own name might be emblazoned there, nor when the cockaded guard of the Committee of Public Safety might halt at the door with the dread summons:

"In the name of the Republic of France!"

That morning I called on Laurier, the Chevreuse advocate. He had returned from Touraine the preceding afternoon. But I got slight benefit from the visit. Old Laurier declared himself utterly at a loss.

"For months I have been at work on the case," be said in doleful perplexity. "It seemed moderately simple at first. Indeed, I cannot say why it has not remained so. But at every turn some new and unforeseen obstacle blocks my way. Some legal quibble due to the changed conditions, or else a setback of a clerical sort. It seems as if some wily foe were working in the dark against us."

"You spoke in your letter," I suggested, "of another claimant, who had vowed to fight my claim to the last ditch. Can you tell me who he is, and where I may find him? I may as well settle with him soon as late. If there is a duel to be fought—"

"I am not yet at liberty to give you the information you ask," he interposed. "You see, I am the lawyer of the estate; not your personal advocate. So I must do justice alike to all legal claimants. Personally, as I wrote you, I believe your claim just, and yourself the natural successor. But, until I can fully establish those facts and hear in full the pretensions of—"

"I understand," I broke in, rising.

I knew well the dreary, long-winded technicalities of French law. It could not be hurried.

"Moreover," he added, "even though you are proven the rightful wearer of the title 'Vicomte de Chevreuse,' it will not only be an empty honor in these days of equality, but may even implicate you as an aristocrat. I speak unprofessionally, of course," he finished nervously. "You see, I—"

"I know," said I, "yet I am minded to claim the title. For myself, it means nothing. I am an American, born and bred; and to America I shall return, when this business is at an end. Yet," thinking of Elise and her father, "I wish to prove my right to the title, none the less. As for the estates and the money, I shall need those for the same cause. I beg you will use all diligence in my behalf."

When I reached the outer office, where Shadrach was awaiting me, I found him doubled up on a high stool, poring over a shabby little book, his lips moving noiselessly, his forehead puckered. It was not the first time I had caught him thus engaged. Now, as always before, at sight of me he thrust the book into his deerskin blouse.

But he saw that I had noted his action. As we passed out into the street, he cleared his throat, and remarked, with some nervousness:

"Know what I was doin'?"

"No," I answered. "What?"

Instead of replying directly, he drew a long breath, and then burst forth into a jumble of fearsome sounds.

"Thar!" he ended, with sheepish pride. "How's that?"

"Is it a Choctaw war-whoop?" I asked, "or—"

"It's *French!*" he retorted, deeply offended. "An' you pretend to know the language, an' can't even understand it! What I said was French for 'Have you the pen, ink, an' paper of your gran'ther's wife?'"

"Oho! It was a French text-book you were studying? Good for you! Now say the sentence again, a little slower this time. French people don't talk quite so explosively."

"*Avvy—voo—lay—ploom,—l—*" he began pompously. Then, with a rueful sigh: "The whole measly thing's slipped me ag'in! But I'll git it some time or other. When you goin' to call on Miss Elise?"

I consulted my watch.

"It is nearly noon," I answered. "I'll go as soon as we reach the hotel."

"You were silly not to take her home from that convent place last night. She'd likely 'a' squealed 'I'm your'n!' the minute she clapped eyes on you, an' found it was you that let her out of the convent."

"I've told you once that I want her love, not her thanks," I replied. "And—"

"An' I've told you twice you're foolish. Trouble's li'ble to come from that breed of nonsense."

I laughed at him, and ran up the broad stairs of the hotel to the door of the De Périer suite. To the answering *"Entrez!"* I swung open the door and entered the spacious old drawing-room.

Elise and her father were seated near the window, deep in talk. A glance showed me that Elise had been weeping. On her white face I read, too, that harassed, almost heart-broken look which had so distressed me the night before.

At sight of me, both father and daughter sprang to their feet. I hurried forward eagerly, then halted. For, instead of the welcoming smile I had looked to see, De Périer's pale old eyes were ablaze with wrath. Elise had shrunk back at my advance, as though I had struck her.

And thus, for an instant, we three stood. It was De Périer who broke the silence.

"It is well you have come, monsieur," he said, in a voice shaking with rage, "though I scarce expected such effrontery. It is a peace, however, with the rest of your conduct."

"M. de Périer!" I cried, doubting my own ears.

"It is well!" he repeated. "For you can hear from our own lips how we regard such as you. If—"

"*Mademoiselle!*" I exclaimed aghast, turning to Elise, "has your father gone mad?"

But she vouchsafed me no answer. Her gentle eyes were full of a cold scorn that had no place therein. Yet, behind it, I seemed to read a sorrow greater than her outward contempt.

I drew myself together, facing De Périer again.

"Will you do me the honor to explain, sir?" I asked stiffly.

"Hypocrisy will not help you now," he retorted. "We know everything. I only grieve we did not know sooner."

"What do you mean? On my soul, this is Greek to me."

"I mean," snarled De Périer, "if I were a younger man, I should kill you, as I would kill a cur. As it is, leave our rooms before I forget my own dignity. Another will soon be here who will know how to deal with you. Though it were unbecoming a gentleman of France to soil his hands on such *canaille!*"

Elise had crossed to where the shaking, furious old man stood, and laid an appealing hand on his arm. The touch momentarily calmed him.

"Go!" he repeated, pointing again to the door.

In reply, I folded my arms, and stood stock-still.

"I shall not go," said I as quietly as might be, "until this absurd misunderstanding is cleared up."

"Misunderstanding!" he mocked bitterly. "The misunderstanding has been all ours, *monsieur.* It no longer exists. Nor do you, so far as concerns us."

"*Mademoiselle,*" said I, again ignoring him, "I seem unable to obtain any explanation from your father. Will you do me the honor to tell me what this all means?"

"I forbid you to address my daughter!" quavered the irate De Périer.

"I have been honored by your acquaintance, *mademoiselle,* and by your father's," I went on, unheeding. "To the best of my knowledge, I have done nothing to forfeit that honor. Yet today—"

Elise checked again an outbreak of De Périer's rage. Speaking with an effort, yet in a curiously dead, calm voice, she turned to her father.

"It would be better to end this. It cannot but be painful to us all. Tell M. Braith why we forbid him our rooms, father, as briefly as you can."

"M. Braith," said the old man, quieter now, and bowing acquiescence to his daughter's request, "I welcomed your acquaintance because I believed you a gentleman. I allowed you to meet and converse freely with my daughter, under the same impression. How have you requited us? By causing my daughter's arrest as a political suspect. By having her spirited away from me, and placed in the convent of Our Lady of Montmartre. By—"

"It is a lie!" I shouted, forgetting in my amaze to choose more respectful language toward a man so much my senior. "Who tells so dastardly a falsehood of me? It is absurd, as well as false. I—"

"Your acting is excellent, *monsieur,*" sneered De Périer, "but it will not serve. You know best why you did this thing. At first, I myself was at a loss for a motive to it. But this very day the clue has unexpectedly come into my hands. I understand now only too well why you should wish my daughter out of the way. Have you heard enough? If so, go!"

"I have heard no word of truth," I replied, dizzy with the whole bewildering affair, "nor anything I can understand. You are actually mad enough to claim it was *I* who had Mlle. de Périer kidnaped? I demand to know your authority for so ridiculous a—"

"*I* am his authority," interposed Elise.

"*You?*"

"I went to the *fiacre* to meet my father. I was hurried into it, and the driver started. Then I found it was not my father, but a strange man beside me on the seat. The curtains were down. I could not see his face. I was hurried to the convent. There, they were awaiting me.

"I was led to a cell by two lay-sisters. But no word of explanation was offered. Some hours later—long after dark—I was ordered to go to the abbess's room. The police had ordered me set free."

I remembered angrily the tale I had bade the abbess tell as explanation. Elise went on:

"As the abbess was telling me of my release, she was called from the room for a moment. On the table lay several open papers. One was a *'lettre de cachet,'* consigning me to the convent, 'on request of Citizen John Braith, American, and for such term as he shall designate.' It was signed by Fouquier-Tinville, the public prosecutor, and countersigned by the president of the—"

"*My* name? *Mine?*" I found voice to gasp.

"Your name," she repeated miserably. "I still did not believe. When the abbess returned, I showed her the paper, and demanded to know what it meant."

"And she—"

"She confirmed it. I still refused to believe. Then she showed me the signature 'John Braith, American,' at the bottom of my commitment, and—and described you accurately. She said you had been at the convent that very day."

Naturally enough, the abbess could describe me. She had, at the time, parted from me not ten minutes before. But, even at that, I could make nothing of it all.

Why should a daughter of the church lie about such a thing? No; she had told doubtless what she deemed the truth. Also, she had called me by name on first sight.

Oh, there was no getting to the bottom of the wretched complication! Nor had I just then the heart to try to solve it. All I wanted was to set myself straight in Elise's eyes.

"Well, sir," observed De Périer, "are you satisfied?"

"No!" I declared.

"You still persist in—"

"In declaring my innocence. I do not understand this mystery. But I give you my word—"

"The word of an American!"

There was a slur in the retort that maddened me.

"Yes, of an American!" I flashed back. "Of a race that has yet to be charged with the petty dishonesties and lies that are dragging your Old-World nations to their fall. You use the term 'American' as an insult, Sieur de Périer. *I* wear it as an *honor.*"

"An honor on which your country is doubtless to be complimented," he laughed contemptuously. "But this has little to do with the matter in hand. You have—"

"I have heard you patiently, and I deny the charges. All I ask is the chance to prove them false."

De Périer shrugged his shoulders in disgust, and once again pointed doorward. But Elise now spoke. Her lovely face had softened. I knew she was loath to disbelieve me, and that my vehemence had had some slight effect on her heart.

"M. Braith," she said, "I would rather cut off my own hand than that you should have been thus treated if you do not deserve it. If that is so, both I and my father will make all the amends that mortals can. You must not blame us, nor think we decided overhastily. Surely, the proof stands clear. Can you refute it?"

"He can overwhelm us with lies!" cried De Périer, before I could speak. "If he has *real* proof, let him produce it."

"You have doubted my word, *monsieur*," said I. "Among gentlemen, a sacred word of honor is—"

"My father has doubted your word," admitted Elise, intervening between De Périer and myself, "but he was indignant at what he thought were my wrongs. When he is calmer, he will agree with me in accepting it. I do not ask for proofs, M. Braith. If you will give me your solemn word of honor—"

"Gladly!" I exclaimed, my heart throbbing with joy at her trust, and its triumph over such fearfully condemning appearances. "Most gladly! I—"

"Your word of honor," she continued, "that the abbess was mistaken in thinking you visited the convent and talked with her yesterday—"

My changed face must have warned her. For she stopped, and her own pale cheek grew whiter. Her big gray eyes were luminous with unspoken pleadings. What could I do?

Yes, I know it would have been the part of sanity to say: "I went there to save you." But, even if I could have made her believe the story of my strange interview with the abbess—which my own common sense scarce permitted me to believe—I was still all the more resolved not to come to her with an appeal for thanks, when what I craved was her unbiased love.

And stubborn pride, too, flew to the aid of this resolve.

Her father had insulted me. She herself had at first doubted me—though her strongest reason for that doubt I was destined not to know until many months later—and, in face of all this, how could I pose melodramatically as her preserver? It was out of the question. And, at best, De Périer would never credit my version of the scene at the convent. No; there was no way out of it.

De Périer, who had moved to the window, as though disclaiming any share in his daughter's compassionate weakness, now looked around in some interest. He had noted Elise's pause, and, like her, read my face.

"You heard my daughter's question," he rasped. "Did you, or did you not, go to the convent of Our Lady of Montmartre yesterday?"

I made no reply.

"Did you talk there with the abbess, in reference to my daughter's captivity?"

I did not answer.

"Come, come, sir!" the old man growled. "A moment back, you were eager enough to be put upon your so-called word of 'honor.' Yet, now that we stoop to question you, you are dumb. Surely, there is not so much 'honor' in that same 'word' as to choke back all your speech? Can you find no lies to those two simple queries: Did you go to the convent, and did you talk to the abbess?"

"My answer to both questions," I returned hopelessly, "is—yes!"

A little gasp from Elise, and an ironic chuckle from her father. Then the girl sank down, and buried her face in her hands. There was that in her crushed attitude which went like a knife to my heart.

"I went there," I asserted again, "and I talked to the abbess. But it was not to—"

A jeering laugh from the old man cut me short.

"So the supply of falsehoods has not yet run out, after all!" he remarked. "Have you still others?"

"I have spoken the truth," I urged, casting sense to the winds, along with hope, "and any man with a brain should know it. What object could I have had in the kidnaping of your daughter? Let me tell you one more 'falsehood,' to prove what I say—or to clinch the rest. M. de Périer, I love your daughter. I had hoped to come to you, rich and titled, to claim her hand. Why should I, then, have spirited her away? I love her, and—"

The old man's sardonic humor gave place in a breath to senile fury at my presumption.

"Go!" he shrieked, springing unsteadily at me, cane aloft.

Down came the slender walking-stick, across my unguarded face. Feeble as was the arm that dealt it, the blow was none the less infuriating.

And then I did the bravest deed of my life. I looked De Périer in the eyes—scarce noting Elise's cry of horror, and her hurried rush between us—bowed in silence to both father and daughter, turned on my heel, and left the room.

My whole being throbbed and burned in accord with the sting of the welt across my face. I could not think, save through a mist of red.

I had been struck like a street-beggar—and in the presence of a woman! The woman I loved. I had been struck, and I had been brave enough not to resent it.

I left the hotel, looking not to right or left. Straight onward I went, heedless of distance, direction, or time.

Through deserted byways, and through busy throngs I hurried at unchecked pace. More than one man was rudely jostled in my unswerving progress through the more frequented thoroughfares.

At such times, I came out of my mad daze long enough to hope vaguely that one of the persons thus hustled might take umbrage and pick a quarrel with me.

An angry man is not unlike a child. A man furious as I, and, at the same time, so sorely perplexed and heartbroken, is perhaps little better than an imbecile. And always that reddening welt on my face burned and stung. It seemed to me that the mark must blaze out from my countenance and give notice to all:

"Here is the man who was caned—beaten like a dog—and who did not resent it!"

For many hours this insanity of mine must have waged. Till, at last, by sheer fatigue and lapse of time; it smoldered down, into something like normal mentality, and I came to myself, wondering, at first, where I was.

Dusk had fallen. I was in the Montmartre district. I must have wandered in a half-circle, covering many miles, yet pausing at length only a mile or two from my starting-point.

Montmartre, in those days, as later, was the home of workmen, poor students, riffraff, café politicians, and the "red" political societies.

Not the safest place on earth, after nightfall. But, at that era of agitation, it was the home-ground of the most rabid of all the revolutionary factions.

I loosened my small sword in its sheath, looked about me to fix my location, and, walking in midstreet, beyond the shadows of the rickerty houses, turned my steps homeward.

I was passing a café, when its door was flung open, and one or two men started out. I crossed the broad path of light from within. One of the men lurched accidentally against me, in emerging from the brightly illuminated interior into the dusk of the street.

The impact jarred him, and he gave vent to his feelings in one of those peculiarly offensive epithets for which the Paris pot-house politician is so justly celebrated.

At another time, I might have let it pass. But now, my nerves raw, up flared my temper. Catching the fellow suddenly by the shoulder, I shook him, as a puppy might shake a rag, and then threw him violently against the wall.

He gathered himself together with a volley of lurid curses, pulled out an ugly, short knife, and sprang toward me.

CHAPTER VIII.
A Nocturnal Adventure.

Now, I had done an asinine thing. I had forced a fight in a district where human life was held even cheaper than in the revolutionary courts of the day.

Also, my opponent was no doubt a member of one of the countless Montmartre clubs or gangs, and had probably a score of friends within easy call more than willing to take up their comrade's quarrel. I would be extremely lucky to escape alive.

Still, having brought on the trouble, I would not adopt the one sane course left to me, namely, take to my heels. I stood my ground, half drawing my sword as my assailant bounded forward. Then an odd thing happened.

The fellow halted—almost, as it seemed, in mid-leap. His truculent manner underwent a swift change.

"Pardon, citizen," he said, in brutal attempt at civility. "May I inquire your name?"

"My name is Braith," I replied, surprised.

"Citizen John Braith—American?" with a queer inflection on the last word.

"Yes."

And I made as though to pass on. "One moment," he ordered, barring my way, knife still gripped.

He blew four peculiarly modulated notes on a whistle he had snatched out of a pocket with his free hand. While I was still wondering at the action, and in doubt as to whether to thrust him to one side or to remain where I was, a half-dozen men ran out of the café.

"We are in luck!" cried the man who had summoned them. "And I am glad the meeting was still on in there. It would have been a pity to let such prey escape. And, in my hurry, I was nigh to choosing for my own meat what lawfully belongs to you all. Citizens! Brothers of the Montmartre Branch!" he went on oratorically. "Permit me to present an honored guest. Jack Braith—American!"

I had scarce opportunity to note again that inflection on the word "American." For, at his speech, the half-dozen closed around me.

A little crowd had already collected in the dim street. The café door had swung shut, and we were almost in darkness.

I made as though to draw my sword. Two hands from behind pinioned my arms. I wrenched myself free; but not before another had seized my sword; and pulled it from the scabbard, and out of my reach.

Another patriot, carried away by zeal, threw himself upon me. My fist met his jaw, and he collapsed in the muddy roadway.

But what can one man do against six? I am no hero of Drury Lane melodrama. I struck out in all my strength, and more than one went down before my blows; while others reeled back, bruised and bleeding, into the crowd.

Yet the struggle was short. Others had joined the first comers. Soon I was overpowered by sheer force of numbers, and my arms were pinioned.

"So!" exclaimed the man, who had summoned the rest. "*That's* settled. Shall we carry him inside for his trial, or dispense wholly with the farce, and march straight to the Seine?"

"What does this mean?" I panted, still vainly struggling. "If you are pickpockets—"

"Pickpockets?" echoed the spokesman in high contempt. "Citizen Braith, we are as incorruptible as your beloved friend and patron, Maximilien Robespierre—whom may the guillotine feed upon!"

"Amen!" chorused other voices from the darkness.

"*A bas Robespierre!*" screamed a fishwife in the crowd.

The rabble rook up the cry. Clearly, the "Incorruptible" was not popular here. And I, for some reason, was evidently supposed to be one of his supporters.

"Yell '*A bas Robespierre!*' Citizen Braith," suggested my first acquaintance, "and we may make your end less painful."

The idea appealed to the crowd, and a laugh arose.

"'*A bas Robespierre!*' by all means, if you like," I retorted as unconcernedly as might be. "It is all one to me!"

"See!" commented the man, "his own lieutenants cannot be loyal to the 'Incorruptible.' I'll wager that even Couthon or St. Just would also have—"

"Be still!" ordered a deeper voice, from the other side of the little circle. "That is not Citizen Braith's voice. I ought to know. Bring a torch, some one.'"

A *flambeau* was brought from a nearby huckster-stall. The deep-voiced man—who was taller and better dressed than his colleagues, and seemed in authority—thrust it in front of my face.

"There is some mistake here," he announced presently. "This is not Braith. Duval, you've made another of your stupid, absinthe-bred blunders."

"It *is* Braith," insisted the man with the knife. "He—"

"*I* ought to know," interrupted the other. "It is not he, or any one close to Robespierre."

"You are right, citizen," spoke up another. "This is not Braith. I've seen him a hundred times."

"Well," cheerfully observed the man called Duval, "why not kill him, anyhow, on general principles? It will be symbolic. Like burning Braith in effigy. What do you say, brothers?"

Another laugh went up at the gruesome pleasantry. But the leader intervened sharply:

"Are we patriots, or are we street-assassins?"

Personally I thought the two might amount to much the same.

"A mistake has been made here," he added. Turning to me, and offering me my sword, hilt foremost, he cut short the wrangle by saying:

"Citizen, pray accept our apologies. Ho, there! Give the citizen room to pass on his way. Good night!"

Dazed, my brain awhirl, I returned his bow, took the proffered sword, and passed through the sullenly parted throng, out into the silence of the night beyond.

As a man in a dream, I walked. My wonder is that I did not, in my absorption, fall victim to the first footpad.

Within the past thirty hours I had first been saved from a duel, because I was mistaken, by ill light and other obstructions, for a friend of Robespierre's. Next, I had been able to rescue Elise from the convent, simply because my name was Braith. Now, I had been saved from nocturnal death, because, apparently, my name was *not* Braith.

Was ever mortal man in such another snarl? Was there any head or tail to the absurd, impossible situation?

I had, at first, thought Robespierre mistook me for one of his friends. The same supposition would account for his enemies' assault on me to-night.

But the name "Braith"? Why should it secure me the privileges of the convent-prison, and why should the statement that it was not my cognomen snatch me from death at the hands of the Montmartre Club? Why?

Oh, it was all beyond me. To dwell on it longer, I felt, was like to drive me mad.

But one thing, at least, my Montmartre adventure had accomplished. It had lifted me out of my despondent rage against fate and circumstances in general, and De Périer in particular. I saw that situation now at a better perspective and with saner eyes.

I had played the fool that morning. Instead of insisting on going over the whole misunderstanding quietly and logically with Elise and her father—driving with De Périer, if necessary, to the convent itself, for confirmation of my story—what had I done? I had blazed out like any drunken soldier, seeking, by frantic assertion, to batter down a gate of disbelief that only common sense could unbar. I had bellowed where I should have argued.

As a result, I had crushed Elise's dawning faith in my innocence, and I had subjected myself to a blow from a man too old to give satisfaction. Well, what was done might even yet be undone.

I put my pride and anger behind me—or, rather, both were overwhelmed by my greater love—and decided then and there to humiliate myself, by seeking out Elise and making one more appeal to her. Not for belief this time, but for fair chance to prove myself guiltless.

If she would grant me such chance, I was prepared to seize this baffling mystery by the throat, and—at cost of life, if need be—unveil it.

I reached the hotel, full of my new resolve. Passing the door of the De Périer suite, on my way to my own room, I saw a line of light below the threshold, and heard voices within.

Now that I had fought down my pride, I was minded not to let a night pass before putting my new resolution to the touch. I rapped lightly—for the hour was late—at the drawing-room door of the suite. Then I pulled myself together, determined not to let any rebuff of De Périer's turn me from my purpose or ruffle my wretched temper.

No reply came to my soft knock, the voices within the apartment drowning it. So I rapped again; this time harder.

The door, though I had not noted the fact, was on the latch. The impact of my hand swung it wide. It was ill-hung and its sill warped, or so light a pressure would scarce have opened it. The hotel and its equipment were old, and not in best repair.

As it was, I found myself standing on the threshold, looking into the brilliantly lighted room, whose occupants—grouped at the opposite side, and talking—had not heard even my second and louder knock.

Dazzled by the sudden glare of light after the dark, I stood blinking on the threshold, trying to adjust my eyes to the light, and with my lips parted to apologize for having seemingly flung open the door unbidden.

But, though my mouth remained open, no words came. I stood, like the spectator at a stage-play, gazing speechless upon a scene being enacted at the far end of the long room.

CHAPTER IX.
My Crowning Act of Folly.

A TABLE was spread, whereon lay the remnants of a light supper. At one end of it sat M. de Périer, leaning back with a complacent smile on his withered old lips. His pale eyes were fixed affectionately on two people who had apparently just risen from the board.

One of these was Elise, still pale, but with a happy light in her glorious gray eyes. The other was a man—tall, young, handsome — in traveling dress. On a chair near by lay his cloak, hat, and sword.

The man, with one arm, supported Elise, whose head rested on his shoulder. This was what had caught my eye and held me dumb.

As I looked, she was saying:

"Good night, then, *cheri!* And sleep well. A bridegroom should not look haggard on his wedding-day."

"If the sight of your dear face does not give me sweet dreams, nothing will," replied the stranger, stooping and kissing her. "So I— *Sacré!* who is this?" he broke off, catching sight of me.

With a little cry, Elise released herself from his arm and whirled about, fear in her eyes. De Périer, too, sprang shakily from his seat with a guttural cry.

The eyes of all three were fixed upon me. In the stranger's I read only surprise; in Elise's, a fear so intense that it actually hurt me; in De Périer's a senile fury.

"What do you wish?" asked the newcomer curtly.

"Nothing—now!" I answered, my voice sounding hoarse and strange even to my own ears.

It was the truth. I had no further object in being there. I had just seen that which struck me to the heart as all the horrors of the Reign of Terror had failed to do. For, in the scene I had witnessed, no great acumen was needed to show me my life-hopes lay dead.

Elise was betrothed; was evidently—from her words—about to become a bride. I am glad to recall that even then I did not blame her for her earlier kindly treatment of myself. In none of it, now that I reviewed our happy talk together, had she given me actual encouragement.

I had more than once hinted of my own great love. But she had not coquetted with me, nor offered anything that I could honestly term encouragement.

Yet I marveled that, in our weeks of close acquaintanceship in Paris, I had never before set eyes on this fiancé of hers. Had he but just arrived from a distance? Whoever he might be, and in wherever he might have come, I could see his suit was not only favored by the girl, but by her father as well.

In France, fathers do not sit smiling by while their daughters are kissed by men whose attentions are unwelcome to the family. Elise had told me she was an only child. This embrace I had beheld could not, therefore, be fraternal. No, there was but one explanation, and that the simplest. And the future stretched out before me, dreary and barren as a rainy sea.

All at once I felt very old and very weary.

Hence, as I answered the stranger's brusk query, I bowed, and was stepping back through the doorway, when De Périer found his tongue.

"Nothing?" he queried fiercely, echoing my word. "It seems you add to your other accomplishments the gentle art of spying, M. Braith."

I did not answer. Indeed, I scarce heeded. Nothing mattered now. I was still withdrawing when, at sound of my name, the other man sprang forward to bar the exit.

"Braith?" he cried. "Is this the scoundrel of whom you told me, sir?"

"Yes," answered De Périer. "The cur whom I caned this morning, and who—"

"Monsieur," exclaimed the stranger, "you shall not leave this room before giving me full satisfaction for your gross insult to Mlle. de Périer. You shall be taught that it is one thing to kidnap a young lady,

whose only protector is old and feeble, and quite another to answer for that insult to a stronger man."

"Hush, Maurice!" whispered Elise in alarm. "The door is still open. Any one passing through the corridor might hear or see you. For my sake be prudent. Remember, it is death if—"

"If this *canaille* leaves the room alive," replied the man, but in a more guarded tone, as old De Périer, moved by sudden caution, shuffled across, and closed and bolted the door, near which I still stood. "If he escapes, I have no doubt he will tell the authorities of my presence in Paris. But I do not intend that he shall escape. Both on your account, Elise, and on my own. I have much to live for, just at present."

But Elise had not heeded the latter part of his speech. She was advancing toward me, her hands outstretched, her eyes big with appeal.

"*Monsieur,*" she said brokenly, "we are in your power. Why should you persecute us? If you really came here to-night to spy upon the Comte de Grieux, I implore you to give up your wicked plan. He has not harmed you. He has harmed no one. He was proscribed, as you know, and fled to Brussels. At risk of his life, he has crept back here by stealth. But, on my honor, for no evil purpose. No plot against France. Oh, have mercy on—"

"Stop!" I broke in.

This agonized pleading for the man she loved was more than I could bear.

"Stop!" I repeated. "*Mademoiselle,* you are humiliating yourself to no purpose. I—"

"Oh!" she gasped, shrinking back, in misunderstanding of my words, and clasping her white little hands in entreaty. "But, for—"

"There has been enough of this, Elise!" interposed De Grieux, putting her behind him, and advancing on me. "This is *my* affair, not yours. I—"

But I was not minded to add one more blunder to the long score. I thrust the count aside, with no great gentleness, and again confronted her.

"*Mademoiselle,*" I exclaimed, "when this refugee friend of yours interrupted me, I was about to say you were pleading to no purpose— simply because I had no idea, before I entered this room, that the

Comte de Grieux was here, or even that he was in existence. After I leave this room—which, M. le Comte, I shall do at my own pleasure, and unchecked by you or any other man—after I leave this room, no one shall know from me that M. de Périer is putting his neck in peril by harboring a proscribed aristocrat. Of all this I give you most solemn assurance, which I beg you to believe. Whether or not the others choose to believe me, I care not in the least."

"Oh, thank you!" she exclaimed in relief. "I *do* believe you, and I—"

"But I do *not*," croaked old De Périer. "This man is a spy. Moreover, he has influence with the riffraff that calls itself the French government. Otherwise, he could not have obtained order for Elise's imprisonment in the convent. If he is allowed to leave here—"

"He shall not be!" returned De Grieux. "Rest assured of that, sir. As for his being a spy, and the chances that he may denounce me, I neither know nor care. But, for his behavior yesterday toward Elise, his life shall answer. Stand back from that door!"

For I had already returned to it, and my fingers were on the bolt. I now turned slowly to face him.

"My young friend," I observed calmly, "I had the honor, a few minutes ago, to tell you I should leave this room at my own will. I have not changed my mind. Nor does the fact that you have picked up your sword from that chair deter me the least. I do not wish to fight you—for reasons which Mlle. de Périer will understand better than yourself."

"We will leave Mlle. de Périer's name out of it, if you please," he retorted stiffly. "The matter lies between you and me."

Yet, from the faint flush on her pale face, I saw that Elise understood—she knew I did not wish to fight De Grieux, because he was the man she loved, and because I was averse to harming what she held dear.

"You will fare better with my cane than with your sword, Maurice," jeered De Périer. "A thrashing is more in the fellow's line than a duel."

This, too, I endured without reply—again for Elise's sake. I turned once more to the doorway.

"Well, American," asked De Grieux, stepping, sword drawn, between me and the threshold, "is it true? Will you fight, or must I kill you, as I would any other pestilent vermin?"

"I have told you," said I, keeping myself in hand with difficulty, "that I do not want to fight. Construe my motives as you will."

"There is but one way to construe a coward's motives," he answered.

"Be it so," I said calmly, though my brain was ablaze at the unmerited affront.

"Though," he resumed, in sneering banter, "in your country, I understand, cowardice is more a virtue than otherwise. The example, if I remember aright, was set by your worthy leader, General Washington."

I felt myself go white to the very lips. But I fought back my rage.

"Your ignorance of the greatest man the century has produced," said I quietly, "is ample excuse for—"

"Ignorance?" he mocked, seeing he had struck the right tack to provoke me. *"Ignorance?* No man but an ignorant Yankee bumpkin would attribute greatness to that Virginia farmer who turned traitor to King George. A traitor and—"

He got no further. My sword was out.

"M. de Périer," I cried as I sprang to the attack, "take your daughter to one of the inner rooms. Her *fiancé's* death may not be pleasant to witness."

Then we were at it hot and heavy, sword to sword, up and down the room, overturning chairs, smashing fragile table ornaments, kicking rugs into disarray.

I took the aggressive from the first, but did not fully let myself out until I saw, with the corner of my eye, M. de Périer forcibly draw the trembling Elise to the farther room and close the door on her.

Then I flew at my adversary with all the fury of a man whose country and whose country's idol have been insulted, with all the deadly fencing skill bred of long years' practise under the cleverest *maîtres d'armes* France could boast.

I had endured insults without number—a blow itself—in that room. It was good to be at last free to revenge my shameful injuries. And revenge them I would.

De Grieux was a strong man, and tall. He was a good swordsman, too. Yet, with the mysterious "fencer's instinct," I felt before we had fought thirty seconds that I was his master.

I pressed him back, little by little, forcing him ever to shift his ground, hurling in thrusts and lunges with all the speed and accuracy of an arm trained and strengthened by years of practise.

Now I parried one of his thrusts, feinted and lunged, eluding his guard and touching him on the chest.

It was but a flesh wound I scored, but I knew I would soon or late be able to drive home the finishing thrust. And at sight of the fleck of blood that stained his shirt-ruffle a cold, relentless rage took hold of me, as I have known it to do on the battle-field. And I pressed my advantage the harder.

Brave man as he was, De Grieux knew he had met more than his match. Yet he fought on, despairingly, and with a fury equal to my own.

Our crossed blades grated and whined together, flashing forth long shimmering rays from the candle-light. We were beginning to breathe heavily, too.

De Périer's set, excited face came once into my range of vision. He had left the door of the inner room, and, in his tense interest, had drawn nearer and nearer to us as we fought.

After a series of thrusts, that De Grieux guarded with increasing uncertainty, I saw that all was ready for my final stroke. A bewilderingly swift feint that would leave his guard open to my lunge—and then—

The inner door was thrown open, and Elise advanced into the room. Her father saw her, and seized her shoulders as she would have run between us. But I had seen her face, in the candle-light.

And, at the unspeakable look in those wide luminous eyes of hers, my love surged back upon me, killing the death-hate that had just filled my whole being.

She loved this man, this man who fought at my mercy. Were I to slay him, the thrust that laid him low would kill her heart as well. And I who loved her would then be murderer alike of her lover and her love.

All at once I felt as if it were she, not De Grieux, who stood before me, awaiting death. At the thought, I knew I could not kill my adversary.

Yet I made the feint I had planned. Only, instead of driving my blade to the hilt through De Grieux's heart, I made a light, quick cut that struck from his waistcoat the lowest lapel button.

The button had been directly above his heart. He noted what I had done, and he understood that I held his life in the hollow of my hand, and—was sparing it.

As his sword wavered, in momentary confusion at my inexplicable act of mercy, I made use of another trick I had long ago learned.

With a sudden wrench, my blade slid down his, and jerked it from his hand. His sword flew across the room, and struck the far wall.

Starting back, as I disarmed him, De Grieux's foot caught in a crumpled rug, and he fell heavily to the floor. The impact of his head on the polished boards momentarily stunned him, and he lay motionless.

But, as though in echo to the sound of his fall, a second crash sounded from the other side of the room. The bolted outer door flew open, with a rending of rotten wood, and through the gaping aperture poured uniformed men.

"In the name of the Republic of France!" roared the foremost.

A glance told me these were not mere gendarmes, drawn thither by the sound of fighting. They wore the National Guard uniforms, and their leader's chest was crossed by the dreaded insignia of the Committee of Public Safety.

And then I knew. Word must somehow have reached the government that the Comte de Grieux, proscribed aristocrat, had ventured back to Paris.

His whereabouts being known, a squad of guardsmen had been Sent to arrest him here in his insecure hiding-place. Hence the unheralded assault upon the room, designed in order to give the prey no time nor chance to escape.

Every hotel, every lodging-house had its government spies in those days. De Grieux's love must indeed have been strong, thought I, to lure him here almost to certain capture.

But the French aristocrats ever lacked forethought. Had they not, there need have been no French revolution.

De Périer and Elise alike understood, even as had I, the cause of the intrusion. The lieutenant in command strode toward us.

"Which is the *emigré* Grieux?" he asked sternly, looking in doubt from myself to the man on the floor, who now began to stir feebly.

So! The guillotine was to finish what I had begun! Well, it was decidedly no affair of mine. I shrugged my shoulders, and slipped my sword back into its sheath.

"Which is Citizen Grieux?" repeated the lieutenant more harshly. "Answer in the name of the—"

As ill luck would have it, his eye fell on Elise this time. The question was addressed to her. Like a little child, afraid, her eyes turned to me in what I read for the very sublimity of appeal. And then I committed my crowning act of folly.

"I am the Comte de Grieux, at your service, my man," said I in an offensively haughty tone. "What do you wish of me?"

Elise drew in her breath sharply. De Périer stared unbelieving. At hearing my admission, the lieutenant had drawn a paper from his belt.

"Citizen Grieux," he declaimed in a nasal, singsong tone, "in the name of the French Republic, represented by the Committee of Public Safety, I arrest you. Fall in!" he ordered his men.

Two of them stood on either side of me.

"Citizen Grieux," resumed the lieutenant, in the same singsong, "you are charged—"

"Did you address me?" came a dazed, muddled voice from the floor behind us.

De Grieux had risen on one elbow. Still but half-conscious, and uncertain as to where he was, he had dimly caught the repetition of his own name, and had replied to it. I must act quickly.

"Be still!" I shouted to him in affected contempt, "or must my sword teach you another lesson, American? It is lucky you come in force, lieutenant," I went on braggingly, "or I should serve you as I served that fellow Braith there, who dogged me to this room, and sought to arrest me in the same name of your upstart republic.

"Come," I added, "if I am to be jailed for the crime of being better born than scum like yourselves, let us be moving. There is no need to read me the list of my offenses. I have no wish that this lady and her father should be further distressed on my account. I forced my way in here upon them, hoping to borrow money for my needs. But they are so foolish as to be attached to that same rag-bag republic of yours, and they ordered me away. Come! We waste time."

"March!" ordered the lieutenant, taking my sword from its scabbard, and leading the way toward the door.

I followed close at his heels, my two guards clanking along on either side of me.

"No! No!" screamed Elise, starting from her daze of horror, and struggling to fling herself forward past her father's detaining arms, "you *must* not! Lieutenant, he is—"

But De Périer's hand closed over her mouth, choking back the cry. And so I left them.

"Vive la Guillotine!" shrilled a belated street urchin, as we passed into the midnight darkness of the Rue St. Honoré.

CHAPTER X.
SHADRACH BEMIS, MIRACLE-WORKER.

THROUGH the stillness of the almost empty Paris streets we marched, my captors and I. The tramp of feet and clicking of martial accouterments echoed from the tall houses lining the roadway.

We crossed the Boulevard. To my surprise, we did not turn toward either the Conciergerie or La Force, the two foremost prisons, but in a different direction from either.

"Where are we going?" I asked the lieutenant.

"To jail," he answered laconically.

"Really!" I exclaimed in mock amazement. "I fancied, from your weird costumes, that we were on our way to a comic masquerade."

Now if there was one thing a French National Guardsman adored in those days, it was his gaudy uniform. Many a duel was fought with those who criticized the absurd costume. So, as I had intended, my sneer added tenfold to my escort's hitherto impersonal dislike for myself.

I was glad of this. The more they hated me the surer they were not to suspect they had made any error in my arrest. I wished to be taken to the prison office. To be locked up for the night, if possible, as the Comte de Grieux.

This would give the real De Grieux ample time to escape from

Paris and to take Elise and her father along, if might be.

For myself, now that I had time to think matters over, I had little to fear. I was an American citizen. As such, the French government would think twice before beheading me. All I need do was to make known my plight to the Hon. Gouverneur Morris, our minister to France.

We made our way through an alley or two, and thence northward. I knew now where we must be going. For that way lay the prefecture of Police.

There I was doubtless to be lodged for the night and undergo my preliminary examination next morning, prior to commitment to one of the prisons.

As we came out upon the wider thoroughfare again, beyond the Halles, I descried a figure crossing the street in front of us. One glance was enough. And, despite the lieutenant's sharp order for silence, I called:

"Bemis! Shadrach Bemis!"

The old trapper, on the way home from one of his customary nightly rambles, heard and turned toward me, his lean face screwed up with astonishment at my odd plight.

"Le Grand Sauvage!" laughed the lieutenant, recognizing him.

But Bemis shoved past him, and was at my side.

"How in blazes—" he began.

I cut him short, and told him briefly and in English as much of my story as was needful. This I had to do in decidedly few words. For the guards, as quickly as possible, thrust us asunder.

"Shall I shoot one of 'em, an' give you a chance to cut an' run?" Shadrach asked.

"No," I answered. "I'm going to the prefecture. Go, first thing in the morning, to the American embassy. Tell—"

"I understand," he called back, as the guards broke off my instructions by hustling me away.

And I felt I could safely leave my case in the shrewd old backwoodsman's hands. So, with a lighter heart, I accompanied my captors to the prefecture. There my name and pedigree were demanded by a yawning, blear-eyed desk official. Feigning sullenness, I refused to answer.

The official, eager to get back to bed, gruffly consigned me to a cell for the night. Thither I was conducted. As soon as the iron door clanged shut behind me, I threw myself on the narrow board cot, and in a moment was deep in the heavy slumber of physical and mental fatigue.

It was not yet sunrise when a gendarme opened my cell door, roused me, and ordered me into the outer office. The same sleepy fellow was at the desk. Beside him lolled Shadrach, a court interpreter at his elbow.

"That's him!" observed Bemis, as I was led forth. "Well, young feller," he continued, addressing me with a canting air of disapproval, "a nice mess you've got us all into, ain't ye? What your pore old father'll say, I don't know. I've told them 'ere gentlemen, you can't speak a word of French. So they've got an interp'ter to do the talkin', if any's needed."

I was at sea to explain this cryptic speech. All I could gather from it was that I was supposed to know no French. But why I could not imagine.

"This p'lice officer," went on Bemis, "is goin' to give you one more chance. But I've told him if any of his men ketches you on another spree, they're to lock you up fer a month. Come on home now."

The grinning interpreter kept up a running translation, under his breath, for the official's amusement. Bemis affixed a sprawling signature to two papers, slipped a louis into the interpreter's hand, caught me roughly by the coat, and led me out through the vaulted archway into the street.

There he linked his arm in mine and set off at a tremendous pace.

"What—what does it all mean?" I demanded in amaze.

"It means your plumb foolishness came near gettin' you into all sorts of trouble," he replied, never checking his gait. "Lord, son, what a night you've give me! We're goin' pretty fast now, but it's the slowest I've moved since you an me parted last evenin'."

"'Where have you been? What—"

"Where *ain't* I been? Fust to the hotel, where I makes bold to drop in fer advice on your Périer friends. My! What a state they was in! But Miss Elise manages to tell me all about it. All about your crazy actin'! Son, that business was the wildest, unreason-ablest, worst thing I ever heard on. An'—an' I'd like to shake your silly hand!"

Which he did with muscular fervor; then resumed:

"T'other feller had decamped by the time I got there. He got away with a whole skin, thanks to you. Then I went to the United States Embassy. Minister Morris was just home from a ball, an' I guess he was pretty tired, for it was past midnight. But he saw me."

"I told you not to go there till this morning," I interrupted.

"So you did. So you did. But I'm bad at obeyin' orders. Besides, I had a kind of sneakin' notion that this was a case where a little hurry wouldn't do no great harm to any one. 'Cept, maybe, to the count feller."

"It was on his account I wanted you to wait till this morning, so he might have time to escape."

"Yes. Wa'al, mournin' clo'es is pretty dear. But we needn't 'a' wore any on his account. So off I goes to Gouverneur Morris, like I told you."

"And he arranged my release, of course. I must call today and thank him. But why did you make such a queer scene just now at the—"

"Son, you make more mistakes in fewer words than any man I ever met," answered Bemis. "For one thing, Morris *didn't* arrange your release. For another, you'd better not call on him to-day. An—"

"Didn't arrange my release?" said I in astonishment. "Then how in—"

"It was old Shadrach Bemis what got you off," he announced, with a ludicrous self-complacency.

"Look here!" I cried, angered by his conceited air. "I was arrested last night as the Comte de Grieux, a proscribed aristocrat. That is a case for Fouquier-Tinville, and then the guillotine. Even Morris's influence would be strained, to prove me an American and not at *émigré*—and to induce the French government to take a lenient view of my share in De Grieux's escape. So why do *you* claim you set me free?"

"I don't know *why* I said it, son," he answered ruefully, "unless, maybe, because 'twas so."

I saw at last that there was something more than mere boasting in his words. The trapper was in earnest.

"Tell me about it," I suggested, in doubt.

"I went to Morris," he began, nothing loath, "an' I told him the story. When I got to your name, up he flies in a temper. Says he's sick o' the very name of 'Braith.' Says you're a scoundrel, sneakin' under an American name an' cit'z'nship, an' not entitled to either. He won't git Uncle Sam's fingers burnt in no more of your scrapes, he says, an' th' law can take its course. Then—"

"What?" I gasped. "Gouverneur Morris said this of—*me?*"

"That, an' a lot more jest as flatterin'; an' winds up by stampin' out of the room, an' sayin' he'll hear nothin' more."

"But I don't understand. I never met Minister Morris, and none of my affairs have yet come before him for or adjustment. What can he mean by—"

"Let's git to that later. I've got an idee of my own. Will I go on with this story, or won't I?"

"Go ahead," I said confusedly, my brain sick with bewilderment. "What next?"

"Out he stamps, leavin' me alone in his place. I was just goin' to foller, when I thinks maybe I'll have better luck with some of his sec'taries. So I hangs around, waitin' for one of 'em to happen in on the way to bed. Just to amoose myself, I looks over some of the papers layin' around loose on the study table. Dretful untidy chap, that Morris man is."

"You mean you read his private papers?"

"I don't know how private they was. Most of 'em was in French, an' didn't mean much to me. But I found one, with an English translation pinned onto it. I read that one. It was kind of interestin'. "

"And you read a personal document of—"

"I sure did. An' you'd better be thankful, instead of so stiff about it. 'Cause, if I hadn't read it, you'd still be coolin' them gilded heels of your'n in jail."

"Was it about me, then?"

"Not till I made it so. It was a letter from an American, whose son had got into some kind of trouble over here. The feller was in jail, on charge of insultin' the gov'ment. His father's a Senator, an' he'd got Gin'r'l Washington to endorse his letter, askin' Morris to get the lad off, an' sent it to Morris. An' Morris got a order of release from th' C'mittee of Public Safety, an'—Say, son," he interpolated, "these Frenchies sure don't know a joke when they see one. If they did, they'd a died a laughin' every time they heard that measly c'mittee called 'Safety.' It's about as 'safe' as an angry rattler. I'd sooner—"

"But—"

"Oh, the story? I forgot. Wa'al, the documents was all pinned together, translations an' all, an' tacked to that one long sheet of paper. The order of release was dated yesterday. An' it was made out in blank. Out o' compliment to Morris, I 'spose. I reckon it had come that evenin', while Morris was out, an' he hadn't had chance yet to—"

"So you—"

"I just unpinned the order from the rest, for fear it might fall into some dishonest feller's hands. It was foolish for Morris to leave it layin' about so careless. For all he knew, it might 'a' been used to git some other pore pris'ner out o' jail. To make sartin it shouldn't be misused that way, I jest put temptation out of anybody else's reach by fillin' in *your* name."

"Good old Bemis! Good old boy!" I cried. "But—"

"Or, leastways, *'twasn't* your name, but this mister Dee Groo's."

"De Grieux's?"

"That's the one. I'd made Miss Elise spell it out fer me; an' I wrote it straight. Then, seein' I wasn't wanted at Morris's, an' jest nacherally hatin' to be a unwelcome guest, I leaves the embassy, an'—"

"And came to the prefecture with the order?"

"Not me. I hunted round till I found a jonny-darm that could speak some English, an' I found from him where the court interp'ter lived, an' I routed him out of bed and brought him along. Told him 'bout how I was your old uncle, sent over from the States to bring you back. Said you was a drinkin', dissoloot youngster, an' that you'd got inter trouble before, an' I was goin' to take you straight home. An' I gave the interp'ter a bit of gold every few minutes, to pay him for his bother in gettin' up so early. By the time we got to the jail, he loved me like a white-haired twin brother."

"Oh, you clever old fraud!" I exclaimed. "I'll never—"

"Oh, yes, you will. Next time you git mad at me. But never mind all that. The interp'ter sailed into that feller in charge of the desk in a way to satisfy the most fastijis. T'other feller wasn't fairly awake; an' all he could see clear was a couple of gold looeys I passed him. He had you turned out of your cage, an'—an' here we are! If we'd 'a' waited till later, there'd 'a' been a whole lot of nosey jacks-in-office in charge there, an' we mightn't 'a' got off so easy."

"But De Grieux is a French name," I objected. "Why didn't they know an American wouldn't have such a—"

"What does any of these furreners know about our country? The interp'ter ach'lly asked me was it true we hunted bufflo in Noo York. What'd they know of America or American names? No more than a Yankee p'liceman would know of French."

"Shad," I said, in amaze at it all, "do you know you've committed theft from our own embassy? That you've cheated the French government? That you—"

"That you're walkin' free, instead of takin' a course of guill'tine shavin'?" he supplemented. "That last is all I care about. We'll jest put the rest down to the charge account. But I'm kind o' sorry I had to fool that interp'ter. He was a nice feller. Seemed real int'rested in how I came to lose my scalp. An'—"

"So you told *him* the scalp story, too?" I queried. "What version, this time?"

"The true one," he snapped. "Same as I tell every one. Same as I told Minister Morris last night. I—"

"Did you tell Gouverneur Morris about—"

"I—well—that is, I kind of pleaded with him when he wouldn't help me. I p'inted to my head, where a British shell had took off a part of the scalp, an' begged him, in mem'ry of my patriotic wound, to—*now,* what are you laughing at?" he ended peevishly.

"Shad," I groaned in despair, "that's the twelfth utterly different version of your last scalp that I've—*hallo,*" I broke off, "what's all this?"

We had turned into the square, where stood the Abbaye prison, and were about half-way across the open space. From a street to the right, burst into the square a screaming, cursing mob of men, women, and children. They were fighting, tooth and nail, to break through a tight cordon of National Guardsmen, and to attack some one who walked in the center of the clump of soldiers.

A second glance—even at that distance—showed me the prisoner they were striving to murder was a woman—a young girl.

CHAPTER XI.
A Red Interlude.

FOR a moment my heart stood still. To me, the sight of a girl in the hands of the French law meant but one thing—Elise Périer. And, illogical in my dread, I ran forward toward the oncoming throng.

A statue of "Equality" stood in the center of the square. For better view, I jumped up on its high pedestal; Shadrach scrambled up beside me.

"What ails you, son?" he queried, eying the advancing crowd.

But I had caught a glimpse of the captive's face; and, at sight of it, heaved a great sigh of relief. It was not Elise. It was no one I had ever before seen; yet, my first reaction over, there was something in her look that held my gaze, and that seemed to draw the heart out of me.

It was not that the girl was beautiful, or even because she was in peril of instant death. Her face was not lovely. Not really pretty. But one to compel attention.

She was short—little more than child in stature—but with a rather broad, powerful figure. Her long brown hair had come undone, and poured in heavy masses over her shoulders, framing a dead-white face, whose huge gray eyes glowed with an unearthly light that seemed to illumine her whole countenance.

She was plainly clad. Not as a servant, but as perhaps a small-shop-keeper's daughter might be dressed. Her step had the grace, and her bearing the glad fearlessness of a pagan priestess.

Four deep around her marched the guard, while other soldiers, with bayonet and musket-butts, sought to batter back the surging throng. But the mob threw itself madly on the opposing weapons, shrieking, cursing; mouthing horrible threats, shaking fists and clubs at the barely protected maiden, who, as though unconscious of their presence, strode on amid her encircling captors.

The crowd was made up of the scum of Paris. Frowzy-haired fish-wives, purple of face and streaming-haired; ragamuffins that looked as if they had been hurled from some filthy underworld by an upheaval of Mother Earth. These, and a score of other types of the day, bred of the hideously satiric slogan "Liberty! Equality! Fraternity!"

There was nothing new in the rabble to hold my attention. But I marveled none the less at their presence. A single prisoner, or even a group of such, haled to the nearest jail, was no novelty in those days. Scarce enough so to evoke a stray glance, a handful of mud, or the cry *"A bas les Aristocrats!"*

Yet here were close upon a thousand riffraff, not only accompanying a prisoner's trip to the cells, but trying to tear her to pieces on the way thither.

What did it mean? A larger, more rabid assemblage could scarce have gathered to escort Queen Marie Antoinette herself to the guillotine. The soldiers, on their route to L'Abbaye, passed close by the base of the "Equality" statue, on whose tall pedestal Shadrach and I were standing. The pressure of the throng, eddying about the base, caused, by sheer weight of numbers, a momentary halt in the procession's march.

In that brief rest, before the outlying guards could beat a passage for their fellows through the press, the girl seemed to become aware, for the first time, of the mob's presence. Lifting her head proudly, she faced that yelling, seething crowd, and, in a voice like a silver trumpet's, cried aloud:

"My friends! My brothers! What I have done was done for the Fatherland! For France! I—"

She got no further. A mingled howl and roar from the rabble drowned her clarion shout. At the same instant the guards clove a way through the press, and the ghastly procession took up its march again at faster pace.

A crippled beggar, who had been left behind in the increased rate of speed, paused for breath at the statue base. I leaned over and accosted him.

"Citizen," I asked, tossing him a franc, "who is the prisoner? And what has she done?"

"*I* don't know," he answered impatiently over his shoulder, as he hobbled off, yelling "Down with her!"

But my gift of a coin bath excited the cupidity of one of the street gamin who hung to the outskirts of the mob. Noticing my action, he dashed back to where we stood, and held his cap upward for a similar offering.

"*I* know what it's all about!" he squawked in pride. "For a franc I'll tell you."

I held the silver piece in my hand above his head, but did not drop it into his waiting, ragged cap.

"Speak first," I ordered.

"Citizen Marat," he announced, fairly bursting with the joy of being first to tell any one the great news. "Citizen Marat—the liberator, the friend of the people, the—"

"What of him?" I inquired; shuddering inwardly at mention of the fanatic demagogue's name. "What of him?"

"He is dead! Murdered in his bath. *She*," jerking his thumb toward the vanishing procession, "she killed him. Her name is Corday, curse her! Charlotte Corday!"

CHAPTER XII.
SHADRACH'S IDEAS.

THE fanatic, glorified face of Charlotte Corday still fresh in my memory, I continued on my way, with Bemis, back toward our hotel. I wanted to make one more appeal to De Périer to take his daughter out from this accursed city, ere he and she should become hopelessly enmeshed in the ever-spreading terror-web.

Also, I was human enough to long for an interview with Elise, in the light of the previous evening's happenings. I knew she had noted to the full my quixotic service to her betrothed, and that such service must go far toward wiping from her thought the former ill opinion of me that had been forced upon them.

My act had not been that of a spy or a kidnaper. Even prejudiced old De Périer must recognize that.

Though she was lost to me, and about to wed another man, it none the less gave me a little, miserable thrill of joy to feel I had softened her contempt of me. All I now asked was to guard and serve her.

If she was to be the wife of another, and if my own future life was to be but a grave of love's memories, I was none the less minded to help her to what happiness and refugee existence could offer.

If my unselfishness could not force me to include De Grieux in my kinder feelings, who could blame me? I had acquired a very lively and natural dislike for the graceful, brave young noble. What unsuccessful lover would not?

Shadrach Bemis, as we walked along, broke in on my reverie, bringing me violently back to the present.

"Son," he observed, "from that mooney look of your'n, I take it you're thinkin' of Miss Elise. An' nice and nat'ral it is for you, too. Only this ain't the time for sech sugary dreams. You got suthin' livelier to rastle with jest now."

"What, for instance?" I asked, humoring him.

"Oh, but it must be grand to be a youngster!" he retorted. "To be ramblin' along on the edge of a cañon, half an inch from the prec'pice, an' yet be able to think of nothin' but a pretty girl!"

"You think I'm in danger?"

"I don't *think* nothin' about it," he said grimly, "I *know* it. While you've been mixin' up in love business, *I've* been doin' some figurin' in my mind. An' I've come to two or three kinds o' queer conclusions. Want to hear 'em? Don't trouble to, unless—"

"Go ahead!" I replied. "What are they?"

"Fust of all," he began slowly, "there's some one in Paris who ain't a double of yours, nor a twin brother, nor any of them story-book things, but who looks enough like you to cause a whole lot of—"

"I've gathered that much already," I interposed, "and—"

"An' have you figgered it out any further?"

"No," I admitted, "I have not. Have—"

"Wa'al, *I* have. You don't know anything about him, more'n that he's most likely one of the he-coons of this rev'lootion outfit, an' that some folks—Robbyspeer an' his gang—thinks pretty high of him; an', thanks to that, he stands solid while the Robbyspeer bunch is on top. Likewise, that there's a whole passel of other folks as'd look on it as a reel Sunday-school treat to be able to snuff him out. That's all you know about this 'ere feller who's been gitten you in such a mess of scrapes lately. Now—"

"Yes," I agreed, "that's all I know of him. And most of that is conjecture. But—"

"But *he* knows a whole lot more about *you, son.*"

"About me? Absurd! Why he probably doesn't even know I exist. He—"

"Don't know you exist, eh? I s'pose that accounts fer his usin' your name so free an' promiskus?"

"Good Lord, man! I never connected—"

"Of course you didn't. You was spendin' your val'ble time sighin' about a girl, an' trying to rime 'love' with 'dove.' An' yet, when you're sane, you're a real clever chap. Honest, I wonder at your thickness these days. Wake up, man, if you don't want ol' Missus Guill'tine to put you to sleep for good. Want to hear more of my idees?"

"Yes," I said, all attention now, "I do."

"This myster'ous feller," pursued Shadrach, "maybe hasn't seen you. He mayn't even know you're in France. An' he's passin' himself off as you. He got Robbyspeer an' the public pros'cutor to let him put Miss Elise into that convent place, an' sign your name to the commitment. Now, the prosecutor chap might be bribed to do that; but Robbyspeer's said to be so straight he bends backward. That's what I can't make out. How'd he get such a hold over Robbyspeer, an' by usin' your name? If he's a rev'lootionist boss, Robbyspeer must know all about him, an' must know his real name ain't Braith an' that he ain't an American. Yet he seems—"

"Whoever he is," I put in, remembering the scene at Montmartre, "he is known as 'Jack Braith, American.' And, from the way people add the 'American,' it looks as if they don't believe it, or that they are just quoting his own words about himself. How could he have got hold of my name? And for what reason? We've only been here a few weeks. He must have assumed the name before then. So it can't be that my arrival in Paris has—"

"Jest what I said," chimed in Shadrach. "I doubt if he even knows you're in France. You've been livin' pretty quiet, up to yesterday, an'—"

"But if he doesn't know I'm here—"

"If he doesn't, he's sure to find it out mighty soon. Some of these spies that happens to know him are sure to mention there's another 'Jack Braith, American,' stayin' in town. An' when he finds that out—"

"Then we can meet, and I—"

"Oh, son!" scoffed Bemis, "you're plumb foolish. D'ye s'pose he's stole your name an' nationality jest for a measly joke? Not he. I don't know what his reasons is, but you can gamble they're good, useful ones. So it looks plain to me he won't be over happy at learnin' that the real Jack Braith turned up in Paris. Two Jack Braiths is one too many. An' it ain't much of a stretch to figger out that he's likely to fix up a little guill'tine party for your ben'fit, as soon as he finds you. *Now* do you see you're in danger here?"

"No," I returned, "not in the least. These crazy revolutionists can cut off each other's heads to their heart's content, but when it comes to laying hands on an American citizen, our minister will have something to say. And when Uncle Sam orders 'Hands off!' people have a way of obeying him."

"H'm!" grunted Shadrach. "All you say 'bout Uncle Sam is true, son. But when it comes to your own case, that's a horse of another color. Didn't Minister Morris git madder'n a wet hen the very minute I says your name? I couldn't count on findin' one of them blank release orders *every* time I happen to drop in on him. Next time it might—"

"That's true!" I had to confess. "This man who's stolen my name seems to have used it and my nationality once too often, as far as Gouverneur Morris is concerned. I'm afraid I could look for little help, after all, from our embassy."

"He's imposed on Morris, somehow," went on Shadrach, "an' Morris has found out he ain't American. So, if it came to your usin' that same Jersey name to git you out of jail, you'd be li'ble to stay behind bars all your life, before the minister'd help you. No, son. You see whar you stand. You're jest a coquettin' with the guill'tine, by hangin' on here in Paris. Let this feller git on your trail—which he's bound to before long—an' you're a dead man."

"Upon my soul," I laughed uncomfortably, "you're a cheery companion!"

"I ain't extra strong on refined humor," retorted Bemis, "but I'm talkin' good horse-sense, an' you know it. I'll tell you suthin' else, that any one but a lover would 'a' seen before now. This other feller has reasons for wantin' to git Miss Elise comf'tably out of the way. So he put her in the convent. What them reasons of his are I don't know, not bein' a prophet nor a mind-reader. But they must 'a' been pretty strong ones to make him risk the chance of gettin' nabbed for misusin' state dockyments fer pers'nal grudges. An'—"

"But, tell me, what harm has Mlle. de Périer—?"

"Besides," he went on, unheeding, "it's dollars to doughnuts that it was him who sicked the National Guards onto that De Groo count last night. Must have spies at the hotel. When them spies tell him Miss Elise got away from the convent, he'll start another game to get her locked up, if he ain't done it already. There, son! Don't look so sick. Pull yourself together and face it like a man."

I had quickened my pace almost to a run in my haste to reach the hotel. But the backwoodsman's long, easy stride readily kept up with me.

"He'll most likely ask questions at the convent, too," continued Shadrach. "Then I'd like to see his face when the abbess tells him it was Jack Braith that let Miss Elise out. That'll give him the tip you're in Paris, if he ain't already got it from somewhere else. You got *scand'lous* little time to waste, Jack."

"What do you advise, then?"

"Git your traps together, an' light out o' Paris before night."

"And leave Elise here to—"

"You can't help her any by stayin'. Make her come away, too. If she won't, then kidnap her, if you like. I'll help you. Carry her and the old man acrost the frontier. I'll think up some way to arrange it."

I made no reply. We had turned into the Rue St. Honoré, and I broke into a run. Into the hotel I dashed, and up-stairs to De Périer's suite.

The door swung wide. Within, a man was moving. I entered without ceremony. It was no time for etiquette observances.

I came upon Gelat, the proprietor, taking inventory of some personal effects that lay scattered about.

"Where is—" I began.

He cut me short with a grunt of anger.

"Gone!" he snapped. "He and the citizeness, his daughter. An hour ago. A pretty name this sort of thing will give my poor hotel with the government! To think that—"

"Gone?" I repeated. "They have left Paris?"

"They will leave Paris by way of heaven," he grinned. "They were arrested—both of them—by a squad a National Guardsmen. For the crime of 'harboring and aiding a proscribed aristocrat.' The guillotine deals quickly with such cases."

CHAPTER XIII.
I Begin a Man Hunt.

"WA-AL," drawled Bemis, when I hurried down to him with the black tidings, "that makes it easier. Now we can go."

"Go! Where?"

"Home. Nothin' left to stay here for. They're nabbed, an' neither of us is strong enough to git 'em out of a French prison. I'm sorry, son. Sorrier'n I can say. But you can't do no good by stayin' longer. Any hour your own call's li'ble to come. Let's git our duds packed an'—"

"By all means," I sneered, "if you are afraid. Don't stay on my account. But I am going to get Elise out of the shadow of the guillotine, or else go to death at her side. Laugh if you will, or call me an idiot. *I am going to stay.* What's more, I start this moment in search of the man who is at the bottom of all our troubles. And he and I will settle this once and for all. I shall find him, and—"

"Oh, you'll find him, all right," growled Bemis, in high disgust. "No fear about that. You'll find him as easy as a stray chicken finds a hungry wildcat. An' with about the same chances of gittin' away alive."

"That's *my* affair. I—"

"No, it ain't. That's what I'm mad about. It's *my* affair, too. D'ye s'pose I'm going to leave an addle-pated youngster like you careerin' alone around Paris, with no one to keep him from tumblin' into the first trap anybody takes the trouble to set? Not me.

"You speak like this was the forkin' of the trail. It ain't. We keep right on together. I ain't sayin' I think it's a good trail. In fact, I ain't denyin' it's the worst one—next to that dee-vorce game—I ever yet treads. But we're on it. So, go ahead. *I'm* takin' it, too."

I gripped his gnarled hand in silence. Under his rough, complaining words I read the calm, steadfast loyalty which forbade him to turn his back on a friend in danger. It was the same simple, straight backwoods code that is turning our Western wilderness into civilized communities by the single bond that makes men in trouble stand by one another.

"An' now," he asked, "where first?"

"For you," I said, "a few hours of sleep after your night's work. Meantime, I'll plan our course."

Nothing loath, the tired old fellow went away to our room. I, on the contrary, set off for the modest residence of Citizen Maximilien Robespierre.

Bemis could not have availed me there. Hence my ruse to get him temporarily out of my way. I was resolved to begin my hunt at once, by applying direct to headquarters.

I had little difficulty in finding my way to the modest abode where Robespierre dwelt.

This man, who swayed just then the entire destiny of the French republic, lived in a style more befitting a government clerk than a dictator. Two small, clean, bare rooms on the upper floor of an artisan's house formed his home.

I was ushered, unannounced, into the larger of these rooms. There sat the Incorruptible, trying with difficulty to consume his morning rolls and coffee.

I say "with difficulty," for his landlord's little daughter was sitting on his knee, playfully joggling his arm as it reached for the coffee; while her baby brother was perched astride one of Robespierre's shoulders, using his black queue ribbons for reins in an imaginary but exciting horseback ride.

Thus sat the dictator whose lightest word sent innocent men and women to a horrible death. Laughing with the children, joining in their games, evidently delighted at their presence, he was the counterpart of a nursery-ridden, overindulgent father.

Between attempts at eating, and in intervals of the romp, he would consult a sheet of paper at his elbow, adding or erasing a name here and there. My eyes caught the title written atop the sheet. It was the daily "List of the Condemned!"

"Sing!" the girl was commanding as I entered, unobserved. "Sing, Papa Max! Sing us about the cat that ate the shepherdess's cheeses. Begin now:

"*'Il y avait une bergère.'* Mind me!" she cried imperiously.

"Tut, tut!" laughed Robespierre. "That is a silly, idle song. No, let me sing you one I wrote myself. I composed it before I went to sleep this morning. Just for you two. Listen."

And in dry, cracked falsetto, hideously off key, he began—to a tune, I doubt not, of his own improvisation as well—the following lyric, which naturally loses much by my poor translation:

> "Seek not, dear child, by winsome wiles
>   And coquetry, to please;
> Meek diffidence and modesty
>   By far outvalue these.
> Then learn, while young; to—"

"*No!*" squealed both children in a single breath of highly critical disapproval.

"It's a *horrid* song!" announced the girl. "And you sing it *fearfully*, Papa Max. Sing *'Sur le Pont d'Avignon,'* and we'll all dance in the chorus. Now—oh!" she broke off in sulky surprise at sight of me, where I lingered hesitant at the door, too amazed by this odd scene to announce my presence. "Oh, now we'll have to run away, I suppose, and leave you to talk stupid politics. There's Citizen—no, it isn't, either—it's a stranger."

She and the boy, apparently used to such interruptions, scrambled down from their perches and trotted off, leaving me alone with the Incorruptible.

Robespierre daintily flicked a few stray crumbs from his ruffled shirt-front with a filmy cambric handkerchief, settled his disordered queue ribbons with the air of a dandy, and rose to meet me.

He advanced with a mincing step, a look almost of cordiality on his wooden, greenish face. Midway, he paused.

"Pardon," he said in formal precision, as he halted; "I mistook you, in the bad light, for—"

"For a man who calls himself 'Jack Braith, American,'" I finished. "It is of him I have come to speak. But, chiefly, I have ventured to interrupt you in behalf of two of my friends who—"

"If your friends seek office under the republic," he interrupted, "I can only say that merit is the sole—"

"My friends are the republic's prisoners," I corrected him.

"In that case justice shall be done," said he. "Rest assured of it."

"It is for such assurance that I have come to you," I answered. "Two friends of mine—an old man and a young girl—have been committed to prison this morning for an imaginary political offense. They are innocent of wrong or of intent to harm the republic. I beg their release."

"If they are innocent," he replied calmly, "they shall be released. The republic is built upon justice. If, however, there is a shadow of doubt as to their innocence they shall die. It is better that ten innocents die than that one guilty man or woman go free."

He made this remarkable statement with the assured air of one who states an incontrovertible fact. Then, with a courteous gesture, he waved me to a chair, and himself sat down.

"Who are your two friends, citizen?" he asked.

It was on my tongue-tip to say "M. and Mlle. de Périer." But now, if ever, was the moment for diplomacy. So I changed the form of my reply to:

"Citizen Périer, a French resident of the Barbados, and his daughter, the Citizeness Elise Périer. They are—"

But a light of remembrance had come into his owlish eyes. I saw the name was familiar to him.

"I regret, citizen," he replied, "that you should have such persons for friends. They—the daughter especially—are foes to the republic."

"You are misinformed, citizen," I protested hotly.

"Unfortunately not," he retorted, in no wise offended. "The case is quite clear. The Citizeness Périer was suspected of conspiring against the constitutional government. Until such time as her case could be further investigated she was placed under restraint in the Convent of our Lady of Montmartre. By an error, which even I cannot yet clearly understand—but which shall be duly punished—she was permitted to go free. But—"

"And rightly!" I cried. "Why, use common sense, man! What harm could a young girl do to the mighty French republic? How could she conspire against it, even if she would? It is absurd."

"I pardon your almost treasonable speech," he said reprovingly, "because you seem ignorant. Therefore, let me tell you that many young girls—yes, and mere children as well—have conspired against the republic, and have suffered for their crimes."

The man was in earnest. There was no doubting that. The high, precise voice rang vibrant in its sincerity. This mystical fanatic actually regarded the children in the street as potential foes of his horrible government.

How could I hope to swerve that stubborn faith? I tried another tack.

"Who accuses the Citizeness Périer?" I asked.

"A man high in deserved esteem," answered Robespierre. "A man whom I am glad to call my friend; who—"

"Who calls himself 'Jack Braith'?" I queried at a venture.

The Incorruptible was guilty of a start of real surprise. I took advantage of the momentary shaking of his wondrous calm.

"And on the word of such a man they are imprisoned?" I cried. "The word of a man who uses a name to which he has no legal right! Under an alias he—"

"Again you are wrong," put in Robespierre, with the elaborate patience of one who teaches a stupid child. "His bearing of that name is a thing for which to honor rather than censure him. If you understood—"

"I should like to understand," I exclaimed. "If—"

"He is of a family that was of the *noblesse,*" Robespierre went on, a faint eagerness creeping into his formal tones as he defended his friend. "But he saw early the sin of the old regime, and became heart and soul a republican. So much so that he could not bear to wear longer a name stained with the taint of aristocracy. For further penance he declared himself unworthy the grand title of 'Frenchman.' So, until such period as he shall consider his family faults atoned for, he uses the name and nationality of an American ancestor. One Jack—or John—Braith, whom—"

I heard no more. The crass absurdity of the thing well-nigh wrung a laugh from me. Yet at once I saw how so fantastic a tale of mock-penance might well impose on the fanatic, eccentric belief of a man like Maximilien Robespierre; how the Incorruptible might positively admire such a trait and gain an added faith in its supposed possessor.

It is ever your mystic, your fanatic, who is most easily deceived by the man clever enough to play consistently on his pet hobbies. The fellow who had assumed my name was evidently an antagonist worthy the cleverest brain.

He was making the dreaded Incorruptible his unsuspecting dupe in a personal venture. A risky game, but one wherein he had thus far won. I despaired of opening Robespierre's eyes.

"The suspicion against the Périers," my host was now saying, "was turned last night to certainty, when it was found that Citizeness Périer and her father were harboring a proscribed criminal, here in the heart of Paris itself. At dawn to-day the warrant for their arrest was issued. By this time—"

"By this time," I cut in, "one more of the myriad monstrous injustices of the Reign of Terror is under way."

"That is treason!" flashed Robespierre, rising.

"It is truth!" I repeated furiously. "Perhaps that is why it seems so treasonable a thing under this mockery of liberty, fraternity, and equality."

He had walked to the table and picked up a pen.

"What is your name?" he demanded.

"My name is Braith—Jack Braith. I am an American. I am the man your double-dealing accomplice is impersonating. I—"

"You are lying, of course," announced Robespierre, unmoved, "but one name will serve the purpose just as well as another to fill in a warrant to the Conciergerie."

He went on filling out a blank commitment to prison while he spoke, adding in the same even tone:

"You say you are American. Yet you speak French with no accent. You also pretend to the name of a man high in the government. Of these two falsehoods I say nothing. But your insult to the holy French republic is treason. And treason must be uprooted, even if a whole nation falls. Therefore I am committing you to prison. And upon my deposition you will stand trial for your life."

"Hold on!" I mocked in bitter raillery. "That is no charge whereon to send a man to the scaffold. Your tender conscience will later hurt you for such injustice. Let me give you some *real* and more potent reasons for my commitment."

He looked up from signing the warrant, somewhat puzzled by my tone, but made no comment.

"Offense number one," quoth I: "I secured the release of Mlle. de Périer from the convent, in direct opposition to and against the interests of your cutthroat republic. Offense number two: I shouted '*A bas Robespierre!*' to an enthusiastic Montmartre audience last evening. Offense number three: I arranged last night for the safe escape of the proscribed Comte de Grieux when your guards came to take him. There! I think that is a better list of charges for you to act upon than forcing you to jail me merely for telling the truth. I—"

The door burst open and a man, clad as a small shopkeeper, hastened in. I judged, from his hatless, coatless state that he was an inmate of the house—possibly the landlord himself.

"Citizen," he cried, addressing Robespierre, "terrible news! Citizen Marat has been murdered in his bath! Murdered by a woman!"

A strange light flashed across Robespierre's cryptic countenance. Whether of joy, of grief, or of surprise I could not tell, so briefly did it die, leaving his face wooden as ever.

Yet, if I can read expression, I should say the look was one of triumph rather than wo.

"The murderess?" he asked.

"She is at l'Abbaye. The populace tried to—"

"It is well. Justice shall be done. Citizen Marat has died for France. France shall not forget him."

Thus did Maximilien Robespierre dismiss the news of his strongest—and almost dangerous—colleague's death. Without a pause, he continued:

"Go to the committee-rooms and tell Citizens St. Just and Couthon to await me at my private office in the Bureau. If they are not yet there, find them. On your way, summon a file of National Guards to come here in haste to take this man to prison."

His orders were given as unconcernedly as though he were ordering a dinner. The man bowed and departed.

"You seem very confident of your ability to keep me here at your convenience," said I, when the Incorruptible and I were alone once more.

"Perfectly," was the quiet reply, as he set to sorting over some papers in a drawer of his table.

Again I laughed. I stand almost six feet in height, and am accounted strong, even among strong men. Robespierre, with his long head and spindling body, was no more a match for me, physically, than a puppy for a mastiff.

Yet he spoke as though he had a thousand men at his back. I marveled at his utter fearlessness.

"You will pardon me, I'm sure," said I, monstrous polite, "if I refuse to impose longer on your hospitality? It will be fully fifteen minutes before your National Guard friends arrive. And I am not minded to taste prison life just yet. Adieu, *M. l'Incorruptible!*"

I strolled to the door and placed my hand on the knob. Then, moved by some unexplained impulse, I glanced back over my shoulder.

Robespierre still leaned over the table in his former attitude when searching the drawer. But his right arm was extended toward me, and that outstretched arm gripped a big pistol whose muzzle covered my retreating body.

"I beg that you will wait, citizen," observed the Incorruptible in that gentle, precise voice of his that I had learned to loathe. "I beg that you will wait. It is a prisoner the republic desires, not a corpse."

CHAPTER XIV.
CHECK AND COUNTERCHECK.

THE man with the loaded pistol always has an unanswerable argument on his side—an argument that seldom brooks contradiction.

So it was that I halted instinctively at Robespierre's order, and stood hesitating by the door, facing his leveled weapon. Providence never created anything else so terrible as an armed man. And not one other, perhaps, of all his creatures, is so helpless as a man who is unarmed.

What a mess I had made of it all! I had gone there to plead. I had remained to taunt. I had wantonly won the ill will of the most powerful, the most deadly man in France.

I stood in his dread power, in the guillotine's grisly shadow. My last hope of saving Elise was gone. My own life lay forfeit. And by it all, what had I gained? Nothing. Absolutely nothing.

Shadrach Bemis had been right. I was not fit to be trusted to manage an affair like this. At every point, the man who had stolen my name had counterchecked me. And ever I had buoyed myself with the hope that the game was not yet played to an end, and that I might in time outplay him.

But now—before me stood a pitiless man with loaded pistol. On the table lay a warrant committing "Jack Braith" to the Conciergerie.

A sudden fury filled me. Robespierre held my life in his hand. And he would not spare it. But I was not minded to wait passive for the guard, and then be led like a sheep to my pen. If I must die, I would give this vile republic something whereby to remember my name.

I recalled how, at Cowpens, a farmer boy with a bullet through the lung had yet lived long enough to pull to earth and slay a British dragoon. My mind was made up.

Slipping my hand behind me, I turned the key in the door. Now we were moderately safe from outside interference.

Robespierre, hearing the click, probably thought I held a pistol concealed behind my back. For he took a stride forward, and I saw his forefinger contract on the trigger of his weapon.

"Would it not be just as well," I observed with affected sarcasm, "to cock your pistol before firing it?"

As ninety-nine men out of a hundred would have done, the Incorruptible momentarily glanced down at the hammer of his pistol—which, by the way, as I had observed, was correctly cocked—but, brief as the interim was, it sufficed.

For with one mighty spring, even as I spoke, I was upon him. In the impact of my attack, his finger dropped from the trigger.

But, like an eel, he slipped nimbly to one side again, leveling the pistol—barely six inches from my face—and pulled the trigger.

"Click!"

The hammer fell against the flint-holder, and both struck resoundingly into the priming-pan. But the sharp jar I had given the man's arm in my first assault had dislodged from its holder the bit of flint necessary to a spark for igniting the powder and exploding the weapon.

The flint, insecurely wedged into its receptacle, had dropped out, rendering the big pistol for the time as harmless as a club.

But even a weighted club in the hands of a skilful man is formidable enough. And his failure to slay me did not rob Robespierre of his quick wit.

Leaping back, he caught his pistol by the muzzle and, at my onrush, brought down its butt with a terrific blow for my head. Himself merciless, he doubtlessly looked for quite as scant mercy from me.

It was life for life, with no hope for quarter. But now I was his equal—and more.

For as I rushed I divined his intention. As the blow whistled downward, I checked myself just beyond its reach, and as it whizzed past, a bare inch from my skull, I ran in and grappled.

Pinioning Robespierre's right arm to his side with my left, I caught his lean throat with my right hand and threw into the grip all the strength I could muster.

Wiry he was, and unexpectedly strong for so slender a man. And he fought with the reckless fury of a trapped wildcat. But from the first clinch he was a child in my hands. And I knew it.

It was no prolonged, spectacular struggle. Little by little I forced back his head, my fingers biting deep into the muscles of his throat.

His thin face lost its greenish hue and took on a purplish tinge. His lips blackened and his tongue protruded. Oh, he was not a pretty sight!

Then it was, through my rage, I became aware of a hammering at the door. The handle was impatiently tried. Then the loud knocking recommenced.

Robespierre, half strangled as he was, heard it, too, and redoubled his futile efforts.

But I saw it was time to end the matter. If the guard were already at the door, I had only one chance in a million of escape. I was not minded to lose that single chance.

At such times one thinks quickly. Even a man who, of late, had been so foolishly impulsive as had I.

With one final effort, I threw my enemy from his feet. The pistol fell to the floor from his nerveless hand. He himself collapsed in a huddled heap. Under the strangulation, his senses had suddenly departed.

Picking up the unconscious body, I bore it hurriedly into the bedroom beyond, the increased hammering at the outer door accompanying my progress.

I threw Robespierre on the narrow cot, tore down the stout silken cords that looped back the canopies at either side, and bound him, hastily but securely, hand and foot.

Then, ripping the ruffled front from his shirt, I thrust it into his mouth and bound it in place with his cambric neckcloth. Trussed, bound, and gagged, the Dictator of France lay helpless as a new-born child.

Now for my own safety.

I glanced about in eager search for some other door of exit. There was none.

I ran to the bedroom window. A sheer drop of forty feet to the flagstones below. No hope there.

I was caught like a rat in a drain.

And now a voice—or a dozen voices, for all I could tell—sounded beyond the thick door. The knocking reverberated like a bass drum's tattoo. In another moment they might burst down the door, as the guard had done at the De Périer suite.

I shut the bedroom door behind me, picked up the fallen pistol, found and affixed the missing scrap of flint, gripped the weapon in one hand, and with the other snatched up and stuck into my pocket the warrant for my arrest.

Then I loosened my sword in its sheath, unlocked the outer door and threw it open, prepared to sell my life as dearly as might be.

As the door swung inward, a man who had been hammering heavily against its panels was literally precipitated into the room, and narrowly saved himself from falling to the floor.

Swift as was his entrance, I had time to note there were none others behind him on the landing; and in relief I slammed shut the door. Once more it seemed it was to be a case of man to man.

"They told me below stairs you were in," said the newcomer, as he recovered his balance. "But, faith, you must have slumbered like the seven sleepers. Have you heard the great news? Marat has been—"

He turned and caught full view of me. There, for nearly a minute, we two stood, stupidly eying each other.

Robespierre's visitor was a man of perhaps my own height, though of somewhat slighter, more elegant, figure. He was foppishly dressed—after the manner of such chiefs of the revolution as did not affect in garb the "simplicity" of the rag-picker—and, like myself, wore his long, fair hair loose and untied.

His face was gay, handsome, shrewd.

But what most caught my eye was his marked likeness to myself. As I gazed, this faded into a mere casual resemblance. But at first glance it was almost remarkable.

Less, I think, of feature than of coloring and expression. What is commonly called "family likeness." His eyes were blue, while mine are brown. Yet their shape and general appearance were the same.

His nose, too, was hooked, while mine is straight; and a scar on the left cheek twisted his mouth into a slight but perpetual sneer.

You have often on the street seen some one approaching whom you at first mistook for an intimate acquaintance. As you looked again, the similitude vanished until there was scarce a trace of it.

So it was with this man and myself.

Yet instinctively I felt that even the slight likeness between us was not of the sort to be regarded as mere coincidence.

"Who are you?" I asked on impulse, breaking the stillness of mutual surprise.

"My name is Braith," he answered civilly enough.

"You lie!" I retorted.

His handsome face flushed scarlet and his hand sought his sword.

"I shall be glad to overrule Citizen Robespierre's principles against dueling," said he suavely, "and prove my statement's truth in cold steel."

"You lie!" I repeated fiercely, ignoring his gesture and later words. "You claim to be Jack Braith? And an American?"

"I have that honor. May I ask who you are? Not that it matters greatly; but it is always interesting to know the names of those one is going to kill."

"My name is Braith," I made answer. "Jack Braith, of America."

His sword-arm dropped. After staring at me a second in ludicrous bewilderment, he collapsed into a chair and gave way to shouts of irrepressible laughter that made the whole room ring with the echoes of his mirth.

CHAPTER XV.
The Other Jack Braith.

LONG and loud my strange acquaintance continued to laugh. Nor was there an atom of affectation in his noisy mirth.

The man was genuinely and overwhelmingly amused at what he evidently considered one of the funniest happenings of his life.

And so delightfully infectious was his laugh that, despite my own distress and sore straits, I was nigh to joining in the merriment. It ceased as suddenly as it had begun, and he sat up and eyed me more closely.

"I might have done worse!" he remarked. "'Pon my honor, we're as like as twin peas, at first look. But—if I may say it—you lack something of my deportment, my air. You look more like the real American. More like—"

"More like an honest man?" I suggested. "It may well be. But let us come to the point."

"By all means," he agreed, without offense. "What dolts the wisest of us are! I never dreamed you were in France, or that you'd dare come till after the whole revolution had simmered down. Few tourists travel our way, just now. Not even if a fortune and title are dangled before them."

"You know of my business in Paris, then?" I asked in surprise.

"Naturally. You are here after the De Chevreuse title and the estates. I knew you were nearest of kin, and that old Laurier had written you. And I managed to throw a few trifling obstacles in his way now and then. But I hoped for a full year's time yet before you could arrive. Title-hunting is dangerous sport nowadays. So I looked for a clear field in—"

"Oho! So *that's* why you borrowed my name? You were to palm yourself off on the lawyers as the missing American heir to the title?"

"Not quite so bad as that. The title can wait till it is safe to claim it. But the estates, with their two hundred thousand francs a year income, are another matter."

"Aren't you making a rather open confession of dishonesty?" I asked, amused, in spite of myself, at his nonchalant candor.

"Why not speak frankly?" he returned. "There are no witnesses. At least—"

He glanced about hurriedly. The door into the bedroom, having been too carelessly closed by me in my haste, stood ajar. But the narrow bed was directly behind it, and, with its bound occupant, was quite invisible from where my opponent sat. Thus the little bedroom appeared to him quite empty.

"Where is Citizen Robespierre?" he asked suddenly and with a shade of uneasiness. "I came expecting to—"

"He may be back before very long," I replied. "He had business, I suppose, with the committee, owing to Marat's death, and—"

"The poor Incorruptible!" laughed the other. "To be dragged out of the house on business at sunrise, when he so loves his late rising! One of the penalties of greatness. So you were waiting for him?"

I nodded. An idea was shaping itself in my mind.

"Then let us go on with our business," he resumed. "You say I speak frankly. I do. Why should I not? There are no witnesses. And if you repeat what is said, who will take your word against that of Robespierre's pet protégé? Moreover—again pardon my frankness—it is decidedly doubtful if you get chance to repeat anything at all. For, don't you see, now you have turned up in Paris, I must for my own sake get rid of you?"

There was politeness, even gentle regret, in the pleasant tones. I was reminded of Shadrach Bemis's forecast of the pseudo Jack Braith's probable behavior when he should learn of my presence.

"You seem well posted on the De Chevreuse affair," I said. "From your spies, I suppose?"

"No. From personal knowledge. From the same source that you and I get our mutual likeness. My dear Jack, I have the good fortune to be your second cousin."

I ought not to have been astonished. Yet somehow I was.

"You are—" I began.

"I am—or, rather, I was—the Chevalier Etienne de Chevreuse," he replied. "And, like yourself, I was great-nephew to his very cantankerous old lordship, the Vicomte de Chevreuse. But, unfortunately, your grandfather was his next younger brother; while mine was still younger, the youngest of all, in fact, with another between him and your grandfather. Hence, if the old monarchy had survived, you would have inherited, not I.

"As it is," he went on, "I think I have arranged matters a trifle better. In fact, but for your present appearance here, the whole thing would have been settled within another month. Though," he added reflectively, "it may be just as well you *are* here. It disposes of you."

Now I understood, as I should have done long ago.

Often, as I said earlier in my story, I had heard my great-uncle, the *vicomte,* rail at the wildness, the daredevil dissipations, and the unscrupulousness of my cousin Etienne, whom of all his possible heirs the old gentleman most cordially detested. Of course, Etienne would have all the family history at his fingers' ends.

It was less audacious than it seems, that he should have taken advantage of the revolutionary turmoil to assume my name and, with proofs of his own relationship to the *vicomte,* should lay claim to title and lands. That I should come upon the scene so soon was unlikely. He had hoped that by the time I did arrive, the fortune would be in his own grasp, and he himself high enough in governmental authority to maintain his hold on it. It was a bold stroke, but characteristic of all I had ever heard of him. I remembered a clause in Laurier's first letter, and asked:

"So it was *you* that the advocate warned me would contest my claim to the bitter end? Well, I came prepared to fight, if necessary, and—"

"No," he replied; "that must have been the other claimant. I never bothered old Laurier with my claims. At least, not openly."

"'The other claimant'? Whom do you mean?"

"It doesn't matter. There have been several, as a matter of fact."

I returned to my original idea.

"How could you, an aristocrat by birth, bamboozle Robespierre into trusting you? Into believing your—"

He laughed again.

"The worthy Incorruptible is as easy to lead by the nose as any other donkey," quoth he. "There are ways—and ways."

"You relieve me!" I declared in seeming contentment I was far from feeling. "I feared that you—a De Chevreuse—actually believe in this wild, revolutionary nonsense Robespierre and the others are preaching."

"I do," he laughed. "Oh, I do. I believe in it more than any one else. Why shouldn't I? To me it means all the difference between safety and the guillotine. It isn't every ex-aristocrat who enjoys so easy a berth as mine."

"So you are a republican 'for revenue only'?" I quoted.

"Quite so. Like all the rest. Except, maybe, Robespierre himself. But I've managed so to trim my sails that when the monarchy comes back—as come back it will—I shall be able to enjoy the title of 'vicomte' as much as I now despise that of 'citizen.'"

"You would help overthrow the republic, then?"

"If there were a ghost of a chance. But just now there isn't. The revolution is a disease that has not yet run its noisome course. All in good time. I am still young."

"Do you realize what you are saying? If I should repeat it—"

"If you should repeat it, not a soul would believe you. For—since you force me to mention such matters—you will spend to-night in prison, as a suspect, a Girondist, or whatever else I chance to denounce you for. My favorite spy is posted, as usual, in the entry yonder across the street. When I signal him from the window—"

"When you signal him from the window," I finished, drawing Robespierre's pistol from the folds of my coat, "he will be taking a last farewell of a master doubtless as honored as he is honorable—and honest."

"American manners!" he scoffed. "And yet you wear a sword."

"For gentlemen," I explained urbanely, "not for vermin. In America we shoot such. Sit down, I beg. We must not be premature."

"It is just as well," he assented; "for I should have had to fence with my left hand. My right arm was broken, some time back, by a fall from my horse, and is not yet wholly strong. While I fight quite well enough with my left to kill any American yokel, yet I could not deal the *coup de grâce* as gracefully as with the right."

"Since we are being so charmingly frank in this cousinly reunion," I remarked, coming at last to the subject closest my heart, "what was your aim in kidnaping Mlle. Elise de Périer?"

He sat up straight in his amazement.

"Now, where did you chance to hear of Elise de Périer?" he exclaimed in genuine surprise.

"That I can make clear later. Why did you kidnap her? And why—"

"I thought at first I might perhaps do well to marry her," he answered with a candor which I instinctively felt cloaked some hidden evasion. "But it has since seemed simpler to let the guillotine take her off my hands. You see, she was arrested this morning for harboring an *emigre;* and I could not blot my pure revolutionary escutcheon by taking so disloyal a wife. So I fear it must be the guillotine."

"But why should you wish to marry her?"

"For various rather important reasons. Therefore, I took her—or had her taken—to the Convent of Our Lady of—"

He broke off with a little cry of pain. He had moved his right arm somewhat suddenly, and the gesture caused him to clap his hand to his elbow as though he had wrenched it.

The gesture gave me a clue and called up to my memory in a flash a former pose bewilderingly like to it.

"And once before, I think, there was some such attempt," said I. "Off the West Indies, when you had the good fortune to be cruising in a pirate ship, and the bad fortune to be shot in the right elbow by that same young lady."

He was on his feet, mouth open, his nonchalance for the instant gone.

"You know too much!" he cried, moving toward the window.

"I know too little," I retorted, keeping between him and the casement. "For instance, I fail to see why you should risk death to win the hand of a girl who had never seen you, and with whom you cannot possibly be in love. Also, why you should now wish her death."

His only reply was to press closer to the window. With my open hand I struck him across the face, sending him reeling toward the center of the room.

He whipped out his sword, mad with fury. I, quite as wrathful, but far cooler, covered him with my pistol.

"You coward!" he screamed. "Drop that thing and draw your sword! Meet me like a man!"

"No," I snarled back at him, coldly murderous. "I don't fight carrion. I kill it."

He crouched as for a spring. But of a sudden he straightened himself, and a smile crossed his rage-distorted face.

For an instant I was puzzled. Then I heard the stamp of many heavy feet on the stairs and the clank of sabers on the landing.

The file of guards sent for by Robespierre had arrived. In our excitement neither of us had noted their approach, until now the foremost of them stood without the door.

A rap on the panel was followed by Etienne's exultant shout of: *"Entrez!"*

In marched a guard officer, his men behind him. No doubt the soldiers were not a little surprised at sight of Braith, drawn sword in hand, and of myself covering him with my—or rather Robespierre's—pistol.

But they had little enough time for conjecture. The instant the door was open—before the triumphant Etienne could speak—I had lowered my weapon and stepped up to the officer in command.

"Citizen Lieutenant!" said I with all the air of stern authority I could summon up, and pointing at Etienne as I spoke, "do you know this man?

"Yes—why, yes!" answered the puzzled lieutenant. "It is Citizen Braith—"

"Quite so," I cut him short. "Citizen Robespierre ordered me to hand you this."

And I thrust into his hand a paper I had drawn from my pocket—Robespierre's warrant for the commitment of "Jack Braith" to prison on a charge of treason.

The officer glanced it over, squinted at the Incorruptible's signature, then stepped toward Etienne. The latter, puzzled by my unexpected maneuver, and by no means understanding it, met him halfway.

"Lieutenant," he began, "arrest this man! I charge him with—"

"Pardon, Citizen Braith," interrupted the lieutenant stolidly, "your sword, if you please!"

"My—my sword?" shouted Etienne in blank dismay.

"Fall in!" commanded the officer. People had a way of obeying Robespierre's warrants to the letter.

His men surrounded the amazed Etienne. One of them wrested the sword from his hand.

"March!" ordered the lieutenant.

"Curse you!" yelled Etienne, struggling vainly to get at me. "What trick is this?"

"The odd trick I needed to win the hand," I retorted in English, as they led him struggling and protesting from the room.

Yet I knew that, though at least half of the plan I had hit upon early in the interview had succeeded, I was, if anything, in a tighter fix than ever.

CHAPTER XVI.
ROBESPIERRE'S TRUMP CARD.

PERILOUS as was my plight, I felt a glow of pleasure as I heard the guards shuffling down the stairs with their raging prisoner.

From the beginning Etienne, working in the dark, had thwarted me at every turn, had always outwitted me and turned my best plans to naught. It was a humiliating thought, but true.

And now, at our first meeting, I had bested him, had outpointed him in our verbal duel, pumped him dry, struck him, and ended by sending him to prison. I, a mere outsider, had jailed a chief of the republic!

Small wonder, after my recent rebuffs, that the reflection was as balm to my bruised self-esteem!

But this was only half of my plan. I had yet to learn how the rest had worked.

Whether Robespierre still was unconscious, or whether, helpless to move or speak, he had none the less heard his protégé's sneers at himself and at the republic, the open admission of guilt, and of the longing for the monarchy's restoration. If so, I had dealt to Etienne a blow that almost atoned for what he had wrought against me and mine.

Could I but find Robespierre ready to accept this view of the case I had some faint hopes of inducing the Incorruptible not only to remove the ban from myself, but to release Elise and her father.

I knew I was staking all on a very tenuous hope. But I had no other alternative.

At worst, I would only be sent to share Elise's fate. At best, I would be freeing her for another man. But I had laid down my course of action, and I would follow to the foot of the guillotine itself, if need be.

I once more locked the outer door, slipped the key into my pocket, and returned to the bedroom.

There lay Robespierre, where I had thrown him. To my boundless relief, I found his big, luminous eyes were wide open. They stared at me over the muffling gag with a concentrated malignity that was fairly appalling.

The man's wooden mask of a face was twisted into an expression I still sometimes see in my nightmares. Yet, though I stood before him, pistol in hand, he showed no trace of fear.

I knew he believed he was about to die, even as his colleague, Marat, had died that very morning. But the Incorruptible knew no cowardice.

I was of two minds as I stood there, fingering my pistol. That I would be doing humanity a service by putting an end to this man's life I well knew. Nor should I be committing any great crime. He would assuredly compass my own death were it ever in his power to do so.

Yet, it is one thing to adjudge a man guilty of death, and quite another to slay him as he lies at one's mercy. I could not do it.

Besides, there was always the chance I might yet bend him to my will and persuade him to save the woman I loved.

So I dropped the pistol into one of my pockets, and, bending over, unfastened the neckcloth and gag from his mouth.

"Citizen," said he the instant the gag was removed—and his choking, falsetto tones were not without a certain solemn dignity—"citizen, it is not Maximilien Robespierre you are murdering. It is France. It is the fair land that without my guidance must fall back into its ancient sins and decadence."

"And whose sons will call me blessed for checking the Reign of Terror," I supplemented in the same vein.

"This 'Reign of Terror,' as you miscall it, is the sacrifice needful to save the whole body politic from death," he croaked. "Not as that hypocrite termed it, a 'disease.'"

I could have shouted for sheer joy. So he had heard our talk! He had heard Etienne de Chevreuse condemn himself. The bound man read my unspoken thoughts.

"Yes," said he, and there was just a tinge of sorrow in the even tone, "I heard. Thanks to you, I die knowing that the man I loved and trusted is a traitor. Not only a traitor to me—that I could have endured—but a traitor to France. As such, he shall suffer death."

"And the old man and the girl, ensnared by his treachery," I interrupted eagerly. "You will set them free?"

"No. His guilt does not prove their innocence. They have harbored a proscribed *émigré*. That is an offense which calls for death. They must pay the penalty."

"If you live to enforce it," I reminded him.

"Whether I live or die. The charge is made. They are in prison. The proofs against them have been filed. Citizen Fouquier-Tinville has sufficient evidence to conduct his prosecution. My dying will in no way affect them."

"Will your living?"

"You seek to bargain with me?" he asked wearily. "I had hoped my reputation for probity—"

I groaned. There was no help, apparently, from him. Drastic measures alone could aid him now.

I propped him up in the bed, so that he sat facing me. Then I took a seat on the corner of his dressing-table.

"Citizen Robespierre," I remarked coolly, "I want a paper written and signed by you, liberating M. de Périer and Mlle. Elise from prison. Then I desire that you make out a passport permitting both the De Périers and the Comte de Grieux to leave France at once and in safety."

He smiled slightly, as not deeming the request worth an answer.

"You will write and sign both these papers," I continued; "and you will give them to me. I will then leave you bound and gagged here, with the outer door locked. To-morrow, when the servants come to arrange your room, the door will doubtless be forced, and you will be set free. By that time the persons named in those papers—as well as myself—will be far beyond your reach. Do you accept?"

"Naturally not."

"So I expected," said I. "Have you ever heard of Cherokee Indians, citizen? From an American frontiersman friend of mine I have been informed as to one of their most interesting modes of coercing their enemies. I think this is an excellent time to introduce the custom into France. I trust you will not object to being the subject of my experiment."

Now, the tortures inflicted by American Indians have ever been of keen and morbid interest to Europeans. All sorts of hideously exaggerated tales concerning these torments had crossed the Atlantic. Seldom could an American, in the last years of the eighteenth century, talk for five minutes to a European without being catechized on this gruesome theme.

I could see that even the cold-blooded Robespierre was suddenly interested in my words. I hastened to press the advantage.

"I shall gag you again," I went on, doing so as I spoke, "and leave you propped up here. Now, I shall go into the other room, empty both the lamps there into a bowl and bring the oil in here. I shall saturate your clothing and the sheets with this oil, light a candle and place it on the floor. To a point a little way down the candle I shall attach a fuse made of paper—also soaked in oil—and lay the other end on the saturated sheet near your head. Then, when the fuse begins to burn, I shall go, locking the door behind me."

I wandered slowly out into the next room. There, as soon as he could no longer see me, I emptied a quart or so of water from the jug into the washbowl, pouring into it just enough of one of the lamp's contents to give the mixture a strong odor of oil. By no means enough to make it inflammable.

Returning to the bedroom, I set hurriedly to work on the program I had described. It was quickly completed. Then, fastening the fuse to the wax of the candle about an inch below the flame, I resumed my seat and, smiling benignly on the gagged, bound victim of cold water,

I began my vigil.

It is one thing to brave immediate death, and quite another to watch death in its most agonizing form creep slowly nearer and nearer, with no power to move hand or foot to avert one's fate. Show me the man whose steel nerves can endure such suspense, and I will acclaim him either a world-hero or else insane.

My plan was worth a cleverer brain than mine.

Robespierre, for all his calm courage, watched the burning candle on the floor with a growing, irresistible fascination. Its mild little flame seemed to mesmerize him, as bit by bit the wax-rim sank lower and lower toward the dingy twist of paper fuse.

Had I not known that the soaked condition of the sheets and of Robespierre's clothing would at once put out the fuse as it came in contact with them, I myself could not have borne the sight. As it was, the gradual breaking down of a brave man's stoicism was well-nigh too much for me.

For the Incorruptible's greenish face was growing ghastly. His bright eyes were filmed. Involuntary tremors convulsed his bound limbs. Yes, the man who was the most responsible for the Reign of Terror was now tasting for the first time in his strange life the pangs of that same terror.

Perhaps he then understood—if he had any thought at the moment for others than himself—the horror that had gripped some of his victims as the black shadow of the guillotine had fallen athwart their innocent life-paths.

"It will only be a few moments longer, at most," I reassured him cheerfully. "I am told that after the first five minutes or so it does not cause much suffering. By that time—"

A spasm contorted his ghastly face. The candle-rim was within a quarter-inch of the fuse.

"It is so easy to avert all this," I went on. "A few strokes of your pen, and—"

A violent writhing of the lean body, and a look of wild appeal in the dark, maddened eyes.

"You accept my terms?" I queried, without especial show of interest.

He glanced once more at the candle. The fuse was beginning to sputter. He nodded, and his eyes grew wet with the tears of fear and shame.

Between thumb and forefinger I pinched the sparks from the fuse and blew out the candle.

"We will leave these here," I said, indicating the "properties" of my grisly farce, as I undid the gag. "They will be useful in case you should change your mind when you are removed from their influence."

"I agree, not through fear," he croaked tremulously, "for I am above fear. But France needs me. I have no right to die. The fatherland's fate hangs on my life. It is better that a few traitors go free than that the republic be left defenseless to its foes."

"I fully appreciate your high patriotism, citizen," I answered, smothering a grin at his pompous sophistry. "And I compliment the wisdom and unselfishness of your decision."

I lifted him bodily and carried him into the outer room, where I seated him at his writing-table. There I unbound his right arm and placed pen, ink-horn and paper before him.

"I beg you will not be so indiscreet as to call for aid," I suggested, as I saw him glance furtively toward the outer door; "for at first sound I shall be obliged to stifle your voice and carry you back to the impromptu funeral pyre. And next time there will be no hitch in the proceedings. Now, write! The release first, then the passport."

"You hold me in your power," he muttered, "but my arm is long. Beware how you venture again within its reach, when once you leave here to-day."

"Thanks," I said flippantly; "but I am not likely to put my head into the same hornet's nest twice. We waste time. Write!"

He took up the quill-pen. But a swift reaction from his late peril overcame him. A shudder shook his thin form, and the pen he held trembled so he could not make legible characters on the paper before him.

"Here!" I exclaimed, throwing away a spoiled page, "this will never do. Brace up, man! Get control of yourself."

But he only glanced helplessly about, unable to check the tremors that now shook him from head to foot. The man was apparently in the throes of a severe nervous chill. When strong nerves do break, they break completely.

He looked up appealingly at me, then drew open a drawer of the table and plunged his hand far into its recesses. I suspected a trick, and stood ready to snatch his wrist should he be reaching for a weapon.

But he presently drew forth a small, wicker-covered flask, stoppered with an enameled porcelain cork.

"I—I am abstemious," he muttered through chattering teeth; "for drunkenness and wine-bibbing are vices that blast a nation's strength. Thus, no intoxicants are kept in my rooms. But, when ill or weary—when the weak body will not obey the mind's command—"

"Why, at such times," I finished mockingly, "we dive secretly into that drawer and bring forth a little artificial stimulation, eh? Purely for the ultimate welfare of the republic."

"Yes," he assented, my satire quite lost on him. "May I trouble you to reach me a glass from that stand behind you. I cannot move far enough myself. And"—with a courtesy that was rather winning—"will you honor me by filling a glass for yourself?"

I had eaten nothing for nearly twenty-four hours. Constant excitement had kept me keyed up, and had robbed me of all desire or need for food.

Now that the strain was over, and victory in my grasp, I began to realize that I was very tired and faint. A dram of brandy might well stimulate me for what yet remained to be done.

Yet I disliked the idea of drinking with this arch-blackguard, or of becoming thus, in a measure, his guest.

"You are perhaps used to coarser liquors in your savage America?" he asked sneeringly, seeming again to read my unspoken thought. "This is an old brandy of '47, and may be too weak and smooth for your uncultured palate."

He had been pouring out a generous measure of the golden liquid for himself as he spoke. And, without mental comment, I noticed that already his hand was firm again.

His slurring words angered me. He had sneered at my country and at myself. Well, I would return the insult.

I snatched up the flask, half filled a glass, and tossed down on the table a silver five-franc piece.

"We Americans can appreciate good vintage in liquor quite as well as can a French ex-attorney's clerk," I retorted. "But we—I, at least—

do not choose to be the guest of such *canaille.* So, I pay good money for what I drink. Keep the change for a tip, honest clerk. I drink to the speedy downfall of that most accursed of upstart institutions—the French republic!"

I drained my glass at one swallow, placed it back on the table, then turned to Robespierre.

He was looking calmly at me, apparently not in the least incensed at what I had said. The brandy he had poured out for himself was still untasted.

"If the mere sight of liquor has steadied your hand," said I, "suppose we get back to business. Those papers—"

"All in good time," he replied, with one of his rare, dry smiles, as his hand once more plunged into the deep drawer. "You may have observed it took me some time to produce the flask, for the simple reason that I was first obliged to uncork it and empty into the brandy the contents of this vial, which I always keep there for emergencies. Some day it may be necessary for me to die. And, when that time comes, I wish a painless end. I do not think you have drunk enough of its contents to kill you. But you will sleep well, and soon. So, why trouble me with the papers now?"

I leaped to my feet, in furious surprise, and took a step toward him. But, even as I moved, I all at once realized that I was very weary, and that he was unaccountably far away. Also, that sleep is the sweetest thing on earth. In fact, the only thing that matters.

So I sank back heavily into my chair, a delicious sense of comfort and drowsiness encompassing me. And I slept.

CHAPTER XVII.
In the Conciergerie.

I HAD slept long and hard. I came slowly to my senses. Little by little I remembered.

I was at Robespierre's. I had checkmated Etienne and sent him to prison. I had forced the Incorruptible to agree to Elise's release.

Had Robespierre signed the release yet? I must have dozed in my chair while he wrote. I—

My eyes opened drowsily. Some one was betiding over me. Something was brushing my face.

What was Robespierre up to now? I felt a dull resentment at him for disturbing my deep slumbers. What did he—

I looked up in drowsy irritation. What I saw drove the sleep-mists from my brain.

Elise de Périer was leaning over me.

"Elise!" I muttered thickly. "Here at Robespierre's own house!"

"Yes," she answered sadly, "at his own 'house.' Like yourself. But don't try to talk, now. Wait till you are—"

"But how did you come here?" I insisted, rising on my elbow. "Did he send for you? Are you free?"

She smiled—a little heart-broken smile that hurt me. But she made no reply save to repeat:

"Don't try to talk. Drink this."

She held a cup of water to my lips. I drank eagerly, for my throat was parched and my lips were dry and cracking.

Never once since I awoke had I shifted my eyes from Elise's face. It seemed my one hold on life. I fell idly to wondering at its dainty, girlish grace, its wavy crown of sun-kissed hair.

Then I remembered all this loveliness belonged to another, and the thought brought me to myself with a start.

I was not sitting in a chair at Robespierre's, as I had supposed, but was lying at full length on a rude pallet on the floor. Nor was the room Robespierre's. It was a great, bare, vaulted apartment, into which the light filtered from narrow, grimy, barred windows.

"What place is this?" I asked, starting up.

Elise, who had been kneeling at my side, now rose and stood looking down at me, a world of pitying wonder in her eyes.

"Don't you know?" she said. "It is the Conciergerie."

I stared at her blankly. The Conciergerie! The huge pile with its thousands of sightless windows that had given me a thrill of horror as I passed it daily. The infamous prison-house where herded the republic's luckless enemies, and whose only door of exit for nine out of ten of these unfortunates was the guillotine!

But what was *I* doing there? Only a minute earlier, it seemed, I had been watching the efforts of Robespierre's trembling hand to write Elise's release.

Yes, his hand had shaken. He had drawn forth a flask—liquor to steady his nerves. Then he—

Ah! Now I remembered everything. The man had trapped me finely. He had put me to sleep with his drugged brandy, and at his leisure had summoned help and had me sent here to prison.

At my very moment of triumph he had conquered me. His was the winning hand, after all. And from a man of his colossal vanity I could expect no mercy after the way I had tricked and tortured him.

Not only was I lost, but my last hope of saving Elise de Périer was gone. At best, now, I could only share her fate.

"How long have I been here?" I asked the girl.

"You were carried in about four o'clock. That must be nearly an hour ago. You were senseless. They did not take you to your cell, but put you down here in the exercise-room. Are you badly hurt?"

"And you, of all people, took pity on me and tried to bring me back to my senses?"

She flushed and turned away her head, saying hurriedly:

"Why shouldn't I try to help you? It is on our account you were arrested. The least I could do—"

"On your account? Then you know—"

"I know you were noble enough to pretend to be M. de Grieux and that you were arrested in his place—"

"But that was last night—"

"And you were injured trying to escape?"

"Escape? No. And I'm not injured. I—"

"But you were carried in here, senseless. I supposed you tried to get free at the *prefecture,* and in the struggle—"

"There was no struggle," I interposed in bitter self-contempt. "I fell asleep and was taken as easily as a roosting chicken."

"I don't understand."

"Need it interest you, *mademoiselle?*"

"Pardon!" she returned, wounded by my hopeless query, "I had no wish to offend."

"I am sorry I spoke so brutally," said I, "but my self-conceit has received a nasty blow. Overlook my boorishness, I beg. Your father is here?"

"Across the hall, *monsieur*. Talking with one of his old friends whom he met here to-day. This is only the exercise-room for the trial prisoners, you know. Those who have been condemned are housed in the opposite wing. Our chance for seeing it will come soon enough. There is little legal delay in such matters, I fear."

"Your father permits you to speak with me?"

"My father realizes as well as I," she replied, "the debt under which you placed us both last night."

"Then, it is simply through gratitude—"

"M. Braith," she interrupted impulsively, "I don't understand you. I don't *understand* you! Last night you bore yourself like a hero. Can it be possible that such a man is—"

"A kidnaper and spy, and several other equally noble objects?" I finished as she broke off in embarrassment. "I have twice before sought to prove to M. de Périer and yourself, *mademoiselle,* that I am innocent of the crimes with which you both charge me. You refused to be convinced. It is not for me to press upon you a statement you cannot credit. So sha'n't we let the whole disagreeable subject drop? Believe me, I am not going to claim any gratitude from either of you for my quixotic feat of last evening, nor force myself further on your acquaintance. Accept my deep thanks, *mademoiselle,* for what you have just done for me. And henceforth—unless at some time I can be of use to you—help me to refrain from thrusting myself upon your notice."

I turned away. But her white hand touched my arm in eager appeal.

"I can't let you go like this!" she cried. "There is some horrible mystery about the whole affair that you must clear up."

"Is it needful?" I protested gently. "What could be gained by it? I would not willingly cause you any further distress."

"It *is* needful," she urged. "Either you are the strangest mixture of heroism and utter black villainy ever born, or else you are a brave, honorable gentleman whom my father and I have fearfully affronted, and who has repaid our insults by saving from death one who is dear to us. Which are you, *monsieur?*"

"Shall we say I'm a little of both, and not too much of either?" I suggested lightly, seeking with all my might to combat the fierce heart-longings wherewith her appealing eyes filled me. "Believe what you will. Only be certain of one thing: While I can be nothing to you henceforth, or you to me, yet I stand ready to serve you to the end of my life. To stand between you and danger with all the puny power that in me lies. May I take you back, now to. M. de Périer?"

"No!" she insisted, her lovely eyes swimming with unshed tears. "I must know the truth. I can't believe you guilty, no matter how strong the proofs are. Something tells me you are innocent of every vile charge we brought against you. That—"

"It seems almost a pity, *mademoiselle*," I answered miserably, "that that same intuition did not come to your aid yesterday when you and your father—"

"It did!" she sobbed. "It *did*. In my heart I kept saying, 'It is not true!' even when reason pointed all the other way. Even when you yourself admitted you had been to the convent, and—"

"I went to the convent to secure your release," said I.

"You did?" she exclaimed in amazement. "Then, why didn't you tell us? Why—"

"Because at that time I was mad enough to dream of winning your love, and did not care to bias your mind with a weight of gratitude. While now—"

"Now?" she asked, her voice sinking to a whisper.

"Now," I resumed harshly, to hide the hopeless affection that was crying for utterance, "I have no longer hope for love, nor desire for gratitude."

She shrank back. It was as though I had sworn at her.

"Since you wish the truth, *mademoiselle*," I added, refusing to note her pain, and speaking fast to crush down my own grief, "I will tell it to you, and you may believe as much or as little of it as you choose to."

Hurriedly I outlined my visit to the convent, my talk with the abbess, and her unexpected compliance.

Elise listened in wide-eyed wonder to the well-nigh incredible tale. Yet I saw she believed. And that knowledge—even though she was now lost forever to me—gave me a certain morbid satisfaction.

"This man—this Frenchman who impersonated you?" she said when I had finished. "Who is he? Have you—"

"Who is he?" echoed De Périer, who, unobserved, had crossed to where we stood and had heard the greater part of my recital. "He is a myth! And a rather clumsily constructed one. I—"

"Permit me to correct you, Citizen Périer," interposed a suave voice at the old man's elbow. "He is not a myth, but quite solid flesh. Permit me to present him to you."

We all three looked around in surprise. Before us, bowing, debonair, and handsome as ever, stood Etienne de Chevreuse.

CHAPTER XVIII.
Tangled Trails.

DE Périer glanced in cold rebuke upon the foppishly dressed stranger who thus broke in on our talk. But this expression suddenly changed to wonder—a look that was reflected from Elise's face.

Then I saw the girl's eyes lighten from amaze to gladness, and the sight thrilled me. Already she had believed. Now, with woman's adorable lack of logic, she deemed her faith vindicated.

"You are—" began De. Périer.

"Either Jack Braith," replied my cousin, "or—if you prefer old-world and discarded titles—Etienne de Chevreuse."

Elise started violently. Even De Périer was plainly astonished.

"You are, then, my second cousin, *m'sieu?*" began Elise.

"Pardon," I interposed, "but it is *I* who have the ill fortune to be this—person's—'second cousin.'"

"You?" exclaimed De Périer. "Then, you must be—"

"It seems," observed Etienne amusedly, "that we are all in more or less of a tangle. Perhaps you will permit me to straighten matters out? The Conciergerie has the undeserved honor of sheltering, at the present moment, all three—the three only—direct descendants of the ancient house of Chevreuse."

"I don't understand," said I, forgetting my detestation for the fellow in my interest in his cryptic words.

"There are many things your Yankee brain has not the wit to grasp, my worthy cousin," returned Etienne. "For—"

"Yet it has smashed your promising career," I answered in the same mocking vein. "And that was more or less of an achievement for even a 'Yankee brain.'"

"We can come back to that later," he replied with a shrug. "As I understand it, we are at present on the theme of genealogy. Let me expound in true heraldic fashion."

He dropped into the dry, precise manner of a pedagogue and, with evident relish of his role, went on:

"M. le Vicomte de Chevreuse, of apoplectic memory—he of Louis Quinze's youthful days—had four children. The eldest succeeded, naturally, to the title on his father's death. He was the great-uncle who lacked the wit to appreciate my own undeniable charms. He had no children. His wealth and name would thus have gone to his next younger brother. That brother, however, had emigrated to America in early youth, and changed his name there to Braith, and was dead. He," addressing the perplexed De Périer, "was the grandfather of Mr. Jack Braith—American."

"Is it true?" cried Elise, looking at me, her great eyes alight.

"It chances to be," I answered dryly. "But—"

"But we thought—we always supposed that branch of the family was extinct. We—"

"Permit me," intervened Etienne. "The 'Louis Quinze' *vicomte's* fourth and youngest child—his third son—was my grandfather. Hence, but for my young American friend—and the revolution—the title of Vicomte de Chevreuse would have descended direct to *me*."

"The estates of Chevreuse—" broke in De Périer hotly.

"I said nothing of the estates, sir," corrected Etienne. "I spoke only of the title. The older *vicomte's* third child was a daughter. By French law, she and her children could not, of course, inherit a title. But the estates—again, but for this inconvenient Mr. Jack Braith and the rev-olution—would have descended to this daughter and her heirs. Of whom," he added, turning to me, "Mlle. Elise de Périer—her daugh-ter's only daughter—is the sole survivor. Now, do you begin to see why I wanted either to marry her or get her out of the way?"

Yes, I saw clearly enough. With my own claim out of the road, and Elise's disposed of, Etienne's path would have been free. For the hun-dredth time, I marveled at the fellow's devilish ingenuity and fixed-ness of purpose.

"I expected little trouble from you, as you know," resumed Etienne in that same nonchalant manner; "but our secret-service men in the Barbados brought word that M. de Périer, at news of our great-uncle's death, was preparing to sail with Mlle. Elise to France, aboard one of his own ships, to claim her heritage. That was quite another matter, and one I wished to put an instant stop to. So I took a brief cruise aboard the privateer craft of a very good friend of mine who chanced to stand somewhat in need of my kind offices with Robespierre. We—"

"It was *you?*" panted Elise. "You were the man in the mask? The—"

"The man in the mask; the man at the convent; the man who held the game in his own hands, but for this blundering Yankee," admitted Etienne, a tinge of bitterness underlying his lightness of manner. "My dear M. De Périer," he went on, "I beg you will not clench your fist and glower at me like that. Take the fortunes of war as a French noble should."

"Quite so, M. de Périer," I caught Etienne up in like strain. "The punishment of the man in the mask chaced to be placed in my hands. And that punishment is quite as complete as even you could wish. Not a death-blow from a gentleman's sword, as I at one time hoped to make it, but even more certain."

And I thereupon told all that had taken place in Robespierre's rooms that morning. With a sort of unworthy pride, I related the whole tale.

De Périer and his daughter listened in open-mouthed amazement, Etienne with absolutely no expression on his handsome, mask-like face. He did not even betray interest when I finished by saying:

"And Robespierre had heard our conversation from beginning to end. On the strength of it, M. Etienne is in as hopeless a case as any of us. You did not know that part of the story, did you?" I sneered, glancing at him.

"Oh, yes!" he said wearily. "I knew it before noon. I had a message sent to Robespierre, telling him where I was, and how I chanced to be brought here. He sent me back a note—a wonderpiece of incorruptibility, and it told me."

That was all. This man who, when arrested by mistake, had screamed and cursed, was as calm, now that his game was definitely lost and his fate settled, as though in a drawing-room instead of the antechamber of death.

Once more I realized keenly the splendid, gay courage that animated the doomed French aristocrat. There was something sublime about it. Almost, in this case, it blinded me to the crimes of Etienne de Chevreuse.

For he had played for glittering stakes. Played for them with an audacity and disregard of peril that I never had seen paralleled. And, having failed, he was yet light-hearted and seemingly free from ill-feeling toward any of us who had helped compass his ruin.

Yet his attitude was that of most prisoners who loafed about the great room. Some were chatting, others reading or writing. But all, save some half-score or more of the *bourgeois* element, were serenely calm. One would have thought himself in the assembly room of a great hotel.

If one must die, thought I, it was some satisfaction to leave the world in so gallant a company. Stained with the sins of centuries of pride and oppression, they none the less bore themselves—men and women alike—as heroes. At the lower end of the room, leading to the street, ran a grating. On the opposite of this were gathered a group of riffraff, indulging in their customary daily sport of mocking and reviling their captive foes. But the prisoners heeded their taunts and insults no more than would a forest stag the buzzing of so many flies.

De Périer, seeing himself unable to chastise Etienne, had turned his back upon him and walked away. Etienne, the same half smile on his lips, followed, to continue the torment. Elise and I were left standing alone.

"So this was your holy 'mission' to France?" I asked. "Was it not a trifle more financial than sacred?"

"No," she answered, unmoved by my words. "It was worthy, and we would do it again if we might. The mere money we did not crave, though we are not rich. But one who is dear to us was ruined by the revolution. Stripped of his estates and his name, he was in hiding, with a price upon his head."

"M. de Grieux?"

"Yes," she returned, surprised at my guess. "This wealth would raise him from poverty, would restore to him what he lost by his loyalty to the king. It was the noblest use to which the fortune—"

"But why sacrifice your own riches to—"

"He is very, very dear to me. And then, he—"

"I understand. Pardon me. I forgot, for the moment."

"There is something else," she added. "Something I want to tell you in regard to that miserable heritage. The morning after I was released from the convent my father and I drove to see the Chevreuse advocate. One of his clerks told us M. Laurier was at that moment engaged in his inner office with 'M. Jack Braith,' a claimant for the estate. So we came away. My father thought you had tried to get me imprisoned so you could claim our fortune. That you—"

"So this explains his true reason for refusing to believe me?" I cried. "I begin to understand. And you did not know I was claimant for the—"

"No. How should I? My father, thinking you were powerful in the government because you had presumably been able to have me sent to the convent, imagined you were using that same power to secure my fortune. Forgive him. He is an old man, and his love for me—"

"But it is strange Laurier never told me—"

"He wrote us there was another claimant, but—"

"Why, that's what the secretive old fool wrote me!" I broke in. "And I crossed to France quite prepared to fight a duel with this mysterious 'claimant.' And it was *you?* Oh, what a muddle!"

"At all events," said she sadly, "we need trouble no longer about it, any of us. The fortune, belonging to 'traitors, stands forfeit to the Republic of France.' But, oh, are you sure you forgive my father and myself for the abominable way we both—"

"Don't," I begged, unable to endure her contrition. "That's all past and gone, like everything else. And the sooner the wretched farce is played out the better I shall be suited."

"You are not afraid to die?" she asked timidly.

"No. It is not bravery. But I have nothing left that is worth while. It is different with you, *mademoiselle,*" I added, forgetting my own hopeless misery for the moment in her great sorrow. "You have everything to live for. And," I went on, "it is perhaps even harder for the Comte de Grieux. On the very eve of his wedding—"

"Is it not?" she exclaimed eagerly. "How you learned about the wedding I don't know. It was largely for that, as well as to restore him to fortune, that we came to France. He couldn't very well have got married if we hadn't, you know."

"No," I agreed, with an angry lack of sympathy for the poor little jest; "naturally he couldn't. Perhaps his lot is harder than mine, after all. For he must live on, remembering always what he might have won. While soon *I* shall fall asleep and forget the bitter lack of what could *never* have been mine. Yes, his is the harder lot. Heaven help him!"

Her eyes were full of tears. Impulsively she laid her soft hand on mine. Then came an interruption. And luckily did it come.

For, in another instant, the armor of outward cold indifference wherewith I had encased my heart must have burst asunder beneath the tender, infinitely compelling spell she cast upon me.

As I have said, the *sans culottes* and other ruffians had been clamoring at us from the free side of the grating. The afternoon was merging into night, and one by one our patriotic tormentors had slipped away, in search of supper or more lively sport than aristocrat baiting.

One tall fellow, however, had held his place, and had never for an instant ceased to roar half inarticulate curses at us. Now his voice rang out like a panther's cry.

"*A bas!*" it bellowed. "*A bas! Jack Braith, you young numskull, come over here! A bas! A—*"

I fairly ran to the bars. There stood the unkempt rowdy, a bright new *sans culotte* cap jammed down rakishly over one eye, his leathery face smudged with dirt. I looked a second time in crass bewilderment, then gasped:

"Shadrach Bemis!"

CHAPTER XIX.
A Voice in the Darkness.

"YES," he chuckled, "same old Shadrach Bemis. An' on the right side of the bars, as usual. But, son, what on airth are *you* doin' in there? When I woke up an' couldn't find you, I guessed you'd run into trouble. So I've been making the rounds of the jails an'—"

"But those clothes—"

"Want me collectin' a crowd after me, like I always do when I go out? Not me. I wasn't advertisin' my business that way. So I—"

"It's good-by, I'm afraid, old friend," I said. "This time there's no other door to the trap. I'm—"

"Quit that!" he ordered sharply, winking very fast. "Now, tell me all about it. An' tell me quick, before those guards happen to stroll past an' lock me up fer swappin' lies with a wicked pris'ner."

I told him all. He listened without comment. But when I came to the story of my pseudo-torture of Robespierre, his lean face took on a look of infantile delight, and he rubbed his hands together as might a proud teacher whose stupidest pupil has at length evinced signs of intelligence. Yet he did not interrupt.

At the conclusion of my narrative he seemed about to speak. But the clank of a returning *gendarme's* saber on the stones warned us that the interview could not safely be prolonged.

"*A bas!*" bawled Shadrach, shaking the barred gate furiously in his effort to get at me.

The officer, noting his apparent rage, paused to laugh at the lanky *sans culotte's* attempt to seize me. Then, noting Shadrach's growing savagery, he motioned the sham ruffian to move away from the gate.

Bemis, with a farewell shake of the fist at me, slunk off.

"You see how true citizens regard you aristocrats," remarked the *gendarme,* glancing contemptuously at my clothes.

A hot retort was on my lips, but I choked it back.

"How long shall we have to wait here before we come to trial?" I asked him.

"You won't wait long," he scoffed. "Citizen Fouquier-Tinville finished up with the cases at La Force to-day. Tomorrow morning, at dawn—or maybe earlier—he begins on the Conciergerie. Last time there were more 'trial prisoners' here than now, and he finished by afternoon. Before to-morrow night you'll have a fine chance to observe the architecture of the 'condemned side.' Sweet dreams!"

And he sauntered away, grinning at his own subtle wit.

I returned slowly to the farther recesses of the great room. Well! The delay was not to be so long as I had feared. To-morrow—perhaps by daylight—Robespierre's vengeance would have begun.

I was sorely tempted to go to Elise, to stay close by her side on this last evening, to carry to my mock trial and condemnation the memory of her dear face and words. But I fought back the impulse.

To what effect should I do this thing? She loved another man. Her words would be for me, but her thoughts—her heart—would be with the absent De Grieux. I could not bear this.

Better far to keep with me her look of gratitude, of gentle remorse—the light, tender touch of her white fingers on mine. These would accompany me through the dark hours far better than could human society.

I wished, though, I had had a chance to grip Shadrach Bemis's brave old hand before the officer had come up. But perhaps I should catch another glimpse of him at my trial, or possibly on my way to the scaffold. I knew I could not speak with him again. For the condemned were guarded far more closely than the trial prisoners.

I made my way to a dark alcove of the exercise-room, near the corridor branching off into the cells; and there I threw myself down on a stone bench, alone with my bitter thoughts.

I sat there long and silent, trying with closed eyes to bring to mind Elise's eyes as she had turned them on me when I so nearly lost my carefully schooled self-control.

At last, in the gloom, close beside me, I heard a stifled sob. I turned hastily. A little girl—scarce past early childhood—was crouched on the farther end of the bench. She was crying softly to herself, her face in her hands. Instinctively, I moved toward her.

"Can I be of help, *mademoiselle?*" I asked.

She looked up, frightened, and peered at me through the gloom.

"I—I am sorry I am not brave," she whispered. "But it is so hard—in the dark—and—oh, I *don't* want to die. I don't *want* to!" her voice rising to a wail.

"Poor, *poor* little girl!" I muttered, a lump in my throat. "Perhaps you will be acquitted. Perhaps—"

"I didn't mean to complain," she said, fighting back her tears. "But—you see, I'm not very old. And it is so dark—so lonely—"

"I know—I know!" I comforted her. "Let me stay beside you here for a while. I won't disturb you, and it may not be so lonesome when you know somebody is close by who is sorry for you and who wants to help you."

Her hand—cold and trembling—stole into mine, and I held it. She was such a child! I wanted to take her in my arms and soothe her to sleep—to make her forget for a time the horrors in store for her.

Consoled by my hand-grasp, she drew nearer to me.

"Are you afraid, too?" she asked.

"Not very," I answered. "I think it will come out right for you."

I slipped an arm around her and drew her to me. Her head nestled against my shoulder.

"Try to sleep, if you can," I suggested. "I will wake you when they come to put us in our—our rooms—for the night. If you can get a little rest, you'll feel better."

We sat silent for a space. Then—

"Tell me a story," she said drowsily. "Maybe if you talk very slowly it will put me to sleep."

"Once upon a time—" I began in obedience.

"Not that kind of a story, please," she objected. "I think I am too old for those. I'm nearly thirteen. Tell me about some place—where you live, for instance—and speak very slowly. That is how my father used to put me to sleep when—" Her voice shook ever so little, and she ended more quickly: "Before he went away."

"I live in a country called America," I began slowly and monotonously. "In the mountains. The place I live in is called Pompton. There is a lake at the foot of the lawn below my house, and there are woods all about the house, and the wind in the trees sings me to sleep every night. And all around the lake there are mountains—low, green, gentle mountains—that seem to watch over us and to shut us in from all the noise and danger of the loud world outside.

"And at night the big white stars shine down on our little valley as if they loved it. I think they do. And at sunset—the sun sets about a mile from our house, just across the lake—at sunset there is a golden light that turns the lake to molten fire and—are you sleepy yet?"

She roused herself with a slight start.

"I—I was dreaming," she murmured disconnectedly. "I was dreaming about—a—nice lion."

"I'm sorry I—"

"It was a spotted lion," she went on, with drowsy accuracy of detail. "It—"

"Go to sleep again," I suggested, smothering a smile, "and maybe this time he will let you pat him."

But my words roused her. She sat up, drawing her head away from my shoulder.

"I'm not a baby," she said with dignity. "I don't like to be talked to as if I was, please. I'm nearly grown. I was to have been a bridesmaid—not a flower-girl—a bridesmaid at my sister's wedding this week. So you see I—"

"I didn't mean to be silly," I answered with contrition. "I'm sorry. So you were to be a bridesmaid?"

"At my sister's wedding. She was to marry Comte Maurice de Grieux."

"*Who?*" I cried, startling the child by my vehemence.

"Comte de Grieux," she repeated. "But why are—"

"Listen, dear," I said. "Are you *quite* sure it was Comte Maurice de Grieux?"

"Why, of course I am. What a question!"

I sank back, dazed. The man Elise was to have wedded!

"What is your sister's name?" I queried, bewildered.

"Sophie de la Roye. I am Daphne de la Roye."

And on such a man had Elise lavished the love for which I would have bartered my soul! A man who came by stealth to see her—embraced her—was willing to profit by her fortune—and all the time was planning to marry another!

I had had his worthless life at my mercy—and I had spared it!

"Is that you, M. Braith?" asked some one who had approached the bench unseen by me.

It was Elise de Périer. All at once a wild fear sprang into my brain. She must not know! Let her go to death believing her lover true! Not die a double death by knowing him false!

I dreaded lest by unguarded word little Daphne should let fall some hint of the vile secret in her presence.

So, as Elise peered doubtfully at me in the shadows, I shrank farther back upon my bench and rasped out jeeringly:

"Not the M. Braith you seek, my fair cousin. But a far better man—Etienne de Chevreuse, to wit. At your service."

Elise turned away with an involuntary gesture of contempt that cut me to the heart. In that dim light the deception had been ridiculously easy.

Yet it had banished my one sweet memory. Instead of her handclasp, I must now recall henceforth her last motion—one of loathing.

Through the long, dark night of summer I lay sleepless. The great prison was never silent. Now I would hear a sigh or moan from some slumbering captive, now the slouching step of a guard.

Midnight rang out from a distant city clock. Then one, two, three, and four. It must be growing light outside. Yet in my cell all was dark.

We were not locked in at night, as were the condemned prisoners, and I meditated, rising and going forth into the better air of the exercise-room.

A sleepy guard, somewhere outside, was humming the hateful "Marseillaise." Carts were rumbling past. The city was beginning to awaken.

Then I heard a sentry's challenge. The barred outer gate of the exercise-room clanged open. A voice bellowed through the gloom:

"The Citizen and Citizeness Périer! Citizen Jack Braith!"

So the trials were already beginning! And we three were the first to be summoned forth. I felt a little glow of pleasure as I hurried out in response to the call. Elise and I, by lucky chance, were to go to our fate side by side.

It was a ray of light before the last great darkness, and I thanked God for it.

Into the gray daylight of the exercise-room I hastened. I had scarcely arrived there when Elise and her father joined me.

No word was spoken; but Elise and I somehow found each other's hands, and thus we walked down the long room toward the waiting jailer.

The turnkey was examining some papers. We halted until he should be ready to pass us out to the carts that were to bear us to our trial.

Elise looked through a grimy window at the pale sky beyond.

"This was to have been Maurice de Grieux's wedding-day," she murmured, half to herself. "Poor Sophie!"

"What?" I exclaimed in genuine amazement.

"I didn't know I had spoken," she said in confusion. "Sophie de la Roye, a girlhood friend of mine, was to have married—"

"But it was *you!*" I cried—"you to whom he was betrothed. You said—"

"*I?*" she repeated in astonishment. "Why, Maurice de Grieux is my half-brother—the son of my mother's first husband. Marry him? Why—"

"Elise!" I insisted, my brain awhirl. "Do you mean to say—"

"He would not marry Sophie while he was penniless. (My mother made *me* her heiress, you know, for Maurice inherited a title and a good fortune from his father.) So I was going to share the Chevreuse inheritance with—"

"Silence, there!" ordered a guard officer. "March!"

"I love you, Elise," I whispered madly, regardless of the gruff command. "I *love* you! *I love you!*"

Our eyes met. And—then our lips.

"Hold on!" called a voice from behind, and Etienne ran across the hall from the cells, drawing on his coat. "I am the 'Braith' called for in the guard's list. I—"

He got no further. As he strove to push past me and out through the door, I caught him by the throat and hurled him back into the room.

No man was now going to rob me of these few last hours of life by the side of the woman I had won—not if the whole French republic sought to part us.

Recovering, Etienne whipped from his sleeve a short knife he had managed somehow to secrete there, and flew at me like a wild beast.

His knife-blade, as I shifted deftly to avoid it, laid open my coat and shirt from shoulder to wrist, raising an ugly graze on my arm.

But, even as he stabbed, my fist shot out. It caught him on the point of the jaw, and he collapsed, stunned and bleeding, on the stone pavement.

"There seems some competition as to who shall first be honored with presentation to the gentle Fouquier-Tinville," laughed the officer, unmoved by the brief battle. "Pass out, you three!"

Out into the chill of early dawn we walked, De Périer ahead. I followed, my right arm pressing Elise close to my side. Never did man go to his bridal with more gloriously joyous heart than I to my probable death.

Whatever might come now, Elise was mine—all mine—here and beyond the grave. What mattered the trial-room, or even the guillotine?

We passed, with our guards, across the courtyard to the outer office of the prison. There an official met us, glanced us over, made an entry in his desk-ledger, and curtly motioned us to the street without. A *gendarme* opened the door for us. We glanced at each other in wonder. This was strange procedure for trial prisoners to undergo.

In the roadway just outside stood a closed traveling carriage, its top piled high with luggage. Out of its capacious depths dived Shadrach Bemis.

By sheer force, and without a word in response to my amazed questions, he hustled us inside the vehicle, nodded to the driver, then sprang in after us, and closed the door. Off we went up the ill-paved street at a tremendous pace, the clumsy carriage swaying perilously from side to side.

"What—what does it all mean?" I asked in a daze of utter bewilderment.

"It seems," chuckled Shadrach, "that you three Babes in the Woods are bein' kidnaped by old Shad Bemis, an' that this 'ere travelin'-ark is goin' lickety-split fer the nearest frontier. That's all."

"But—"

"Everything's all right. Passports—release—everything. No danger now, so long as we keep movin' fast till we cross the frontier."

"*Shad!*" I yelled, seizing him by the shoulders, "is this a wonder-dream or—"

"It's your own trick, son," he retorted. "I jest took the—"

"*My* trick?"

"Why, sure," he answered calmly. "That business of knockin' Robbyspeer in the head an' then tyin' him up an' fixin' a little Cherokee fire torture for him—that was all yours. I jest took the liberty of copyin' it. It was better'n anything else I could think up at the minute. The man who'd show the white feather oncet was pretty sartin to show it twice. That's how I figgered."

"You mean that you—"

"I dropped in on Robbyspeer along about midnight, rigged up in them *sans cullotty* clo'es of mine an' ketches him by the throat before he knowed I wa'n't an earnest patriot with a list of folks to be denounced.

"He'd jest come in when I got there. I'd waited fer him in the street since eight o'clock. He speaks English fine. So I hadn't much bother with him. I guess, too, he seen I meant business. Which I sure did. He yielded like a little babe lamb—by the time the fire began to scorch him. Fer, it was *reel* ile I poured on the sheets. I had a tur'ble time puttin it out."

He grinned as at a pleasant reminiscence. Then he said:

"He's tied up good an' comf'table now, all right, an' no one's li'ble to find him where I've hid him for a day or two. Jest the same, it will be best to hurry.

"You kin bet I didn't do no drinkin' while he made out them papers. An' I told him if there was any legal mistake in makin' out them same dockyments, I'd be back with tinder and steel an' start that comfortin' little blaze a goin.'"

"You actually got the release and passport, and then left him there, Shad?"

"Wa'al, I didn't leave him right off. He'd been a lookin' sort of curious at my head. So I made bold to stay long 'nough to tell him 'bout how I happened to lose my skelp. It's an int'restin' story,' miss," he broke off, addressing my shining-eyed sweetheart. "Maybe you'd care to hear it?"

THE END.

<h1 style="text-align:center">Appendix</h1>
Original source publication

This novel was serialized in four issues of Argosy, from April through July of 1909.

It was not illustrated.

April 1909

Front text:

Author of "From Flag to Flag," "On Glory's Trail," "With Sealed Lips," etc.

A story of Paris in the Reign of Terror, with an American for its central figure and his sweetheart in the grip of powerful foes.

May 1909

Front text:

Author of "From Flag to Flag," "On Glory's Trail," "With Sealed Lips," etc.

A story of Paris in the Reign of Terror, with an American for its central figure and his sweetheart in the grip of powerful foes.

SYNOPSIS OF CHAPTERS PREVIOUSLY PUBLISHED.

ACCOMPANIED by Shadrach Bemis, an old ex-scout and trapper, a young American, Jack Braith, sets sail for France with the purpose of claiming the title and estates of his late granduncle, the Vicomte de Chevreuse. He knows nothing of his French relatives except of his cousin, Etienne de Chevreuse, a wild youth who is said to resemble him greatly in looks. On the voyage he meets and falls in love with Mlle. Elise de Périer, who, with her father, is taken aboard from a sloop wrecked by a privateer after a narrow escape from being kidnaped by the privateer's mysterious captain.

Arrived in Paris, where the Revolution is raging, Braith, Bemis, and De Périer take lodging at a small hotel in the Rue St. Honoré. Two weeks later Mlle. de Périer is abducted by some unknown enemy; but Bemis succeeds in tracking the cab in which she is carried off to a convent in the suburbs. Under the guidance of Bemis, Braith goes to the place and demands to see the abbess. Her words of greeting leave him dumfounded with amazement.

* Began April ARGOSY. Single copies, 10 cents.

June 1909

Front text:

Author of "From Flag to Flag," "On Glory's Trail," "With Sealed Lips," etc.

A story of Paris in the Reign of Terror, with an American for its central figure and his sweetheart in the grip of powerful foes.

SYNOPSIS OF CHAPTERS PREVIOUSLY PUBLISHED.

ACCOMPANIED by Shadrach Bemis, an old ex-scout and trapper, a young American, Jack Braith, sets sail for France with the purpose of claiming the title and estates of his late granduncle, the Vicomte de Chevreuse. He knows nothing of his French relatives except of his cousin, Etienne de Chevreuse, a wild youth who is said to resemble him greatly in looks. On the voyage he meets and falls in love with Mlle. Elise de Périer, who, with her father, is taken aboard from a sloop wrecked by a privateer after a narrow escape from being kidnaped by the privateer's mysterious captain.

Arrived in Paris, where the Revolution is raging, Braith, Bemis, and De Périer take lodging at a small hotel in the Rue St. Honoré. Two weeks later Mlle. de Périer is abducted by some unknown enemy; but Bemis succeeds in tracking the cab in which she is carried off to a convent in the suburbs. Under the guidance of Bemis, Braith goes to the place and demands to see the abbess, who readily accedes to his request to have Elise sent back to her father. But his amazement at this is as nothing to his feelings when M. de Périer charges him with having abducted his daughter, and does not seem to realize that, far from this, it is Braith who has restored her to him. To add to the American's perturbation, a young Frenchman, Maurice de Grieux, suddenly appears on the scene, and seems to be engaged to Elise. He and Jack quarrel, fight; and just as Braith disarms the Frenchman, a company of the Committee of Public Safety appears with a warrant for the arrest of Citizen Grieux. For the sake of Elise, Braith passes himself off for the fellow, and accompanies them to prison, whence he is released through the efforts of Shadrach Bemis, who declares that Jack's French cousin must be at the bottom of the mysteries that are puzzling him. They hurry back to explain matters to the Périers, but Braith is horror-stricken to find their rooms deserted and to learn that father and daughter have been arrested by a squad of the National Guard, charged with harboring a proscribed aristocrat, for which crime the guillotine is the penalty.

Began April ARGOSY. Single copies, 10 cents.

For the following song:

> "Seek not, dear child, by winsome wiles
>   And coquetry, to please;
> Meek diffidence and modesty
>   By far outvalue these.
> Then learn, while young; to—"

...this footnote appeared on the same page:
*This poem was actually written by Robespierre for his landlord's children.

July 1909

Front text:
Author of "From Flag to Flag," "On Glory's Trail," "With Sealed Lips," etc.

A story of Paris in the Reign of Terror, with an American for its central figure and his sweetheart in the grip of powerful foes.

General notes:
A few obvious errors were corrected in this story.

A Bout

With the Man

APT

of Destiny

A Bout with the Man of Destiny

by Albert Payson Terhune

A COMPLETE NOVELETTE

SCP ət̄əT-Bêche
Book V

Silver Creek Press

2021

CHAPTER I.
The Sandy-Haired Man.

I PICKED my way along Pennsylvania Avenue toward the President's house. I say "picked" my way advisedly. There was no sidewalk. The red mud was inches thick, and half-wild pigs were rooting in it at the corners.

Our capital city of Washington was still in its infancy. And an awkward, hideous, wide-sprawling infant it was. The nation's capital, shifting from New York to Philadelphia, had just settled into its permanent home on the Potomac's bank.

The future "City of Magnificent Distances" already possessed the distances, and but little else. Its few houses spread over an unbelievably large area. Its five thousand inhabitants must needs travel far, and over vilely constructed red roads every time they visited one another.

Scattered, half-built houses; miles of dreary expanse of mud and scanty herbage; wide-cut streets, most of which contained no habitation. Pigs, grazing cattle, flocks of wandering geese and chickens, were at large. Truly, the baby city of Washington in 1802 was not a spectacle to strike foreign diplomats with awe.

I came at length to the President's house (they call his abode the "White House" of recent years, I am told) and mounted the steps.

Except for a negro who was clipping grass in the yardway, no one was visible around the executive mansion. No sentry bade me halt. No flunkies demanded my business.

Remembering the "divinity" and formal pomp that hedge the abodes of European potentates, this lack of ceremony surrounding the dwelling of the President of the United States struck me with redoubled force. In no way did the house's outer aspect differ from the domicil of any fairly well-to-do merchant.

And with amusement I bethought me of a newly coined political

phrase that of late had been in all men's mouths: "Jeffersonian simplicity."

As I reached the front door it was not flung open to me. The hour was early, and perhaps that accounted for the absence of ceremony. From somewhere within the house came the strains of a violin, monstrous well played.

I lifted the big bronze door knocker and let it clatter harshly against its brazen plate. The sound of the violin ceased and steps came shuffling down the hall. Presently the door was opened. In the threshold stood a man whom I will describe, by your leave, just as he appeared to me.

Tall, lean, angular. Sandy gray of hair, greenish hazel of eye, sallow and somewhat freckled of complexion. The thin face was strong, alert, preeminently intellectual. At that especial moment, however, it would have been little the worse for a shave.

The man's dress rather than the man himself caught my eye just then. He wore a frayed lounging coat that was more like a short dressing gown and whose surface was spotted with tobacco-ash and snuff.

A shirt, frilled but none too fresh, and loose at the neck; a pair of baggy, shabby trousers, and huge, ill-fitting old carpet slippers completed the down-at-heel costume.

Any respectable linen draper's wife would have been horrified that a servant thus arrayed should answer her door-bell. But this was no servant.

Instead, it was one of the world's greatest men. No less a personage than His Excellency Thomas Jefferson, third President of the United States and framer of our immortal Declaration of Independence.

Perchance you who read this, and who revere the memory of the illustrious Jefferson, may cry out upon me for thus scurrilously depicting your hero, and for telling that he answered his own door-bell in the executive mansion of the United States.

Then let me refer you not only to the news sheet of that period, but to the famous letter of the British minister who, on his first morning call upon Jefferson, was met at the front door by his host, attired exactly as I have described; and who wrote to inquire of the British government whether or not such treatment of a foreign minister plenipotentiary should be regarded as a national affront.

At sight of me the President's alert light eyes brightened, and he held out his hand in cordial welcome.

"Come in, Alwyn!" he exclaimed heartily. "I finished reading your report last night. I expected you a day sooner."

"I crave your excellency's grace for my delay," I answered, as I followed him into his big, book-and-paper littered study. "I was still in the forest garb that I had worn direct from the West; and I dared not present myself at the executive mansion in such rags. So I waited until my civilized clothes could reach me from New York."

The President glanced at my blue broadcloth coat; pearl-gray skin-tight trousers, Hessian boots, and immaculate linen; then at his own slovenly attire. Our eyes met and, moved by some uncontrollable impulse, we bot laughed aloud.

"Our Federalist friends," said he, "would make the obvious retort that in your forest costume you would have been more in keeping with your host's appearance."

He pushed his beloved violin to one side of the desk, and took out a sheaf of official looking papers.

"Alwyn," he said abruptly, as he sorted them over, "I want you to go to France for me."

Now, I had done all the traveling I cared to, and I had planned to settle down to a period of pleasant idleness. Yet, at his order, I found myself athrill with eagerness. For the life of me I could not at first understand why.

Then, of a sudden, I seemed to hear a girl's voice say, somewhere in my memory: "We sail next month for France." And I knew why I was so willing to be gone across seas.

"Livingston is doing what he can," went on President Jefferson. "But he is minister. And that hampers his actions in a network of diplomacy. I have just sent Monroe—former Governor Monroe, of Virginia—over there. But Monroe is a statesman and—"

"And I am not."

"Quite so. The fox may make his way where the lion cannot. You have worked under my supervision for so long that I know what you can do and what you can't. This is one of the things you *can* if any man can."

I bowed. The great Jefferson was not given to flattery. And,

secretly, I was delighted at his praise. Yet I made shift to look formal and unimpressed.

"You know Paris," he continued. "You know French life. You know the etiquette of courts, and, for all our hot temper and over-quick tongue and faculty of fighting, you've a good, shrewd brain of your own. You know what I want?"

"You want the Louisiana territory."

"Get it for me."

It was characteristic of the man that he should so have judged me as to give me this brief command, instead of overwhelming me with a flood of petty details and instructions. In the latter case I should have argued and reasoned—with myself if not with him—and should have felt hampered.

As it was I was thrown on my own resources. And, as ever in such a crisis, I felt my spirit and wits rise to meet the task.

"Here is your commission," he went on. "It appoints you as an envoy extraordinary. It is useful to you only as it proves that our government authorizes your actions and protects you. Here is a rough memorandum of what we can pay, and under what con-ditions. Memorize and then destroy it. Then help Livingston and Monroe to drive the best possible bargain." Once more I seemed to hear Lorraine de la Roche's exclamation: "Oh, you *are* a nation of tradesmen!"

"Theirs will be the authority, the gold lace, the lion's share of the glory," continued Jefferson. "Yours will be the work, the under-ground progress. A division of labor that will suit you better than most men."

"Our only hope is in Napoleon Bonaparte's need for money to press those eternal wars of his," said I. "If he can raise such money elsewhere, he will stick to his original golden plan of establishing a mighty French colonial empire here on the Louisiana tract. It is all a toss-up."

"All life is a toss-up," retorted Jefferson, "but the wise man is he who jostles Destiny's 'tossing' arm at the crucial moment."

"By the way," I remarked, "Pinckney tells me folk in France have begun to nickname Bonaparte the 'Man of Destiny.' They say noth-ing short of Fate could have shot him upward from penury and

obscurity in six short years to the head of the French republic, nor could have made him conquer half of Europe before he was thirty years old."

"Then," suggested the President, "instead of jostling Mmme. Destiny's arm—rude treatment, forsooth, toward a lady!—yours is to be but a contest of wits and persuasion with her henchmen."

"A bout with the Man of Destiny," I amended. "Who could have thought little, spindling, big–headed, shrill-voiced Nabulione would one day bear so mouth-filling a title!"

"You speak as if you had known him," commented Jefferson, in some surprise at my unconsciously reminiscent tone.

"I did," replied I. "Did I never tell your excellency? My friends have joked me about it ever since the Corsican flashed into world fame."

"Joked you about it? I had sooner thought they would deem it a matter for envy. Few dwelling here in America have so much as had a glimpse of him."

"I do not boast of the acquaintance," quoth I. "And, faith, I've scant cause to. Were its details known in France, I doubt me I should be greeted on my landing by a deputation of ardent Bonapartists, who would escort me, as a guard of honor, to—the nearest guillotine."

"You offended him?"

" 'Offended' is scarce the word, your excellency. I *spanked* him."

CHAPTER II.
ANIWAYA.

"WHAT?" gasped Jefferson in crass incredulity.

" 'Twas at Brienne, back in 1782. My father, as you know, had sent me to France to be educated. I went for two terms to the Brienne military school. I was but twelve, but I was big and strong for my age. So, one day, when I found a group of my classmates teasing and pinching an undersized thirteen-year-old youngster, on the playground, I cuffed one or two of them and rescued him.

"Small boys are veritable Indians, when it comes to tormenting an unpopular schoolmate. And this big-headed, spindle–shanked, down-at-heel Corsican was, perhaps, the most unpopular boy in the whole school."

"You are speaking of Napoleon Bonaparte?" asked the amazed President.

"Of Nabulione Buonaparte, as he was known in those days. He hated the rest of us, and took no pains to hide the fact. He sulked in corners by himself. He wrote letters of complaint to the principal and to the French government. He did a score of other things to make himself disliked.

"But he was also a laughing-stock with his queer clothes and his queerer face and figure. He spoke French brokenly, and with a barbarous Italian accent (I am told he still speaks French with a strong accent), and when he was excited his harsh, weak little voice would crack like a peacock's screech. The boys used to tease him for the fun of hearing his voice break; the young beasts!"

"But, if you rescued him from his tormentors," suggested the President, "surely—"

"Surely his admirers would not want to guillotine me? But they would. After I drove off the other boys I tried to explain to Nabulione, as gently as possible, and all for his own good, that he was foolish to antagonize bigger lads, and to bring ridicule on himself by his fits of shrill rage. I thought to help him by such advice. But ere I had half finished my lecture he snatched up a wooden stool and made a highly industrious and praiseworthy effort to brain me. Called me an 'interfering Colonial whelp' and other endearing terms."

"And you?"

"He was too little to thrash, for a he was a year older than I. So I gently took his squirming, writhing skinny body across my knee, and spanked him."

The President broke into a laugh of boyish enjoyment.

"Sacrilege!" he cried. "And you are the man I am sending to cajole him! You of all others! Heaven grant he does not recognize you or remember! Well?" he broke off, as a negro servant in livery hesitated at the library door.

"Yo' excellency," reported the servant, under obvious excitement,

"an Injun—a monst'ous big Injun—is at de do'. Ah tried to sen' him away, but—"

"It must be my servant," said I, embarrassed. "I left him at the tavern. How he came to track me here I cannot guess, except that he follows me everywhere, like a dog."

"An Indian servant?" queried the President. "A novelty, I should say, in a land where negroes are within the means of men of your estate. How came you to engage him?"

"I didn't. He engaged me. Some trappers were torturing him. I suppose I was moved by the same silly meddlesome impulse as when I rescued Nabulione from his tormentors, for I got him away from them. Then the trappers returned the compliment by arresting me. I was shut up for the night in an outhouse in the De la Roche stockade. This Indian tied and gagged the sentry, and helped me escape. He has followed me ever since, out of sheer gratitude."

"Lo, the poor Indian!" quoted Jefferson, from a poem of Master Alexander Pope's with which, luckily, I chanced to be familiar.

"Also," I supplemented, "lo, the poor Indian's luckless master! It seems he considers his life mine since I saved him from torture. And I can't get rid of him. Some of those savages have a most *un*-human idea of gratitude. He even went through the Cherokee ceremony of adoration, much to my disgust, touching my foot with his forehead and casting snow upon his breast, for lack of dust; and intoning a formula I could not at all understand."

"If he speaks no English, how do you and he get on?"

"He speaks a very barbarous French. He picked up the language in Canada."

"He is a Canadian Indian, then?"

"No. A Cherokee. His name is Aniwaya. Cherokee for 'the wolf.' An odd character. If your excellency will pardon me a moment, I'll send him away."

"No. Have him in," insisted Jefferson, and he nodded at the liveried negro.

A moment later, wrapped in his blanket, his gigantic form filling the whole doorway, Aniwaya stalked calmly into the room. His open hand rose in salute to me. He glanced carelessly at the President of the United States, then stood in stony unconcern, awaiting my

orders.

"What are you doing here, Aniwaya?" I asked in French.

"I found the master gone. I feared he might go into ambush. I followed," came the guttural monotone in response.

"But," I urged, "you did not see me leave the tavern, did you?"

He shook his shaven head.

"Then how did you follow?"

He looked puzzled, as might one grown man should another ask him how to read a printed page. I repeated the question.

"The master's left shoe," he said, "has a nail on the heel longer than the other nails."

"And," broke in Jefferson wonderingly, "you tracked him two miles through the mud in that way?"

Aniwaya deigned no reply. He seemed to think the reply self-evident.

"Aniwaya!" I said in some irritation. "Why don't you answer his excellency?"

"No answer needful," he returned. "Any fool knows."

"Aniwaya!" I rebuked, in a horror only a little assuaged by Jefferson's ready laugh. "This is my sachem—the Great White Father."

I expected to see Aniwaya abase himself in lowly reverence to the President as I thus melodramatically made known our host's identity.

Instead, he merely glanced at Jefferson in the same imperturbable fashion as he might have noticed an oddly shaped tree or boulder pointed out to him by me. Then he grunted and looked out of the window once more.

Jefferson was great enough to enjoy the rebuff hugely. He turned on the Indian and added to my introduction:

"And I am also your master's warm friend and well-wisher, Aniwaya."

Up went the red giant's hand in the quick "friendly sign" toward the man who had just honored his master by naming him his friend.

"Perhaps," I suggested gravely in English, "your excellency would care to take him into your service? Since I am to sail at once for France I shall have no further use for him."

"Thank you, no," smiled Jefferson. "But I wonder how he will

take the news of your departure? Tell him."

"Aniwaya," said I in French, "within seven days I cross the great water to the other side of the world."

"I am ready," stonily answered Aniwaya, without changing a muscle of his copper face at the momentous tidings.

"Ready?" I echoed in dismay. "But *you* can't go, man!"

"Where the master goes," he answered quietly.

I looked at Jefferson in despair, only to meet a twinkle of merriment from the hazel-green eyes.

"You see your fate, Alwyn," said the President solemnly. "To the grave you are to be dogged by a giant red shadow. If you leave him at the dock he is quite capable of swimming after you."

"But what am I to do?"

"Take him along, of course. The ownership of such a servant will make you the most talked-of man in Paris. It will stamp you at once as a celebrity. It will go far toward making you popular and famous. Just as Napoleon Bonaparte's Egyptian Mameluke, Rustum, is said to add to his august master's fame.

"Seriously, I advise you to take him. Such novelties mean much to the French. And it may well happen, lad, that ere you win your way back to America you may more than once have need of a loyal heart and a strong arm to stand 'twixt you and trouble. Take him."

"Aniwaya," I said in French, turning to the savage, "I am going to take you across the world with me."

"I know," he answered, as though the matter had long since been settled.

"We go to dangers," I added, purposely making the worst of it; "perhaps to death. In a far land—far from your own people."

"I am ready," replied Aniwaya simply and with no faintest show of interest.

CHAPTER III.
THE FIRST CONSUL.

THE huge assembly salon of the Tuileries was a scene worthy of a

mask ball as Launay and I entered. Men in gaudy uniforms that would have put Joseph's coat of many colors to the blush elbowed civilians whose costumes were scarce less garish.

The era of somber-hued dress for men was approaching. And here in Paris the "Incroyables" were battling against its advent, even as autumn leaves flaunt a gallant red-and-gold defiance to the numbing approach of winter.

Coats of green, of scarlet, of maroon, of peach color, of old gold—in fact, of every conceivable hue and shade—mingled with the scarce-gayer uniforms.

As for the women—their garb beggared all description. Horrifying décolletée, their directoire gowns were absurdly high of waist and narrow of skirt. Their style was modeled on the ancient Greek. (But I gravely doubt if Greece would have recognized its own descendant.)

It was the fad in post-revolutionary France to shape actions, speech, dress, and names upon classical models, as evinced, for instance, by the title of "Consul." And, while of late the hobby had largely died out, it still obtained in feminine styles.

Launay and I stood for a moment on the threshold while those just in front of us were announced. And we occupied the time in surveying the kaleidoscope of color and motion that shifted and blazed before us. It was the evening of the first consul's monthly levee. And it was but the second of these affairs that I had attended since my arrival in France.

I had worked hard during the past six weeks, as had we all. And at times success had seemed very near, while at others our mighty ventures seemed utterly hopeless. Diplomacy, especially in France of that day, was an intricate and heart-sickening game.

"M. le Marechal Lefebvre. Mme. la Marechale Lefebvre!" intoned a flunky as a stocky uniformed man and his florid, rather overdressed wife passed into the salon just ahead of us.

"See there!" whispered Launay in my ear, indicating the woman with an imperceptible nod. "She is a celebrity just now. They've nicknamed her 'Mme. Sans-Gene' because she dares to smash etiquette and tact, like so many Sevres cups and to speak her mind on all occasions. She was a laundress and Lefebvre a sergeant when they were married. She—"

"M. le Colonel Alwyn of the United States Embassy!" intoned the flunky, "M. Launay of the United States Embassy!"

In our immediate vicinity as we entered there was a slight stir. And many pairs of eyes were turned upon me in right flattering interest. But at once the interest faded and the heads were turned away again, while I heard Mme. Lefebvre say loudly and pettishly:

"Pshaw! He has left his *grande sauvage* at home!"

It was highly mortifying to be of interest only because of one's red servant. Yet I recognized now, as never before, the wisdom which underlay President Jefferson's whimsical command that I take Aniwaya to France with me. The giant Indian had assuredly gone far to make me a celebrity—by reflected glory.

Launay and I found ourselves confronting two people—a man and a woman—who stood side by side beneath a canopy, with a crowd of officials behind them. We bowed low as a second flunky announced our names when we moved into the open space directly in front of Napoleon Bonaparte (First Consul and virtual dictator of France) and Mme. Josephine, the gay creole widow he had married.

The consul jerkily returned our bow. Mme. Josephine, on impulse, held out her hand to me.

"Your *grande sauvage?*" she queried. "Have you brought him along?"

"No, Mme. la Generale," I answered respectfully. "Yet if it causes you disappointment I am desolated at my neglect."

"I *am* disappointed," she laughed.

"Nonsense!" snapped the consul, his French strongly tinged with Italian accent. "Dogs and servants belong in kennel and kitchen, not in a salon. Eh, Murat?"

A dashing officer in cavalry uniform who stood just behind Bonaparte colored redly at the seemingly innocent query. And good cause had he to feel the sting.

For, high as Murat had risen—and was yet to rise—on fame's ladder, Bonaparte never let him wholly forget that the cavalry chief's father had once been a poor innkeeper and that Murat himself had begun life as a tavern waiter and dishwasher. Bonaparte had ever a playful way of saying things that touched his friends on the raw.

The first consul at this time was in his thirty-fourth year. A hun-

dred people here in America had asked me to describe him. I cannot do so. Nor can any one else. Read what his various chroniclers write of his aspect and you will understand my reticence.

One says he was undersized; another that he was slightly above medium height. One that he had bad teeth and thin, yellowish hair; another that his teeth were dazzling and his hair thick and dark. One that his face was pasty and his eyes a pale blue; another that his eyes were deep gray, almost black, and his face swarthy.

Read the diametrically contradicting descriptions given by Bourrienne, Las Casas, Talleyrand, and others who recorded their impressions.

Look at the various and varying portraits in the Louvre and at Versailles. Then blame me, if you can, for refusing to enter the lists of portrayal.

Even were I to try to depict him in mere words my description would in no way tally with your own idea of him. Nor would your notion agree with another man's.

For each person has his own mental picture of Napoleon Bonaparte—a picture that will not fade and cannot be altered. It is enough for me to say he had the hardest eyes, the most beautiful mouth, and the most discordant voice of any mortal I ever met. On this night he wore the bottle-green, white satin-faced dress uniform of a general of the French Republic.

Josephine—former widow of the guillotined scoundrel, the Vicomte de Beauharnais—is far easier to picture. She was short, slender, vivacious, a brunette, with decaying, blackened teeth, somewhat irregular features, and yet with a nameless charm and graciousness that enabled one to understand how Bonaparte six years earlier had gone temporarily mad over the already fading loveliness of this fickle, shallow-brained woman, so much older than himself.

She was in pale green silk. And for the occasion the whole salon was hung and decorated in pale green, a detail that was about to be impressed right strikingly upon my notice, for even as Launay and I passed on, the flunky at the door announced:

"Mme. la Generale Leclerc!"

This time there was a veritable stir in the room. Pauline Leclerc— later the Princess Borghese and model for the famed Venas Victrix

statue—was Napoleon's best-loved sister.

But between her and Josephine raged a feud as bitter as ever Corsica or our own Kentucky mountains had produced. They hated each other as bitterly as only two ambitious and not overgood or overintelligent women can.

Whenever they met there was more or less certain to be a clash better fitted to Billingsgate circles than to a court that aped the virtues of Greece and the dignities of the old French monarchy.

Mme. Pauline swept into the salon with the air of a stage queen. A lane was opened for her by the other guests—less, it seemed to me, through respect than from a street crowd's impulse to clear away all obstacles to an impending fight.

Pauline was clad in a robe of vivid blue satin, and a jeweled bandeau of the same material and color bound her glorious hair. She looked like a goddess.

But, as she advanced farther into the room, even my untrained eye could see that her bright blue gown was horribly out of accord with the soft green hangings and with Josephine's green dress. It was a color crime in such surroundings, and it changed Pauline's classic beauty into momentary ugliness.

She reached the canopy where Bonaparte and his wife stood before giving any special note to her surroundings. Then as the consul, with one of the rare smiles that so beautified his hard face, took a step forward to greet his best-loved sister, Pauline halted.

In a single glance she grasped the color keynote of the place. Then her face went crimson and her eyes blazed. Halting, she glared for an instant in dumb fury at Josephine, then wheeled upon her brother.

"She *knew* it!" shrilled Pauline in a rage-shaken voice that filled the suddenly silent room. "She *knew* I was to wear blue. I wore it because this is the blue salon. And she changed the hangings to humiliate me! To humiliate *me,* the sister of Napoleon Bonaparte, the wife of General Leclerc! The creole minx! I—"

"Pauline!" exclaimed Bonaparte.

And in his harsh, high voice there was all at once an indefinable something that made me understand how daredevil fire-eaters could cringe like whipped curs under his explosions of rage.

He said no more. But Pauline Leclerc checked her tirade as

though a hand had been clapped across her pretty mouth. She looked doubtfully about her; then, with a choked little sob, wheeled and made her way blindly from the room.

Truly, I was in strange quarters. Was there ever, since the birth of time, such a court as this? A court of world-famed notables, the bulk of whom had begun life as laundresses, waiters, plowboys, ill-paid tradesmen, *et cetera,* and who now mingled the manners of the tavern with a preternaturally lofty dignity borrowed from the classics!

I recalled the stately, infinitely graceful courtiers of the old monarchy, and I winced as at a discord in music.

There was a momentary lull in the arrival of guests. Launay and I started to make our way onward toward the refreshment buffet.

"Shades of the *ancien régime!*" whispered Launay. "Bonaparte looks as though he had lost a battle. He hates the coarseness that he cannot prevent. He would give up half his conquests to persuade some of the old-time aristocracy to attend these awful functions and to raise the tone of them. But the aristocracy shun him as a plebeian upstart. Not one of them will come near the Tuileries."

As if to contradict the young attaché's words, the flunky at the door intoned pompously: "M. le Sieur de la Roche! Mlle. de la Roche!"

My heart gave a great jump. I turned breathlessly to face the door. Then an audible snicker ran through the salon.

CHAPTER IV.
WHEREIN I MEET AN OLD FRIEND.

INTO the room strode a figure taken bodily out of the old court days whose passage I had just been deploring. I looked twice ere I recognized my one-time captor and wilderness judge in the portly Louis XVI courtier who advanced so mincingly into that roomful of self-made celebrities.

The Sieur de la Roche wore a much-too-tight suit of peachblow satin, with the wide-skirted coat, small clothes, silken hose, and dia-

mond buckles of ten years back.

His black, shaggy hair was covered by an enormous white periwig. A silver-hilted court-rapier hung at his side. His florid face was adorned with black, star-shaped beauty spots. The whole effect was just a little like that of a dancing bear in ruffled petticoats. At his side moved Lorraine, her free, forest walk sorely impeded by her scant, white directoire gown, her air of outdoor freedom cramped by her artificial surroundings.

Yet her costume was of the present mode. And her dark beauty and lithe grace far more than atoned for her unfamiliarity with such clothes and environments.

The titter that greeted her father's advent changed, so far as the men present were concerned, to a stare of real admiration at the daughter. "Jove!" muttered Launay under his breath. "A forest goddess! And escorted by a satyr!"

"No," I answered. "The loveliest girl I have ever known, forced to accompany an old fool who does not know he is an anachronism."

"You know them?" he asked in wonder.

"Only well enough to have been marked for death by the father and succored by the daughter. Look!"

The De la Roches had reached the canopy, and there the second flunky repeated their names. Bonaparte was looking keenly at the oddly dressed seigneur. And I could guess what was in the Corsican's usually fathomless mind. For once he seemed in doubt.

If this queerly dressed old fellow were really a member—perhaps an advance guard—of the ancient aristocracy (at whose social barriers Bonaparte had so long and so vainly battered, though he affected to despise the once powerful régime), it behooved the first consul to make him welcome.

If on the contrary, the guest were merely a provincial or a renegade from his class, he must be properly snubbed for the benefit of the self-made aristocracy who were present.

Wherefore Bonaparte hesitated as the forest lord minced forward. De la Roche bowed before the Bonaparte with stately dignity and Lorraine, at his side, curtsied low.

"Sieur de la Roche," said Bonaparte in his best manner, "this is the first time I have had the pleasure of greeting you here, I think?"

"It is my first visit to France, M. le General, in many years," returned De la Roche, evidently pleased by his courteous reception. "I arrived but a few days since. From America, where my fur-trading has—"

"Quite so!" rasped Bonaparte, frowning slightly. "Quite so. Murat, go and find Curée for me. He is fairly certain to be near the buffet."

De la Roche's florid face darkened and his engaging smile went blank as the first consul abruptly turned his back upon him. As for Lorraine, her big eyes went wide with wonder at such gross discourtesy.

I strove to make my way toward her as she and her father moved uncertainly away; but the crowd was dense and my progress was slow. Launay, divining my purpose, kept close to my side.

Several minutes elapsed before I could reach my goal, as the De la Roches were going in an opposite direction. Once or twice I even lost them in the throng.

When at length I came upon them they were in a shallow alcove or niche in one end of the great room, far from the canopy. Lorraine had sunk into a seat, and her father was standing in front of her like a grizzly at bay.

And, faith, he *was* at bay. Facing him were a knot of three or four gaily clad men who had marked Bonaparte's cold reception of the forest lord, and who were thus safely singling out the old man as a butt for their jest.

The spokesman was a dashing cavalry colonel with whom I had some slight acquaintance—Du Fresne, by name—favorite *aide-de-camp* to Bonaparte himself; a man who had long and laboriously sought fame as a wit. And, as is usually the case with such men, he had found a number of folk willing to accept him at his declared value.

Wherefore, the lesser humorists were standing by, leaving their leader a free hand in the baiting of this bewildered old provincial. And, like buzzards to the feast, others were drifting toward the group to participate in the rare sport.

"Yes, *m'sieu'*, " De la Roche was saying angrily as Launay and I drew near, "it was in fashion when his sainted majesty ruled here, and I need no bewhiskered jackanapes to advise me as to my dress."

"I stand properly rebuked, O Nestor of the Wilderness," laughed Du Fresne; "and for a smile from your fair if somewhat provincial daughter I—"

"M. le Colonel du Fresne," I said very softly, laying a hand on the humorist's gold-laced arm, "may I humbly call your august attention to the fact that this gentleman and Mlle. de la Roche are friends of mine, and that it will afford me infinite bliss to thrash you within an inch of your worthless life if you address another word to either of them?"

My voice reached him and those immediately around him. Yet, as I had planned, it did not penetrate to where Lorraine de la Roche sat.

The railing grin left Du Fresne's lean face, to be replaced by momentary wonder; and this wonder was reflected in the faces of his cronies.

I knew why. The man was a redoubtable duelist. Even in that day and country of incessant and murderous dueling his fame was established.

As a garment his air of mocking gaiety fell away from Du Fresne. So did the surprise that had at first replaced it, leaving him cold and deadly.

"Did I hear you aright, Mr. Alwyn?" he demanded.

"If you did not, *canaille*," I repeated in the same gentle undertone, "I shall be glad to repeat my words loudly enough for even deaf old M. Berthier to hear."

"It is not needful," he replied. "My seconds will—"

"Send them to M. Launay at the American embassy," said I, "or let them talk with him now in one of the retiring rooms. Sieur de la Roche," I went on, approaching the old provincial, "may I recall myself to your memory?"

De la Roche had been glowering doubtfully at us during my brief colloquy with Du Fresne. Now, as the group of scoffers all at once dwindled, he seemed for an instant in doubt as to whether I might not be also seeking to bait him. But he seemed reassured by my gravity and by the genuine welcome in my tone.

"Your face, *m'sieu'*, " said he as he returned my formal bow with one whose Old-World grace no American could hope to imitate—"there is something familiar about your features and your voice; but you will pardon me if for the moment I cannot place you."

It was not peculiar that he could not recognize the well-dressed and smooth-shaven man before him as the unkempt, bearded wanderer of the Mississippi forests.

"My name is Louis Alwyn," I returned. "I am an American. I was the recipient of your hospitality in the West some months ago."

He looked puzzled. Then a gasp and a change of color showed he remembered. Ere he could speak I went on: "May I have the honor, monseigneur, to present my fellow American and dear friend, Mr. Guy Launay, of the United States Embassy?"

As De la Roche and Launay were bowing, I slipped past the old man into the alcove, where Lorraine had risen from her seat and was staring at me in amazed recognition.

I felt again that strange little thrill as our eyes met. And it rejoiced me mightily that she had known me despite the complete change in my appearance.

"You will let me thank you now," said I, "as I had no time to before, for your wondrous goodness to a ragged prisoner in your father's domain?"

"*You?*" was all she could say for the instant.

Then, rallying her self-control, she went on:

"Oh, it is *good* to see a familiar face in this desert of strangers! My father insisted on coming here to-night. Was it not terrible the way Bonaparte and—and the others treated us? Even our Indians would not treat a guest so abominably."

She paused suddenly, as though recalling the treatment I had received in her father's hall. But I gave no outward heed to her embarrassment.

"No one shall treat you rudely again, *mademoiselle,*" I assured her, as if comforting an ill-treated child. "Of that you have my assurance."

Impulsively she stretched forth her hand toward mine. And our fingers clasped. In that magnetic contact I quite lost sanity.

CHAPTER V.
A Fool and His Folly.

"TELL me," she asked in sudden recollection, breaking in on the brief pause that followed my fall from sanity. "How did you escape that night? About half an hour after I left you there was a great commotion out in the enclosure. And Raoul rushed in to tell me you were gone and Plagge was tied and gagged."

Briefly I told my story, adding the tale of my mission to France. I learned of her own voyage from New Orleans, of her arrival at Paris, and of the futile efforts her father had made during his brief stay to recover the confiscated property that was the cause of his journey hither.

"That was why he brought me here to-night," she went on. "Everywhere we learn that General Bonaparte is all-powerful. My father thought we might get his ear in this way. You see, my father is eager to secure the property or its money value, because it is mine, not his. He wants to get it for me."

"For you?"

"It is my grandmother's estate. She left it to me. It is valued at two hundred and fifty thousand francs. Fifty thousand dollars of your American money. It is all the dowry I shall have, and, I'm afraid, all the heritage. For my father's estates in the West are fearfully mortgaged. And now, it seems, we are not to get it, after all."

"Have your father send the title deeds and the other documents in the case around to me at the embassy in the morning," I said. "And I will see what I can do. Uncle Sam's influence may help, even though you are not technically an American subject. Launay has the legal mind of the embassy. I'll turn the problem over to him to solve. By the way—"

I broke off as Launay came toward us. The Sieur de la Roche was deep in talk with a white-haired officer whom, it seemed, he had known in early days. And Launay, being relieved of the burden of conversing with him, had turned to us.

I introduced the young attache to Lorraine, and for a space we all three chatted right pleasantly together—though with all my heart I wished my very good friend Launay were anywhere else, just for the time. I felt a strange distaste to sharing Lorraine de la Roche's attention with any man.

Presently Mme. Lefebvre came to the entrance of our alcove and beckoned me imperiously to her.

"You are Alwyn?" she asked abruptly.

"Yes, *madame*," I made puzzled reply—for I had never until that night set eyes on the woman.

"Good!" said she. "I hear much of you this evening. Notably that

you have insulted Du Fresne for daring to speak lightly of that pretty provincial maid in there. You are in love with her?"

"Yes, *madame*," I replied frankly, amused and yet somewhat swept off my feet by her blunt impudence.

"Good!" she exclaimed again. "I think I like you. And I think I like her. And I more than think she may have need of some one besides that old fossil of a father of hers to look after her here in Paris. Take me to her and introduce her to me.

"Introduce *her* to *me,* remember. Not *me* to *her.* For, while it is quite possible I may have washed clothes for her grand-parents, yet I am a general's wife now, and she is but a stranger. And etiquette must be observed. We, who have very little dignity to stand on, must needs stand very hard on the very little we have."

She rattled off this somewhat bewildering speech without pausing to catch her breath. And, flighty as her words sounded, I read the good heart and sound commonsense that prompted her offer of protection to the lonely girl.

Yes, and I saw the value such protection might be. Especially if Du Fresne's sword should prove nimbler next day than mine.

With what thanks I could summon I conducted her into the alcove and presented Lorraine to her.

"My dear," said Mme. Lefebvre, "you are pretty. And you are lonely. And I am ugly and lonely. So we can both help each other. And to-morrow I am coming to see you. And very often after that. You will hear odd tales of me. You will even hear unmannerly folk dub me 'Mme. Sans-Gene.' You will hear also, however, that I am an excellent watch-dog; and that Napoleon Bonaparte himself does not care to risk a tongue-lashing from me.

"Alwyn, you two men can go away and amuse yourselves. This young lady and I are going to be friends. She had ancestors. One sees that from her hands. I had none. No ancestors, I mean. Not hands. But I *am* an ancestor, which is infinitely better—for the ancestor. Run along now, like good youngsters, and leave me to tell Mlle. de la Roche how best to be on her guard against such men as you both."

And in the kindly eccentric woman's care I left Lorraine—well satisfied that so powerful a personage had taken the luckless girl under her wing. Paris was a treacherous place in those days for an

unguarded and beautiful woman. More so than either Lorraine or her old-fashioned father could realize.

"Well," observed Launay, "you have managed to get yourself into more trouble in a brief time than I could have imagined. What was President Jefferson thinking of when he sent a marplot like you over here to help us? As wisely try to put a fire out by pouring oil on it!"

"If you mean the duel I'm to fight to-morrow morning—" I began.

"No," dissented Launay, "I don't. Duels are fought every day here in France, and no one the worse for it, except the man who chances to get killed. But, with Du Fresne, of all men—"

"Why not? He is a clever swordsman, I'm told. One of the cleverest. But I have been trained from childhood to the use of saber and rapier. And—"

"Don't waste breath in boasting. Don't you understand? Du Fresne is Bonaparte's favorite *aide-de-camp*."

"Well?"

"And you are here to do all you can to win Bonaparte over to the sale of the Louisiana region."

"Well?"

"And just as we seem to be overcoming a very few of his countless objections you must needs undo all our work and win his hatred by publicly insulting his favorite."

I understood for the first time what an unforgivable diplomatic blunder I had committed. A diplomat must be above—or below—all personal feelings. Instead of putting a stop to Lorraine's humiliation at Du Fresne's hands, I should have joined heartily in the laughter his brutal sallies evoked.

I saw it now. And—and I thanked Heaven I had been enough of a man and little enough of a diplomat to do exactly as I had done. Yet, manlike, I said nothing of this to Launay, but looked glumly at him, awaiting his next rebuke.

"Yes," he pursued, "you have muddled everything. And if you had done otherwise I should have done my best to cane you. Now for the arrangements."

"You must make them to-night?"

"They are made."

"When? You've had no time to—"

"These things take little time nowadays in France. As I quitted the Sieur de la Roche, Captain Grieux stopped me and said: 'I am acting for Du Fresne. Will the rear gardens, an hour from now, suit you?' I told him they would. And we have just eight minutes to get there. Come!"

"But surely—"

"It seems Du Fresne must start for Milan at daybreak on official business. Hence the hurry. And"—he added—"if you kill or disable him and thus interfere with the military errand on which he is sent, you will make Bonaparte your foe for life."

"You're a cheery comrade, Launay," I laughed. "I cannot now recall another man who would put such heart into me. If I kill Du Fresne, according to you I am ruined. And if he kills me—"

"If he kills you he will have the pleasure of killing me afterward, before he can start for Milan."

Our hands gripped and we made our way from the salon. A minute later we were leaving the palace by a rear entrance. We went along a gravel path, between high and fantastically clipped hedges.

And presently we came out in a cleared space, hedged in by shrubbery, and lighted for the Tuileries fête by a string of red paper lanterns that shone glowingly on the white busts and statues which stood around the central enclosure.

Two men were already awaiting us. They were Du Fresne and Grieux. As we approached both of them saluted in cold courtesy. We returned the salute in like fashion. Then Grieux and Launay stepped aside to confer.

CHAPTER VI.
Wherein I Fight for My Life.

I STOOD punctiliously aloof where Launay had left me. On the far side of the red-lit enclosure stood Du Fresne. Launay and Grieux were whispering together in one corner.

It is not the fight—in any walk of life, I think—that requires true

courage. It is the suspense of waiting. And that same suspense began now to twitch at my nerves. I had time to think. And, in a man of action, too much time to think is often fatal to success.

As I waited now, through what seemed to me the interminable time that the two seconds took in arranging the simple preliminaries, my thoughts were not pleasant. I was still in the early thirties. I was splendidly strong and well. I was comfortably rich. I had a glittering career ahead of me. I was in love.

I had so much more to lose than have most men! And yet, because a beast of a soldier had done something for which I should merely have horsewhipped him, the foolish ethics of dueling gave him an opportunity to kill me.

If I should fall, what would become of the mission on which so much of my country's future greatness depended—the mission President Jefferson had intrusted into my futile hands? What was to become of my high hopes, my love, my career?

At thought that Du Fresne wrongfully held all my fate on the point of his sword, a fierce and wholesome rage against him and against the absurdity and injustice of the dueling code dwelt over my nerves, tightening and calming them.

Launay advanced toward me, a saber in his hand. Grieux, similarly equipped, went to Du Fresne.

"Du Fresne insists on *combat à l'outrance*—to the death!" reported Launay. "Grieux got hold of a pair of sabers and a pair of rapiers, from the *salle d'armes*. I chose sabers. I don't know that you're any better with one than with the other. But I do know he's better with the rapier. And as the choice of weapons was ours—"

"Quite right," I assented, cool and ready now that the actual test was at hand; "I could wish for better light. But I have fought under worse. We are safe from interruption?"

"I think so. Grieux tells me he has given two louis to the sergeant of the guard on duty in the garden to-night."

"Good."

"Any—any commissions or message in case—"

"I shall live," I answered tartly. "It's a way I have."

We advanced toward the center of the cleared space, where the two others joined us. I tested the temper of my saber by bending it

across my hands and ran my fingers along its shining blade. Then I moved my feet along the turf. I found it more slippery from a recent rain than I could have wished.

Handing the saber to Launay I divested myself of coat, waistcoat, and stock, and rolled back the soft cambric shirtsleeve from my right forearm. Then, taking my weapon again, I stood ready.

Du Fresne, similarly stripped and armed, was awaiting me. He was as tall as I, but more slender and wiry.

Dueling was to him a delight—his favorite pastime. Whereas, to me, the thought of slaying a fellow man in cold blood has ever been abhorrent. I think this difference in tastes must have showed in our tense faces as we stood awaiting the word to begin our fight to the death.

"En garde, messieurs!" called Grieux.

Our blades came together with a ring. The scarlet light from the lanterns above turned the burnished steel to whirling lines of red fire. Yes, and red fiery sparks leaped in air from that first swift clash of the weapons.

From the beginning I felt, by the mysterious "fencer's instinct," that I was opposed to a swordsman of rare skill and strength. And the knowledge exhilarated me strangely. Gone now were all nervousness, all thought of consequences. For the time I was no longer a rational man, but a primitive battling animal.

Up and down the small enclosure, forward and back, we raged, my foe and I. Our swords smote and whined and slithered, grinding and clicking in thrust, moulinet and parry.

Ever we sought for an opening, ever we were met by a flying red wall of steel. Like sentient things our blades wound and writhed about each other, clashing, slashing, lunging, guarding. Around us, in the lurid lantern glow, rose the high walls of shrubbery that hid us from prying eyes. The sightless white eyes of the statues gazed with benevolent blankness on the scene of strife before them.

Our feet slipped and stamped for firmer grip on the slippery wet turf. Our seconds, crouching and darting here and there to get a better view of our ever-shifting positions, were kept well-nigh as active as were we.

I parried a deadly thrust for my bared throat, and *riposted* with

a lightning downward cut that was aimed for Du Fresne's head. He sprang nimbly aside to avoid it, and my blade only shore off the gilded epaulette from his left shoulder.

Angered, I suppose, that a foreigner should come so close to wounding his redoubtable self, Du Fresne flew at me with a rage and force that well-nigh beat down my guard.

But that very fury of his served me well. In every crisis of life the angry man is at disadvantage. I watched my chance and, bounding back as he sent in one of a dozen mighty lunges, I caught his sword blade obliquely.

Throwing all the strength of wrist and forearm into the effort I pressed downward and outward in one motion.

His saber flew from his too-far extended arm and fell to the grass ten feet away. In a trice I had reached it and placed my foot upon it.

The disarmed man stood dazed and bewildered for an instant, as if trying to understand just what had befallen him. Then with a yell like a mad cat he rushed bare-handed at me.

I verily believe he would have flung himself bodily upon my sword-point in his rabid craving to get at me and kill me.

The two seconds, crying out in horror, sprang forward to intercept him. But they were too late. Ere even I was aware of his mad intent, his breast had well-nigh touched my upraised sword.

His yell, his rush, the cries of the seconds had all followed so closely upon one another as to seem simultaneous. I scarce was able to toss aside my saber in time to prevent its point from transfixing him.

Then, with the same hand that had just flung away the sword I struck. He was so close upon me that his gripping fingers had already touched my throat when my short-arm upper-cut reached his jaw.

Delivered at such close quarters the blow lost half its force. Yet it was strong enough to send him reeling backward with wildly-clawing, upflung arms—to overcome his balance and lay him sprawling on the wet turf.

As quickly as a panther he had regained his feet. And he would have made for me again had not both our seconds thrown themselves between us and seized him.

"Du Fresne!" cried Grieux in dire chagrin, as he grappled the struggling man, "are you stark mad? You have broken every rule of

the *duello*—you, a veteran duelist! I am ashamed of you."

"A duelist!" I mocked, forgetting in my excitement and disgust the rigid rule which forbade two combatants to address each other except through their seconds. "A duelist! You are more like an unwhipped nursery child. Before you venture to challenge a grown man again learn to control your silly temper."

"Alwyn!" muttered Launay, leaving Du Fresne, as the latter ceased to struggle, and speaking rapidly in my ear. "Shut up! Do you want to make them think we are tyros at this game? "

"M. Alwyn," called Grieux, "in my principal's name and my own, I most humbly apologize for this shameful breach of the code. I can explain it only on the ground that no man until to-night has ever succeeded in disarming Colonel Du Fresne. He has grown too accustomed to victory to accept defeat as gracefully as he should. When calmer he will join in my apologies."

"I shall *not!*" mouthed Du Fresne, no whit calmed mentally, although he no longer strove to get at me. "I apologize to no Yankee—"

"Du Fresne!" cried Grieux aghast.

"I demand no apology," I made reply. "He was insolent to friends of mine. In return I outfought him with his own weapons and then knocked him down. As far as I am concerned, honor is satisfied and the incident is closed."

I turned to pick up my discarded outer clothing.

"Wait!" ordered Du Fresne. "Grieux, the Yankee is not going to get away from me like this, to boast lyingly through Paris that he has bested Maximilien Du Fresne. By the terms of this duel we were to fight *à l'outrance.* I demand that right."

"But surely—"

"I demand that right!" stormed Du Fresne.

"He is within his rights," whispered Launay as Grieux vehemently sought to dissuade his principal. "By the code, when two men agree to fight *à l'outrance,* either one can insist on doing so and the other is obliged to consent. I should have thought Du Fresne would have had enough. But—"

"Messieurs," interrupted Grieux, despairingly, "M. le Colonel will not be turned aside from his intent. And, as you know, by the laws of—"

26

"Oh, very good," I said, stooping and picking up the two swords, one of which I handed to Grieux for Du Fresne; "have it your own way. We have perhaps argued overmuch already over so small a matter as two human lives."

Grieux handed Du Fresne his saber, and once more we two fell into position, awaiting the word.

"*En garde, messieurs!*" called Grieux again.

And for the second time I and my opponent crossed swords. From the start in this new encounter Du Fresne took the aggressive. Yet now his former fury had turned to a cold purpose that made him doubly formidable.

Unused of late to such violent exercise, I found myself beginning to breathe heavily, and the speed of my arm slackened ever so little.

Du Fresne noted these failings as quickly as did I. With a fiercer ardor he hurled himself into the attack.

CHAPTER VII.
A Foe and a Strange Friend.

THROWING myself wholly on the defensive I husbanded my strength. I knew that no mortal man could long maintain such speed as Du Fresne was exhibiting. Soon he must tire. And in the mean time I contented myself with parrying his hailstorm of blows and shifting my position only as occasion demanded.

And soon I could feel, with the fencer's instinct, that the force of his attack was slackening. My time had come to resume the aggressive.

Parrying a head slash I lunged for his heart. He warded the blow—but a fraction too slowly. Seeing that my point must reach him if he remained where he was, he gave ground.

And, in his sudden backward move, his foot slipped on the wet, greasy turf.

Down he went, asprawl, the saber falling from his hand. I stood over him, my own blade drawn back. The fight was over. And I was glad, for I was beginning to tire.

"Get up!" I ordered. "Take up your sword and use it hereafter to

better and more honorable purpose. I give you your life."

"Strike!" he snarled, melodramatically, crouching there in the damp grass at my feet. "Strike! It was *à l'outrance!*"

"Where I come from," I said quietly, "we don't hit a man when he's down. And most assuredly we don't stab him. Get up!"

"Good for you, Louis!" applauded the irrepressible Launay. "Sounds vastly like a stage play, but 'tis rare good sense. America forever!"

With a sudden motion Du Fresne gripped his fallen sword and leaped to his feet.

"*À l'outrance!*" he cried. *"En garde!"*

"Good Lord!" I growled in disgust, "must I—"

But he was at me like a wild beast, and I saved further breath for fighting. Back and forth we stamped and slashed once more. But only for a bare quarter minute at most.

Then down swept his blade in a stroke that, had it reached me in full force, must have cloven my body to the girth. Up went my saber to guard the direful sweep.

Our swords met in a clash that sent a shower of tiny sparks flying in every direction.

And the blade of my saber, under that fearful impact, snapped short at the hilt.

Luckily the bulk of his downward blow's power was spent ere the breaking of my blade. Luckily, too, the weapon turned in his hand. The flat of his saber struck my bare head with sufficient power to make me see stars and to stagger me.

Almost at once my eyes and my brain cleared. Just in time to see Du Fresne break away from Grieux's detaining clutch and rush at me, blade aloft.

"*À l'outrance!*" he panted.

And again, according to the laws of the duello, he was technically within his rights. But, as it chanced, those "rights" were never to be exercised.

As Du Fresne leaped at me something strange and uncanny in that elusive red glare glided with the speed and silence of a snake from the tall hedge behind him.

The mysterious thing caught Colonel Maximilien Du Fresne in

mid rush and whirled him high in air as lightly as though the tall Frenchman were a child.

Then, before any of us could move or speak, the newcomer dashed the writhing colonel to the ground with terrific force and, stooping, picked up his inert victim's saber.

"Aniwaya!" I cried, dumfounded.

"À l'outrance!" calmly observed the Indian.

He stooped and wound the fingers of his left hand in Du Fresne's long hair, lifting the unconscious man's head clear of the turf and bringing the saber carefully downward toward it.

"Aniwaya!" I cried again. "Stop, man! What are you doing?"

"Left knife at the lodge," he answered, his dull voice portraying a trace of apology for such inexcusable neglect. "Do best I can with sword!"

"Good Heaven!" I gasped, throwing myself upon him in stark horror and fending off the saber's edge from the senseless duelist's head, "were you actually going to—"

"Scalp him," finished Aniwaya pleasantly. "À l'outrance," he said. "À l'outrance let be!"

A murmur of unbelieving dread burst from the two seconds. I seized with tighter grip the arm that held the descending sword blade.

"Aniwaya!" I ordered, sick with the thought of what he contemplated; "drop that saber! Stand clear of him."

Reluctantly, but with no show of resistance, the savage obeyed me. He dropped not only the sword but Du Fresne's head as well. And now I noted the fallen man had come to his senses during our colloquy. The look of dumb terror in his eyes showed he understood Aniwaya's awful intent.

"Master," said the Indian curiously, "how you kill him now?"

"Kill him?" I echoed. "I'm not going to kill him."

"No? Why you fight him then? In papoose-play? He looked like kill you. Did *he* play, too?"

"We don't scalp men in a civilized land like France! We are not savages!" broke out Captain Grieux, finding his tongue at last.

"No?" queried Aniwaya. "Then what use you make of guillotine my master showed me? That for play, too?"

"It is to cut off the heads of criminals," replied Grieux; "not to—"

"Oh!" grunted Aniwaya, "cut off *all* his head—that is France and civilized. Cut off only scalp of his head—that is Indian and savage!"

And oddly enough none of us at the moment could voice an argument to confute this patently absurd deduction of Aniwaya's.

A groan from the injured Du Fresne drew our attention. Grieux knelt beside him, running a practised hand over the wounded man's body.

"A broken collar bone and two fractured ribs," he reported presently. "That is all the damage I can find. It is a miracle he was not crushed to death. That flower-bed broke his fall."

"Now we torture him?" pleasantly suggested Aniwaya. "Lighted splinters between fingers, and then—"

"*Silence!*" I roared.

My nerves could not stand much more of this sort of thing. Grieux, looking up from Du Fresne who had cried aloud at the Indian's suggestion, thundered:

"We do not torture helpless people, we French. We are not savages!"

"The master," remarked Aniwaya to no one in particular, "showed me prison yesterday. Women there, with big chains cutting wrists and ankles. Men starved and put in dark with rats till they confess crimes. No torture? Maybe they like it."

"Come!" said Grieux, "help me lift him. We'll put him in a guardroom then and I will send for a coach to take him home. I can say he was thrown from his horse as he left the Tuileries. I think, gentlemen, we are all agreed it is best for every one that this night's happenings be kept secret among us?"

"With all my heart," I agreed.

And a ray of light shot through my depression. I had not wrecked my mission after all. Bonaparte would never know. Du Fresne, of all men, was not likely to talk of that scene in the shrubbery. Once more I had a chance of success!

CHAPTER VIII.
Wherein I Score a Blunder.

THE next week was the happiest I had ever known. Daily I rode or drove or walked with Lorraine de la Roche, showing her the wonders of Paris, enjoying her utterly artless joy in it all, living in a glorious fool's paradise.

Launay, too, managed to spare overmuch time from official duties, to my way of thinking; and most of that time was passed with Lorraine.

But I did not let this worry me seriously. With all my will and all my heart and all my soul I had resolved to win Lorraine de la Roche's love. And I refused to recognize any chance of defeat. I knew she liked me. I knew in all probability she guessed at my love for her; and if she did she gave no sign of being offended thereby.

The time to speak was not yet ripe, as I realized. But every day was bringing me closer to that wonderful moment.

Already had I won the good will of the Sieur de la Roche by promising to do what I could to press his claim for the confiscated estate. Indeed, I was working over that claim well-nigh as hard as over my own mission.

What with these two tasks and my hours with Lorraine, my days were filled to overflowing. In behalf of the Louisiana region I was sounding politicians, enlisting the services of such of Bonaparte's satellites as could be approached by any means at my command, and pulling all of the thousand wires of French politics that came within my reach.

And little by little I felt I was nearing success. Pressure was brought to bear from a dozen minor sources upon the first consul. My line of action was laid out. With Launay's help I was at last shaping it toward success.

So far had I advanced at the end of a week after my duel with Du Fresne that I received a tentative pledge from one of Bonaparte's secretaries that the first consul would make an appointment to receive me privately before long and discuss the weighty matter with me.

Launay was promptly despatched to the Tuileries to see if he could

arrange a definite date for the meeting.

As I returned to the embassy at sunset one afternoon from a ride in the Bois with Loraine, Aniwaya handed me a letter. It was in Launay's scrawling hand. I read:

Dear Louis:

The first consul has consented to see you in his private study at six. He is nervous lest news of the affair get abroad. So you are to come through the rear gate and the rear gardens. The sentinel there has orders to pass you. I will be waiting to show you to the Great Man's study.

He does not want his secretaries to know (which of course they do), so I am to act for the nonce as chamberlain. By the way, remember for once, that you are a diplomat and not a wild man. Bonaparte's nerves and digestion are in bad condition just now, so his secretary tells me. And he flies into a rage at the slightest provocation.

He is more than ever imperial Cæsar and Alexander the Great, thrown into one. So prythee be monstrous careful not to scratch his lofty dignity. One misstep might wreck everything.

I read and reread, smiling over Launay's boyish eagerness, until all at once I realized that my own eagerness and enthusiasm were quite as unbridled as his own.

All now depended upon *me*. And my spirits rose to the task as a cross-country thoroughbred to a stiff fence. Not risk anything by rubbing the touchy consul's indigestion-bred dignity the wrong way? Not I. Talleyrand himself could be no more diplomatic than would I.

My pleas, my arguments, my promises in Jefferson's behalf were all at my tongue's end. Something told me I should succeed this day. The Scotch have a word to express the wild exhilaration that was mine. The word is "fey."

As I busied myself dressing for the momentous interview Aniwaya eyed me dubiously; looking first at the gorgeous raiment I was

donning and then at the letter I had read.

"No," I laughed. "It isn't an ambush. And you are not to dog my footsteps as you did the night I fought Colonel Du Fresne. Stay here, understand?"

"If I stay here *that* night," he argued stonily, "you not here now."

I waved aside this irrelevant speech, and ran down the embassy stairs into the street. Hastily I made my way through the gathering dusk toward the Tuileries.

I was a trifle piqued that Launay had that day seen fit to appropriate the new English greatcoat and hat that I had been saving to wear when I should pay my secret visit to the first consul.

Both coat and hat were of a new and striking design, and I had hoped to impress the finery-loving Bonaparte with them. Indeed, my outfitter had told me that no other such coat and hat had been sold in all France.

And now, on this day of all others, Launay, on going to the Tuileries, had taken advantage of our friendship to deck himself in these prized garments. He was a gay, irresponsible chap with whom no one could long be angry. And he lent his own possessions every bit as freely as he borrowed mine. Yet, through my elation, I was resolved to take him severely to task for this especial misappropriation.

I reached the rear gate, was admitted by the sentry, and started up the deserted strip of walk toward the palace. As I passed I glanced reminiscently over the high hedge into the enclosure where I had so nearly been done to death by Du Fresne.

And, as I was about to move on, I was aware of a man pacing up and down the enclosure. One look, even in that dim twilight, was quite enough. In a single glimpse I recognized Launay's figure. Also, and more to the point, I recognized the long great-coat and hat whose designs were so unique.

Launay, then, was awaiting me in this spot of gruesome memories instead of in a rear doorway of the palace.

Good! There was time to make him give back my treasured garments so that I might, after all, wear them into the august presence.

And my exhilaration giving me for the moment the prankish spirits of a schoolboy, I hit on a plan of whose buffoonery I would, in ordinary moments, have been ashamed.

But, before judging me an ass, pray remember that I had just approached the very pinnacle of my ambition, and that, after many dreary disappointments, the prospect of success had gone to my head like strong wine.

Otherwise I should not have contemplated such horse-play even with so old and so boisterous a friend as Launay.

On silent feet I kept through a gap in the hedge. Launay's back was toward me and he had paused to kick a disturbed bit of turf back into place.

Stealing forward until I was just behind him, I leaped forward and snatched the hat from his head, growling in mock rage:

"You disreputable old blackguard and clothes thief! I've a great mind to treat you as Boney's pet aide was treated on this very spot!"

As I was speaking I had deftly reached over and caught the coat by its lapels. With one herculean jerk I wrenched the loose-hanging garment completely off of its wearer.

My roughly powerful action, unexpected as it was, knocked him clean off his balance, and he collapsed into the prickly heart of a large and intensely thorn-protected rosebush.

"There!" I exulted. "That will teach you another time to steal clothes from me when I'm on my way to cajole Boney into selling us half a continent for one-quarter of its value. I—"

He dragged himself clumsily out of the thorny embrace of the rosebush and wheeled about on me with a shrill, peacock-voiced volley of such blasphemy and abuse as never before nor since have I heard.

I fell back thunderstruck, dumbfounded, horror-stricken—oh, there is no phrase to tell you what I felt.

For, his eyes shining like coals and his face white and hideous, the man I had upset and forcibly disrobed was not Launay at all.

He was Napoleon Bonaparte!

CHAPTER IX.
Disaster!

I STOOD aghast, bereft of voice or motion, even of the power of clear thought. All my stricken senses could realize was that I had smashed to atoms my mission and my every hope of its success.

I had laid violent hands on the inviolate. I had put unforgivable indignity upon the man who personified the loftiest dignity. I had, in short, knocked over and despoiled the Man of Destiny—I, a nameless Yankee.

Dim as was the falling twilight, I recognized him, even as he right assuredly recognized me. For the moment I did not pause to consider how or why he chanced to be wearing the hat and coat that Launay had "borrowed" of me. Out of the maze of utter impossibilities this one impossibility more or less scarce counted.

Then, amid the shipwreck of my hopes, I recalled Jefferson's trust in me, the vast import of this mission to my dear country's future, the bright career that had been mine but a short five minutes before.

Not from ill-fortune or a blow of fate, but through mine own stark idiocy had I ruined everything.

And as a strong swimmer, hurled forcibly overboard, begins to rise to the surface as soon as his feet touch bottom, so did I in my depth of despair grit my teeth and vow that I would yet win.

Faith, one need not have been a soothsayer to declare my chances nil, after a single look just then at Napoleon Bonaparte. His torrent of high-voiced fury had ceased as suddenly as it had begun.

He was still as a statue now, the passion-distorted face once more calm as marble, save for the fathomless eyes where burned a dull red fire. His features were immobile, his whole pose one of lofty command.

Even in that instant of stress I marveled that any mortal could in a trice shift from the most absurdly undignified of postures and rages into an atmosphere of such august majesty. A stage-trick to cover his discomfiture? Perhaps. But no other living man could have achieved it.

Under his baleful, unwavering gaze I felt myself shrink. It was only

by the effort of all my will-power that I forced myself to face him with outward calm.

"*M. le General,*" I said contritely, "I ask ten thousand pardons for—"

"M. Alwyn," he broke in as though I had not spoken, "you requested an interview with me, I believe?"

His icy voice held no faintest trace of emotion.

"I did, *M. le General,*" I made swift to reply; catching the cue from his manner, and realizing that any further reference to his mishap would be a blunder. "And I thank you in my country's name as well as in my own for the courtesy of granting it. I understood that I was to be conducted to your study and—"

"It was overwarm in my study," said he. "I had worked long and I desired a few moments of air and exercise. So I came out here by way of the long window. I left your compatriot, M. Launay, to watch for you at my study door and to apprise me of your coming. As the evening air is raw and as I did not wish to summon a servant, M. Launay kindly lent me his hat and great-coat. Pray return them to him with my thanks when next you see him."

He pointed carelessly at the forgotten garments on the ground beside him as he spoke. I understood. It was his way of explaining the masquerade and incidentally of showing the contempt in which he now held my luckless apparel.

I stooped and picked up the discarded hat and coat, at a loss what to say. Bonaparte saved me the trouble of speech by remarking:

"I understand, M. Alwyn, that your audience with me to-day is in reference to the land-purchase on which I have already been approached."

"Yes, *M. le General.*"

"And for the Louisiana region the United States is prepared to pay, I am told, the sum of one hundred and five million francs? "

"Fifteen million dollars," I corrected respectfully.

"H-m! In francs that is—"

"Seventy-five million."

He looked at me absently for a moment, then murmured, under his breath, as if in reverie:

"Half a continent for one-quarter what it is worth?"

The simple words struck me like a slap across the mouth. For I now recalled uttering them in my moment of crazy exultation when I had seized upon the supposed Launay. And I understood doubly the pit wherein my asininity had plunged me and my mission.

What I could not at all comprehend was the fact that the first consul was continuing the interview and discussing a question on whose refusal he must already have decided.

I could but wait his next words. And presently he went on as though that low-voiced remark about "half a continent" had not been spoken.

"M. Alwyn," said he, "seventy million francs is a goodly sum to pay for a country estate on which is a chateau in fair condition and perchance a mile or so of game preserves. It is even a tolerable sum to pay for a lottery concession. But does it seem to your government a fitting price for nearly nine hundred thousand square miles of land—a territory equal to a great empire?"

I wondered at his unwontedly argumentative tone. But it gave me the opening I sought. Into the subject I plunged, bringing forth all the arguments, promises, and pleas that I had so long rehearsed; explaining why we could not pay more; why the land that was so needful to us was of no use to France; how the money we offered would help fill France's war-chest, and how the purchase would strengthen the bond between the two nations.

Oh, I promise you I talked right eloquently and well. And none the worse because I knew my appeal was hopeless.

Sometimes I think that the knowledge of hopelessness is a spur to a man of spirit to do his best. Yes, and even more than his normal best. Even as I am to-night toiling with my best skill to set down this tale in a way that shall show you of a later day the stirring drama in which I was once an actor; albeit I fear me the chance that it may some time reach the public eye is scant enow.

When I was through, Bonaparte for the moment did not speak. Throughout my recital he had stood, his hands clasped behind him, his chin on his breast, watching me with those inscrutable, hard eyes of his. Whether or not he were attending to my words his sphinx face gave no sign.

"That is all?" he queried at last, as the silence grew embarrassing.

"That is all," I replied. "May I request—"

"In that case," he said, "I will detain you no longer, M. Alwyn. Good night."

He turned abruptly and strode off toward the palace.

"But—" I exclaimed.

"By the way," he observed, halting and glancing back at me over his shoulder, "my aid, Colonel du Fresne, who was to have gone to Milan for me on pressing State business a week or two ago, was prevented from making the journey by a fall from his horse."

He paused. I crossed to where he stood, wondering what new turn the futile talk was about to take.

"Du Fresne's injury," he continued, "caused a delay which robbed me—robbed France, I should say—of a great diplomatic victory. I will not attempt to sketch the affair to one so unversed in diplomacy as yourself. For, being an American and therefore ignorant of the finer points of statecraft, you would not understand. But let it suffice you to know that the delay cost France dearly."

"I commiserate you on the loss," said I awkwardly, fuming at the slur.

"Commiseration from such a source," he returned gravely, "well-nigh robs the loss of its sting. I was, told," he went on, "that Du Fresne was thrown by his horse. But it occurred to me within the last half-hour that I may have been misinformed."

Again I understood. He had not only caught my silly words about "half a continent for quarter its value," but also what I had said about the way we had served his aid.

There was no longer any need to curb temper or to assume a respectful bearing. The Man of Destiny had avenged himself with true Corsican subtlety for the unintended affront he had received at my hands, and which, with all his greatness, he had not been great enough to overlook.

Had he ordered me, cursing, from the gardens in the first instance or sent for his guards to throw me out, he knew I should have had a fine story to tell as to the reason for my ejectment.

All Paris by the next day would have been splitting its sides over the story of the Cæsarlike Napoleon Bonaparte sprawling on the grass, with his coat yanked off his back. And ridicule no man of des-

tiny dares to brave.

As it was, he had made fairly certain of sealing my lips as to the ridiculous incident. He had granted me the secret interview I had sought. He had heard me patiently to the end.

Were I now to tell of upsetting him people would infallibly believe me a liar. They either would think I had devised the story in silly revenge for the refusal of my plea or else would not believe it humanly possible that the great Bonaparte, after suffering such unspeakable indignity at my hands, could have brought himself to listen patiently and at once thereafter to a lengthy diplomatic harangue from me.

Oh, he was clever, this Corsican adventurer! And he knew men as a schoolboy knows his primer. What mortal would credit my tale that I had ripped the coat off Bonaparte's back, upset him into a rose-bush—and then, a minute later, induced him to grant me a long political audience?

He had safeguarded himself beautifully. And, having done so, had not only proceeded to insult me (and my country through me), but to seek to pump me for the secret facts anent his favorite aid's injury.

He had treated me as the school bully might treat a baby. And a cold rage possessed me as I began to grasp the facts. A rage that cleared my mind and cooled my nerves and, for the time; made me feel myself every whit this strange genius's equal in brain and resource.

"Have I been misinformed, M. Alwyn?" went on Bonaparte. "Is it possible, for instance, that Du Fresne, instead of being thrown by a horse, was—shall we say—kicked by a donkey?"

"No," I answered bluntly. "No horses or even donkeys figured in the scene. You must seek still lower in the animal kingdom. The whole affair simply resolved itself into the just punishing of a cur."

Bonaparte made no immediate answer. I could see a red spot flame out on either cheekbone there in the gathering night. And I inwardly rejoiced at the thought that he believed I had been the cause of his aid's injury, and of delaying the Milan message. It helped a little to atone for my mishap. Presently he spoke again.

"M. Alwyn," he said coldly, "the United States has sent a bungler hither. That bungler has interfered with France's best good; has brutally crippled an officer of the state, and has in other ways rendered himself *persona non grata.* You will make arrangements to sail from

this country within three days, M. Alwyn."

"Since I am to be sent home in disgrace," I retorted, checking him as he started again toward the palace, "let me finish out the catalogue of my crimes. I am accused of misconducting myself here. I am accused of impeding France's progress by disabling one of her couriers. Why not add that I am accused of knocking down Napoleon Bonaparte, and of taking a better man's coat from him?"

"M. Alwyn," he began, with regal dignity; but I still barred his way.

"Also," I insisted, "when you add up mine offenses, do not forget to state that once, some years ago, I took that same Napoleon Bonaparte—or Nubulione Buonaparte, as he was then known—over my knee, and spanked him?"

He jumped. No, he did not start back dramatically. He *jumped,* this Man of Destiny. Jumped as though I had stuck a pin in him.

"Perchance," I resumed, "you may have guarded against my telling the tale of the ravished coat and hat. Indeed, I fancy you have. But the story of the spanking will sound right interesting in the opposition prints. And there are a score of men still alive who can attest its truth."

I proceeded:

"*M. le General,* you probably think my case is lost. That I am going to return home a failure. I am *not!* I shall not return home until I have accomplished my mission. How, or when, I do not know. But I do know I am going to win this fight, soon or late. And I shall stay here till I do.

"I am an accredited envoy of the United States of America, and as such, you cannot banish me from France without giving my government your reasons. And, if those reasons are given, I shall give a few reasons of my own to the English and the opposition French news sheets. Here I am! Here I stay! And I am going to win. I have not a card in my hand, but I am going to *win!*"

I turned on my heel and stalked out of the garden, leaving the world's foremost man standing there to digest my words—to ponder over my somewhat blatant defiance.

CHAPTER X.
A Fool, and His Money.

FOR an hour or more I strode the dark, narrow streets of old Paris. Then I went back to the embassy. Launay was waiting for me there.

"A nice diplomat you are!" he fumed, as I entered our rooms. "A fine representative of our government!"

I walked over to the big chair where he lounged, and looked down on him.

"Launay," I said wearily, "I'm a bit tired, but at the next word of blame from you for what has passed to-night, I am going to pick you up, as tenderly as I can, and drop you out of that window. And I chance to recall just now that there is a heap of broken wine flasks in the alley directly below it. I have stood about all I care to for one evening."

He glanced up in quick concern.

"Why," he said apologetically, "I mean no offense, lad. And if some mischance held you from going to the Tuileries—Aniwaya says you had my note—if—"

"What nonsense are you prating?" I demanded. "You speak as if I had not troubled to go to the Tuileries at all."

"Nor did you, if it comes to that," he asserted, the memory of his wrongs again ruffling him. "I waited at the door of Boney's study for you for a solid hour. Then the first consul—he had strolled out into the gardens to while away the time—returned and said to me: 'Your American friend evidently does not think an audience with Napoleon Bonaparte worth his attention. Pray notify your minister that the Louisiana negotiations are quite at an end.' Pretty sort of news for me to hear, wasn't it?"

I made no answer. I was still adjusting my mind to this newest means whereby the Corsican sought to discredit me with my government.

I felt actually complimented that the conqueror of half Europe should have deigned to stoop to the effort of crushing one insignificant American. And aloud I spoke my quizzical thought:

"A giant can readily smash a hornet between thumb and forefinger. But many interesting things are like to happen to the giant ere the

hornet is finally crushed."

"What nonsense are you babbling?" growled Launay.

"I crave your pardon," I apologized. "My thoughts strayed a-maying. As I recollect, you were reproaching me for not going to the Tuileries. May I ask a question in reply? How came you away from there?"

"How came I away?" he echoed. "Afoot."

"With neither hat nor greatcoat on so cold a night?"

"How did you know that? And," he shouted, leaping to his feet, "where got you the hat and coat you are wearing?"

"From my outfitter but a day or two since," I answered innocently. "Surely you remember my showing them to you yesterday?"

He stared, gaping and bemused.

"The first consul," he babbled, "told me he had mislaid them and—"

"He did not mislay them," I contradicted. "I took them from him."

"When? How?"

"During the interview at the Tuileries, which, to your mortification, I did not trouble to attend," I retorted.

And, in brief, I told him the whole story. He listened with the air of one who attends an impossibly entertaining stage-play. Long after I had finished, wonder held him dumb. Then he spoke with enforced calm.

"When do you start for home?" he queried.

"The day after I secure Bonaparte's signature to the Louisiana Purchase," I replied.

"But—"

"If you listened at all to the story I have just told you—"

"*If* I listened! I have—"

"Then you heard what I told Bonaparte? And I meant it. I am going to win. Ere I left America, President Jefferson and I laughed over my proposed 'bout with the Man of Destiny.' Well, that bout has at last begun."

"Begun!" he scoffed. "Ended, you mean."

"My uncle, Anthony Gale, was an officer aboard the old Bonhomme Richard when she fought the Serapis. A score of times have I heard him tell how the British captain called to Paul Jones when the Richard was in flames and sinking, and asked if he had struck his

colors.

"And Jones yelled back: *'Struck? I have not yet begun to fight!'* That, if you like, is my case at this hour. Boney has me burning and sinking. But I mean to win."

Launay gripped my hand in an ardent but horribly painful clasp.

"Louis," he exclaimed, "you have about as much chance of winning against Bonaparte as has a tallow dog to catch a salamander in a race through the Inferno. But somehow you make me believe in you. What shall you do?"

"I shall borrow a leaf from Bonaparte's own book and let Destiny shape my first move."

"You might join the Royalists?"

"The Royalists? Why?"

"Why, you know they are ever planning and scheming to overthrow Bonaparte and place their own beloved, thick-headed Bourbon prince, the Comte de Provence, on the throne as Louis XVIII and—"

"On the throne? Thrones have gone out of fashion here nowadays."

"But they believe that if Bonaparte were done away with, now that he has absorbed the republic in his own person, the republic would collapse and the monarchy come back."

"What nonsense!"

"Perhaps so. Perhaps not. At all events, the Bourbon faction thinks so. And that comes to the same thing, so far as they are concerned. A dense-brained crew at best."

"'The Bourbons,' I quoted, 'learn nothing and forget nothing.' And," I improvised, "they knew somewhat less than nothing to begin with. I wonder they have enough initiative left to plot against any one."

"My dear fellow," laughed Launay, "plots are the cheapest pastimes imaginable in France. And, as a rule, they form an innocent diversion that harms no one. But of late, it seems, the sluggish blood of the Bourbon faction has been quickened by the membership of a reckless element. A band of malcontent adventurers who have fared ill under the republic and seek a fresh chance of fortune."

"But what can one little band of adventurers do?" I asked. "They cannot destroy a great republic."

"No," he answered seriously; "but they can destroy a great republic's greater chief."

"You mean they—"

"I mean that Fouché tells me there have been no less than three such conspiracies unearthed in the past two months. All directed against Bonaparte. And there seems to be a brain working behind it all. Even the first consul is beginning to worry. He dare not stir abroad of late except under heavy guard. Do you know why he borrowed my—I mean your—hat and greatcoat this evening?"

"He told me. Because the evening was raw."

"Raw!" mocked Launay. "He is a veteran soldier. Would a breath of raw air trouble him? No, no. That is the excuse he gave even to me. But I understood."

"You mean that he sought to disguise himself even in the guarded Tuileries garden for fear of assassination?"

"Quite so. Your clothes and the twilight, it seems, proved a sufficient disguise even for—"

"That will do!" I silenced him hastily. "But I am petty enough to be glad he has annoyances. I don't see, though, why you suggest that I join the Bourbons. In the first place, I am not an assassin. In the second, I don't want Bonaparte gotten out of the way. I want to conquer him on his own ground. And I shall."

I started for the door again as I spoke. Aniwaya, who had been crouching as usual in the corner by the grate-fire, rose to his feet. I motioned him back.

"Not to-night, old watchdog," I said. "I go into no danger. By the way, Launay," I asked at the threshold, "there is nothing new about the De la Roche matter?"

"There is," Launay replied gloomily. "Bonaparte utterly refused to restore the estate or its value. He says the old nobility forfeited their lands by leaving France—faith, those that stayed forfeited their necks as well!—and that the republic can take no steps to restore lawfully confiscated property. I had it to-day from Livingston, who has bothered himself most kindly in the matter—so far as a diplomat of another country may."

"That means," I said, turning back into the room, "that De la Roche will soon be turned off of his mortgaged American lands. It also means that Mlle. de la Roche will be dowerless—even penniless."

"Not a pleasant prospect for a delicately reared patrician girl,"

assented Launay with an indifference that was palpably forced. "The more so when her father dies—or is executed."

"Executed?" I cried. "What do you mean, man?"

"He is vaguely suspected of dabbling in the Bourbon plots, the hidebound old aristocrat!"

"The hide-bound old idiot!" I corrected. "Full of dreams, I suppose, for restoring the dead and gone monarchy. And a blind tool for cleverer adventurers. You are certain he is involved in this foolish network?"

"No. No one is certain. If the French government were certain, or even moderately so, De la Roche would be in prison now, awaiting trial. It is only a rumor. And I came across it through one of Bonaparte's secretaries. The one from whom we get most of our underground news for a consideration."

"Listen," I ordered, going over to my own desk and unlocking it. "I want you to do me a great favor. And I want it done without question."

I drew forth a sheaf of papers fastened together with scarlet tape.

"My father," I said, "invested about half of his fortune in foreign securities, chiefly English. Here they are. I got them in England, and brought them across here with an idea of selling and reinvesting. English securities are high just now; though they won't be when the impending war with France is declared."

"Well?"

"To-morrow I want these made over to you."

"To *me?*"

"Get the embassy's banker to manage it. I will make out the transfer in the morning."

"But—to me—"

"Or to the banker—I don't care which, so long as my own name does not appear in it. That's not the favor, though. I want you to tell a lie for me. Livingston won't. Or, rather, I cannot ask him. So I must rely on you. You have been in charge of the De la Roche matter all along. So they won't suspect you."

"Who won't?" he demanded in stupid bewilderment.

"The De la Roches. I want you to have securities transferred first to yourself or to our banker in order to throw any suspicion off of me. Then have them all transferred over to Mlle. de la Roche."

"What?"

"It is not a crazy impulse. I have thought it over carefully ever since they came here. I want you to tell her the French government has consented to pay for the confiscated estate in its estimated money value, and that you have taken the liberty of investing the sum in these safe securities for her. Neither she nor her father has the least notion of business matters. It will appear perfectly natural to them."

"I shall do nothing of the kind!" he exclaimed. "Why, man," glancing over the papers I had handed him, "there are fifty thousand dollars' worth of securities here—a fortune!"

"Just half my own fortune," I amended. "And approximately the sum the De la Roches expected for the estate. By the way, tell them it is a secret transaction and the French government does not want it known, for fear of establishing a precedent. So make them understand they must say nothing. Otherwise old De la Roche will go thanking Bonaparte in public, or—"

"Louis," he protested, "do you realize what you are doing?"

I crossed over to him and laid my hand on his shoulder.

"I realize," I made answer, "that I am securing Lorraine de la Roche from poverty; that I am making her happy and sparing her from future grief. And to do that I would blithely part with everything in all this world. *Now,* do you understand?"

His face went white, and for an instant the hand that held the securities trembled as with ague. Then the nerves grew firm again and the color came back into his face.

"Yes," he said gently, smiling at me in that boyish fashion of his, "I understand, old friend, and—I—I wish you all the luck in life."

He hesitated; then asked in a matter-of-fact tone:

"Are you coming with me to the Tuileries?"

"The Tuileries?" I echoed.

"To the great *bal masque,* of course? It begins in half an hour. My domino and mask are ready in my bedroom. Have you gotten out yours?"

"No," I said; "I am going somewhere else. At least I think I am. Do you know if the De la Roches are to be there?"

"No. They are not. Mademoiselle told me—"

"Then I'm quite certain I am going somewhere else. Good night. I will see you about the transfer papers in the morning."

But, oddly enough, I was to see him sooner.

CHAPTER XI.
Wherein I Enter a Lonely House.

THE night was still young, and instead of hailing a fiacre I set forth on foot for my visit to the De la Roches.

Love is assuredly an odd thing. Here was I, beaten in the first onset of my bout with the Man of Destiny and just self-deprived of half my patrimony. Yet, at prospect of seeing one dark-haired, big-eyed girl, I had clean forgot my woes and was walking on air.

And a long walk it proved, even to a lover. The De la Roches had leased a great, lonely, ramshackle old house in the Montparnasse Quarter—a house that stood by itself in weed-grown grounds, surrounded by a crumbling wall.

The nearest abode was a full furlong distant and the section was a solitary one at best. Scarce less lonely and forbidding, withal, than the log hall in the Mississippi wilderness.

On their arrival in Paris the De la Roches had stopped for a day or two at a pleasant little hotel on the Rue St. Honoré. Then, through a whim of the old *seigneur,* they had leased this out-of-the-way ruin.

I rang the bell at the battered gateway. Presently a deaf old porter appeared and let me in. Up the long gravel walk he preceded me with his lanthorn, and up the cracked marble steps of the house itself.

Admitting me there, he turned me over to a solemn-faced man servant, who, though shaven and shorn, was right easily recognizable as mine olden enemy, Raoul, of the Mississippi days.

And presently I found myself in a little drawing-room, a whit less sepulchral than the rest of the dismal house. There in a moment or two Lorraine de la Roche joined me. And at first sight of her, lover-like, my best rehearsed phrases went to the winds. On bowing over the slender fingers she offered me I found myself saying in the most banal fashion: "You are not at the Tuileries *bal masque* this evening?"

"No," she made self-evident reply. "One must draw the line somewhere, you see; and I draw it by not going where I am not invited."

"You were not invited? Oh, I wish I had known! Through the embassy I could so easily have procured invitations for both of you."

"Thank you. But it would have made no difference. My father would not have gone, nor have let me go."

"But why not? He—"

"He has met many of the old Royalists lately, and they seem to have imbued him with their hatred of the first consul. Besides, the treatment we met with at the one *salon* was attended—"

"It was abominable!" I flashed. "Pray, try to forget it. It was nothing to the treatment I received at the Tuileries to-day."

"You?" she asked in pretty solicitude. "Tell me."

"Another time if you don't mind. The memory is still a painful one. M. de la Roche is not at home?" I asked to change the subject.

The old man, while allowing his daughter far more freedom (thanks to his forest life) than was permitted to most French girls, always made it a point to receive any guest who might visit the house and to remain in the drawing-room for at least a few minutes, and I wondered now at his absence.

"He was obliged to go out immediately after supper," she said. "'Twas on business of some sort, I believe. It could not have been to any *salon,* for he wore cloak, boots, and sword. He told me not to sit up for him."

It was a thoroughly delightful evening for me, and I stayed an unconscionably long time. We talked of my mission, of Paris, of the wild forest life we both loved.

After a while she got down her lute from the wall and sang to me in her rich contralto voice the old *voyageur* songs of the Mississippi.

As it drew near the time for even the most persistent wooer to go home, I broached a subject that I had not intended yet to mention. It was she who made me do it.

She was speaking of the possibility of her return to America and of the strong likelihood that her father's creditors would soon dispossess them from their Mississippi realm. The note of sadness in her voice was more than I could stand.

"*Mademoiselle,*" said I, "I have good news—wondrous good

news!—for you. But for the present you must keep it secret."

"'A woman and a secret,'" she quoted gaily from the old Provence maxim, "'water and a sieve!' But tell me. What is it?"

"Your claim against the French government," I said. "You are to receive the full value of your confiscated estate. Two hundred and fifty thousand francs."

"*No?*" she cried in delight.

"But *yes!*" I laughed.

"Oh!" she sighed rapturously; then: "How splendid of M. Launay! How wonderful of him! He is a genius. I believe no other man on earth but he could have wrested success from such certain defeat."

"Launay!" I repeated, vastly discomfited.

"Why, of course!" she cried. "You told me from the beginning that he was managing the whole affair. And how miraculously he has done it! Oh, if only he were here so I could thank him! Why didn't you bring him with you?"

"Yes," I babbled vaguely, "why didn't I?"

"And," she hastened to add, evidently noting the disappointment that I could not wholly keep out of tone or face, "I thank you, too, M. Alwyn, for bearing the beautiful news to me."

"I am more than repaid," I answered.

"And now," she said naively, "I can marry!"

"What?"

"I can marry," she repeated.

"Why now more than any other time?" I questioned, bewildered.

"Don't you see?" she explained. "A dowerless girl cannot hope for a husband. My father has told me so a thousand times. I was very unhappy about it—now and then."

"Now and then?"

"When I happened to think of it."

"But were you so anxious to marry?"

"It was not that. One is not anxious to visit China. Most of us never expect to. But if a law were passed strictly forbidding any one to set foot in China cannot you see how wildly eager we should all be to go there—women especially? It was the same about marriage and a dowry. Now that I have a dowry, I don't care at all about marrying. At least I don't think so."

Truly I had made a sorry mess of the whole Quixotic affair. For the love of Loraine de la Roche I had happily cut my fortune in half, and for reward all I heard was glowing praise of Launay and the tidings that she did not care to marry! Decidedly this was not my day.

"Perhaps," I said, foolishly enough, "you may change your mind. You have never been in love?"

"I—I am not sure," she answered, troubled. "How can one tell?"

"The man who can define love in one word or in a million words," I returned, "is not yet born. When he is he will solve the secret of the universe. Love is like music. Once you have heard it you know it forevermore. But to one who has never heard music, music *cannot* be explained. I think real love is best defined as the thing that makes one willing to sacrifice oneself and all he has in order to make the loved one happy."

"To sacrifice oneself and all he has," she repeated softly, "to make the loved one happy. That is very beautiful, and when one feels like that one is in love?"

"I think so."

"Are *you* in love, M. Alwyn?"

"With all my heart and soul," I answered fervently.

I thought I read a look of pain in her great eyes. Perhaps it was only the candles, low in their sconces, flickering as the wind drifted through the great tumble-down house.

"And," she asked in a constrained voice, "does—does she love you?"

"I can only hope and pray so."

"But do you mean you have never asked her?"

"No. I have never dared."

"Never dared? M. Launay says you are the bravest man he knows. Yet you are afraid of one woman?"

"Horribly!" I confessed.

"But why?"

"Because if I found she didn't love me life would no longer be worth while. So I am afraid."

"The Book tells us 'Perfect love casteth out fear,' M. Alwyn, and—and perhaps she is afraid, too. Won't you tell her? Please do!"

I had come to her side in one step. What inspired idiocy I would

have poured forth in another instant I know not, but the words died unsaid.

There was a clamor in the hallway. I heard voices—Raoul's among them—raised in sudden commotion. Then the drawing-room door was flung open and two men rushed in.

CHAPTER XII.
When I Hear Amazing News.

LAUNAY was crossing the threshold. Close behind him was Aniwaya. Launay addressed Lorraine in quick, almost curt, apology for the intrusion, then turned to me.

"I am sorry to break in on your call, Alwyn," he said, suppressed excitement shaking his voice, "but important business has come up and I'm afraid I must ask you to come back to the embassy with me at once."

He was in ball dress. The domino still hung from his shoulder and a red half-mask dangled forgotten from his wrist. Hastily saying good night to the puzzled girl—and, I fear me, cutting off the thanks she was trying to voice to Launay for his supposed victory in winning her estate for her, I followed the attaché from the house.

Raoul lighted us down the walk and through the gate to a waiting fiacre. We jumped in, Aniwaya vaulting to a seat beside the cocker, who thereat looked about as uncomfortable as might a man who has a bear for a bedfellow. Off started the rattling vehicle.

"What's up?" I demanded of Launay the moment we were alone in it.

My nerves were still atingle with the interruption of my love avowal. The wonder of Lorraine de la Roche's sweet presence was still strong upon me. And bitterly did I resent the intrusion that had dragged me away at the very instant when my fate had trembled in the scales.

"What's up?" I asked querulously.

"What *isn't* up?" retorted Launay. "Louis, there is the deuce and all to pay. I—"

"There must be," I growled, "if the embassy needs me at this time of night."

"The embassy? That is only an excuse I gave. I couldn't tell the real truth. Listen, man—Bonaparte is gone."

"Gone? Where?"

"No one can say. He has vanished. It is a secret yet. Only a half-dozen know. But—"

"Bah!" I scoffed. "Bid them search the reception-room of Mlle. Georges at the Comédie Française or of Mme. Bacchiochi at the—"

"No, no! You don't understand. He has been kidnaped!"

"Kidnaped? What joke is—"

"No joke. It is Gospel truth—stolen from his own palace in the very midst of the *bal masque.* Oh, it was a clever trick and well worked out."

"A Bourbon plot!" I gasped, unable to believe the strange tidings.

"Yes—another. Instead of killing him at the ball and risking capture and death, they seem to have spirited him away to some place where they can get rid of him in safety. Fouché has given orders to keep the thing quiet until all hope of finding him is gone. His police are scouring Paris now, and the troops. I had the story from the secretary you know of."

"But—but how did it happen?"

"The first consul wore a gold-embroidered red domino and a flame-colored mask. His disguise was an open secret. Fouché thinks one of the conspirators may have worn a duplicate of the domino and mask and have taken the first consul's place in the ballroom for a time to avert suspicion. But when we unmasked Bonaparte was gone.

"A servant told Fouché that he had seen a man in such a disguise crossing one of the passageways with a woman hanging to his arm. Two or three men in dominoes surrounded them, and there seemed to be a tussle, accompanied by much laughter. Then the men hustled the flame-colored masker out through one of the long windows into the gardens. The servant thought it all a bit of gaiety, for mirth had been running high and champagne was plentiful.

"A sentry at the rear gate said he saw several men in dominoes escorting another such man, who appeared to be drunk, into a carriage that drove away at once. It would have been an easy thing, you

see, to drug Bonaparte, once they got him into a secluded part of the gardens. That is all any one knows. But he is gone!"

I sat in the swaying, pitching old rattletrap of a fiacre as it bumped along the dark, ill-paved streets; trying to adjust myself to these startling facts and to see how they might affect me and my mission.

With Bonaparte dead and the government in a ferment, the whole affair of the Louisiana Purchase might well fall through. The new government might not care to prosecute expensive wars as did Bonaparte. And thus it might not be in such crying need for ready money. It might even very probably carry out the old "colonial empire" idea as regarded the West.

"Bonaparte must be found!" I exclaimed.

"Decidedly," assented Launay. "But kindly tell me how. Even if he is not already killed."

I made no answer. There *was* no answer. Launay continued:

"I knew you'd want to be told at once. That is why I came. I guessed where you were spending the evening, and when I got to the De la Roche gate and found Aniwaya standing there I—"

"Aniwaya! The man gives me no peace. He follows me everywhere like a dog, for fear I may be hurt. It is humiliating for a grown man to be tracked by—"

I broke off short. My own complaining words had given me the idea I sought.

"I have it!" I shouted aloud.

To the coacher I called:

"The Tuileries! Rear garden gate!"

"What is it?" queried Launay in surprise.

"Aniwaya!" I repeated. "Can't you understand? If he can track me for miles through the dark, over an unfamiliar road, he can track others."

"You mean—"

"Just that. Paris will be treated to-night, for the first time in its history, to a feat in trail-reading."

"Impossible! How can he—"

"I don't know yet; but it is worth a trial."

I halted the fiacre again and made the Indian leave the box, much to the driver's relief, and get into the interior of the vehicle with us.

Then, as we drove on, I began:

"Aniwaya, do you know who Napoleon Bonaparte is?"

"Chief of the Long-House where you fought the French warrior."

"Yes, and Sachem of France. He has been caught by enemies and taken away secretly. No one knows where."

"H-m!" grunted Aniwaya in disdain. "Not hard to know. They take him to their village and torture him out of life or maybe just burn him. Any man would know that."

"Aniwaya!" I exclaimed, exasperated; "is there no way of making you understand the difference between the Mississippi country and France?"

"Yes," he assented, unmoved. "More people in France—that is all. Do the same things, but say S'il vous plaît,' first."

I was not to be drawn into a useless discussion when time was so precious; so I went on:

"Bonaparte has been carried away from the palace. Perhaps he has already been killed. Perhaps—"

"As I said," croaked Aniwaya.

"Perhaps," I continued, "he is still alive."

"Saved for torture," he murmured with the air of a connoisseur.

"If he is dead," I resumed, "my work here in France will go for nothing. I shall be in disgrace and a failure. If he is alive and I can find him and bring him back to his palace it will probably mean that I shall succeed in my errand here and be famous in my own land."

I paused to let my words sink in. Aniwaya sat speechless, apparently indifferent.

"I mean," I explained, "that all my hopes depend on bringing him back. It means everything to me."

Still no reply.

"Do you think," I asked impatiently, "that there is a chance you could track him?"

"Why, yes," was the careless answer. "You know that. Why make so much talk? I find him."

"You forget, Aniwaya," put in Launay, "that he did not go away on foot. He went in a carriage. How can you track one carriage where a hundred have passed?"

Aniwaya did not seem to consider this remark worth answering.

A Bout With the Man of Destiny

As you may have gathered, he was not a fluent conversationalist.

Presently we came to a halt at the Tuileries' rear entrance. Lights were still gleaming from the ballroom windows and strains of music came to us. For the ball was not yet over; nor did one guest in a hundred know of the first consul's abduction.

Aniwaya, as usual, speedily became the center of a knot of admiring, staring link boys, *cochers,* and idlers. He brushed them aside like so many flies and stalked up to the sentinel.

He made a few guttural inquiries of the sentry in a tone of such assured command that, combined with his giant size, he quite overawed the machinelike soldier and elicited answers that were almost civil. Then the Indian came back to me.

"Traveling coach," he reported. "Four horses. Not coach for gentlefolk. Only one that was here. Rest all carriages. Long journey, maybe."

"Yes," I assented, "they would naturally have taken a strong traveling coach if they had far to go. But—"

He had not waited for me to finish. Staying only to repeat to me what he had gathered from the sentinel, he had moved back to the roadway.

"He is looking for the marks of traveling-coach wheels," I whispered to Launay. "They are broader and stronger than carriage wheels, because more strain is put on them."

"But how can a savage know that?" wondered Launay.

"A man who lives in trackless forests observes everything," said I. "Otherwise, after making a wilderness journey, how could a *courreur de bois* make the return trip so accurately over the same ground?"

Aniwaya was not on his knees in the roadway, nor was he coursing like a dog for the scent. Indeed, to the ignorant onlookers his actions were not such as to cause curiosity.

He was standing idly beside the gutters, glancing with seeming indifference at the countless cuts and ridges and hollows scored in the road by the passage of myriad wheels.

The radius of light from the gate lanthorns was narrow, and presently Aniwaya strayed onward out of this radius into the darkness beyond. Knowing the amazing power of sight possessed by the night travelers of the forests, I felt certain he had picked up the trail.

CHAPTER XIII.
On the Trail.

I MOTIONED to Launay to follow; and I strolled off, as though with no especial interest, in the wake of Aniwaya. Presently we had left the Tuileries and its light and music and its groups of loungers behind us.

So dark was it that Launay often stumbled, and once he fell. My own eyes, accustomed as they were to the midnight forests of the West, could scarce achieve more through the gloom than keep the giant Indian in sight.

This was no easy feat, for Aniwaya strode along at a pace that forced me into a dog-trot. The huge savage never for an instant faltered. His eyes on the ground before him, he maintained that mile-eating stride of his.

To him, who could trace unerringly the invisible footprints of a fur-bearing beast through trackless wanderings in the wilderness, the following of plainly marked wheel tracks was the simplest sort of achievement.

As he afterward told me, the trail more than once crossed that of other and similar wheelmarks of traveling coaches. But ere it did so he had so fully acquainted himself with the dozen minor peculiarities of the particular coach he was following that the tracks of the others did not for an instant confuse him.

To you who read, this performance of Aniwaya on a moonless night may seem little short of miraculous. To him your own ability to distinguish the handwriting of one correspondent from that of another would have appeared infinitely more wonderful.

Each man to his own art. And the art of Aniwaya and of his forebears for ten centuries back had been to read trails and to follow prey and foe through places where the most crafty devices had been employed to throw off pursuit.

On we went, never checking that swift, tireless pace, although more than once I heard Launay panting heavily as the long-sustained speed began to tell cruelly on wind and muscle.

Paris streets by night, save in certain sections, were well-nigh as

deserted as those of a country village. They were not safe; nor were there as a rule many amusements to call respectable folk abroad.

Once, as we rounded a corner, two footpads sprang out on us from the black mouth of an alleyway. One of them leveled a horse-pistol and the other unveiled the swathed light of a lanthorn.

The lanthorn's rays fell upon the huge, awesome figure of the blanket-clad red man. The thief dropped his light with a yell, fearing, I suppose, that he had met with Beelzebub himself, and took to his heels, followed by his companion.

Otherwise our strange progress was not checked. And the few belated pedestrians we met hugged the wall and gave us the road.

We had crossed the Seine and had plunged through a wilderness of mean streets on the Rive Gauche. On and through them and out into roads bordered by fields and trees, and still Aniwaya did not check his steady, swift pace.

"They have carried him out into the country," puffed Launay behind me. "And any minute now we are like to find his body in a roadside ditch."

But his prophecy proved false. Onward we went, and no body did we find. For perhaps two miles we continued after we had passed the last house. Then, at a cross-road, Aniwaya veered sharply to the left.

"He's lost the track," panted Launay. "He's taking us back to Paris again. Hi, there, Aniwaya!"

The savage made no reply, nor did he slacken his swift pace. Hardy and strong though I was, I was beginning to tire. As for Launay, he was in piteous case.

I could not at all understand why Aniwaya should have taken this new turn. But experience had told me his trailing instincts were never at fault.

And finally it dawned on me that this detour into the country might readily have been a ruse on the part of Bonaparte's captors to confuse any possible pursuers.

The phenomenon of the turning back did not seem to worry Aniwaya at all. He was used from childhood to the "doubling" of a pursued quarry, and to him the maneuver must have seemed the most natural thing imaginable.

Whereas the outward trip had been in an almost semicircular

detour, the return journey was straight. No baffling trips into side byways as before, but along the highroad with not a single deviation.

"Slower, Aniwaya!" I ordered as I heard Launay groan with weariness.

The savage abated his long stride, and we moved along, still rapidly, but at a less heart-breaking pace.

At last we were back between rows of scattered houses; then in the city itself, and on at a new angle.

"Have you any idea where we are?" panted Launay after a time.

"Yes," I made answer. "We are passing through the Montparnasse section. We'll be beyond it in another minute or so, and then in the—"

I ceased abruptly. We were traversing a narrow byway, on one side of which were vacant lots. On the other ran a high, rather dilapidated wall. And at a gate in this blank-faced old wall Aniwaya came to a halt."Here," he announced quietly, his deep, guttural voice unshaken by the long journey.

"The coach stopped here?" asked Launay.

"Here," repeated Aniwaya; "then went on."

"Why don't you go on, then?"

"No use. Four got out—went through gate. One was pushed along to gate. Three in boots. One in slippers for dancing. Smaller man. None came back. The coach made lighter marks when it went on—not so heavy. I think only driver left in it."

"Good!" applauded Launay in open admiration of the trail-reader's skill. "Aniwaya, you are a wonder."

"Papoose-work, this," grunted Aniwaya scornfully. "Any child read this trail. What next, my master?"

But I could not at once reply. My heart had stopped beating, and my brain was dizzy at a discovery I had made. Well did I know where we were. We had stopped at the near gate and wall of the rambling old Monparnasse house which the Sieur de la Roche had rented. The house where, barely an hour earlier, I had been interrupted in my avowal of love for Lorraine de la Roche.

And Napoleon Bonaparte was there! A prisoner, perhaps already murdered.

CHAPTER XIV.
Wherein I Play the Housebreaker.

HERE, then, was the end and goal of our night's wanderings. Here at the door of the girl I loved. The girl who, in the wide, blind sweep of French justice, was likely, for this night's work, to find her white neck beneath the guillotine's knife.

Innocent and ignorant of the plot as I knew Lorraine must be, she and all the old house's inmates would assuredly be punished by death were it ever known that the first consul had been assassinated there. Yes, and even were we to save Bonaparte alive, prison was the least penalty she could hope for.

Oh, it turned me sick! To me the whole medieval plot was now as simple as had been the midnight coach-trail to Aniwaya.

The Bourbons, using De la Roche and a few of the wilder spirits as their instruments, had abducted Bonaparte from the Tuileries, wholly or partly drugged him, carried him off by a devious route into the country (doubtless laboriously leaving a score of false trails for pursuers to follow), and had doubled back to Paris with him as the place where he would least likely be sought.

Here in this ancient house, taken for the purpose by De la Roche, they had at last immured their prisoner. I could very easily imagine the reasons why he had not been put to death immediately.

It was not the French—to say nothing of the Bourbon—way to do things without full attention to dramatic effect. The chiefs of the Bourbon party would, of course, come into Bonaparte's presence, revile him oratorically for his misdeeds in crushing the Royalist party and in exalting the rabble, and would, each in turn, melodramatically condemn him to death after the fashion of the ancients whom they aped.

After which the assassins would be allowed to do their work with due heed to scenic elaborateness. All of which would consume time. At daybreak, probably, at the earliest the accusers would be summoned. For they were folk who did not relish the loss of a night's rest.

And hours still intervened before sunrise. Hours during which the captive consul was probably guarded only by a handful of the faction's

desperadoes and by De la Roche himself. For it would be unsafe to fill the house with noisy patriots at such an unusual hour, when the bulk of the servants and Lorraine herself were not in the secret.

"We have till dawn," I said. "There is not much chance that the grounds are guarded. The captors are probably chuckling over the idea that they have thrown off pursuit. You know where we are, Launay?"

"Yes," he answered with a gasp, after a closer look at the oddly carven gate. "Good Lord, man! what—"

"Go back at once to the embassy," I ordered. "Send a carriage here to wait at this entrance, or, better, come back yourself with it. But as soon as you get to the embassy, write out an account of this matter and tell one of the servants to carry it to Fouché at sunrise, if we have not returned before then. Quick! Don't argue. Do as I say."

"But—"

"Hurry!"

"Your own safety—"

"My own safety and Aniwaya's—yes, and Lorraine de la Roche's—will be secured by your obeying me. That written account will be our safeguard. By holding it over the heads of the people here I may be able to work wonders. Or I may not. Anyhow, it is our one chance. Go!"

Reluctantly, and still muttering, he vanished down the road.

"Now," I said to Aniwaya, "to get over that wall. The gate is locked. It would rouse the household if we tried to break it down. Can you climb the wall?"

He glanced up at the ten-foot structure above us. My eyes followed his. Stepping back to get the better view, I saw against the paler gloom of the sky that low, twisted iron spikes fringed the top, and that these were plenteously reenforced by masses of broken glass.

Before I could comment on this seemingly insuperable barrier, Aniwaya had slipped off his blanket and stood clad only in loin-cloth and moccasins.

Folding the blanket thrice lengthwise, he tossed it with a pretty accuracy to the wall-top, where it lay like a buffer along the crest of the spikes and bottles.

Then, with a leap upward, Aniwaya caught the edge of the coping with his fingers and silently drew himself to the summit.

Once there, he crouched on the blanket, bracing himself, and held down his arms to me. I caught his outstretched hands, and partly lifted, partly digging my shoe-toes into the inequalities of the wall's side, I reached the coping.

There for a moment we stood. Tangled shrubbery was below us. Beyond was a sweep of untended rose-garden, and then loomed up the house itself. The lower floors were dark. In a little turret room, at one corner and high up, twinkled a candle.

By the rays of this feeble light I could see the window was barred. Many old houses of France had such upper rooms. They had once served in a way as cells; for the confining of some thieving servant, or even for a refractory son or daughter of the house who chanced to be in temporary disgrace or in need of discipline. Fathers in ancient France had—and often exercised—the rights of jailers.

"In there!" I whispered. "There is where they would have put him. It is probably the only room that has bars. It is too high for escape, and the garden-wall shuts off its view from the road. Even were he to shout for help, he could scarce hope to be heard. And if he should shout once—"

I paused. A shadow had come between me and the candle-light. It vanished and, a few seconds later, reappeared; vanished and appeared again.

Some one was evidently pacing the narrow confines of the room.

As I watched, the shadow became a figure, and the figure stood for a moment at the barred window. Even at that distance I recognized the uniformed shoulders and the big, sternly erect head.

Then, as the form turned away and the candle-light fell for an instant full upon him, my far-sighted eyes told me two more details.

Not only was the captive Napoleon Bonaparte, but his arms were bound behind his back, and his face was disfigured by a bandage across the mouth. Scant wonder he did not cry for help!

In no other window on that side of the house did a light show. But I knew most of the living-rooms were at the front. And such persons as still remained awake were probably gathered there.

While I gazed, Aniwaya had picked up the blanket (he had cleared a precarious space amid the broken glass of the coping for me to stand on), and had wrapped it about his shoulders. Now, stooping over, he

seized the edge of the coping and without a sound let himself down into the labyrinth of shrubbery below. Not a snapped twig nor a rustling leaf marked his impact with the earth.

"Wait!" he whispered as I prepared to follow. "You would crash like elephant. Now, jump!"

I did as he bade me. And noiselessly he caught me in mid air, lowering me to the ground without the slightest sound. The man's strength and powers of silent motion were phenomenal. Never had I realized it so fully as now.

He set off through the shrubbery, I after him, and presently we came to one of the weed-grown gravel paths leading to the rear of the house. There he halted.

"What—" I began.

But he checked me with a gesture, and now I heard what his own quicker ear had already caught—the scurrying pad of feet on the turf coming toward us from the house.

"A dog!" I muttered.

And for the first time I remembered the existence of Belle Annie, one of the three giant boarhounds I had seen in the wilderness hall of the De la Roches'—the only one of the trio they had brought to France.

The huge brute was kept in the house during the day, but roamed the grounds by night as a guard—and a terribly efficient guard at that.

Soundless, after the manner of her kind, Belle Annie was bearing down on us. Already her vast shape was visible through the darkness. In another second she would be near enough to spring.

Then the night quiet was split by a sound—low-breathed and venomous—a long-drawn hiss, followed by a sharp whirring—the warning of the forest rattlesnake.

The hound checked her rush, her wilderness training telling her all too surely the dread import of that sound. All the fight scared out of her as it could not have been by any human foe, she wheeled and slunk away.

I myself had started involuntarily; but a grunt from Aniwaya told me the origin of the dread "rattlesnake call," and on we crept unmolested.

CHAPTER XV.
Wherein I Play Knight Errant.

ABOVE us the house bulked dark and huge. It was not an inviting place at best. Now it looked ghost-ridden.

We walked softly along its base until we came beneath the turret. Then we looked up. The wall above our heads rose abruptly for perhaps forty feet before it was pierced by that feeble bar of yellow light. Aniwaya turned and looked at me for instructions.

"We have no ladder," said I. "And if we had it would not be long enough. The only thing to do is to get in somehow and make our way to the room. Are you armed?"

Lifting the blanket he showed me the long, keen knife at his girdle.

"I am not," said I. "I have not so much as a pocket-knife. But we have not time to go back and raise assistance."

Now, therein I deceived both myself and him. There was probably ample time for such an act of common sense. And in the rearmost recesses of my brain I knew it.

There was probably ample time to return to the Tuileries with my news. In less than an hour the surrounding streets would be choked with cavalry and police. A regiment of infantry would fill the grounds. A thousand troops would burst into the ramshackle old house to rescue their adored general.

And, unless the plotters, on the approach of the soldiers, should kill Bonaparte out of hand, he would be rescued in a right spectacular fashion. Yes, and De la Roche and Lorraine as well as the wilier conspirators would be dragged forthwith to prison, and later, perhaps, to the guillotine.

Which, down in the bottom of my heart, was why I was intent on jeopardizing my own life by entering the house now, rather than to adopt the ostensibly saner plan of sending for help.

Should we fail, Aniwaya and I, and lose our lives thereby, I knew Launay's message to the Tuileries at sunrise would bring the needed rescue party. And I knew, too, that in such event Launay would, for my sake, move heaven and earth to exempt the girl I loved from the wholesale punishment that must follow.

Aniwaya had already started around the house in search of a door or unshuttered window. I followed. But before he had taken three steps beyond the turret he stopped.

His arm, brushing against the bushy growth of wistaria and ivy that covered the south wall of the ancient mansion, now wriggled cautiously into the heart of one mighty clump of vines.

He gripped the twisting "stalk" of a century-old wistaria vine, a stem as thick as my thigh and gnarled and knotted like the fingers of a rheumatic.

With both hands Aniwaya grasped the stalk. And with all his strength he tugged at it. The force that would have dragged a bison bull to its knees did not so much as budge the mighty stem.

For full a hundred years it had grown there, driving its million rootlets into the mortar crevices of the house wall, reenforced by twining streamers of ivy and hardened by a century's growth. Not two yoke of oxen could have ripped it free.

Releasing his hold, Aniwaya stepped back and looked upward.

"Runs to top!" he muttered. "Come. But be slow and make no noise."

I had already divined his plan. With the deftness and silence of a snake he began to climb the thick stem. I followed.

I could not hope to rival his skill either as a climber or in noiseless motion. Yet I was a strong man and active. And the hold given by the surrounding creepers made the climb ridiculously easy.

I obeyed the Indian's command to go slowly. And thus I was able to minimize the rustling and tearing of the leaves about me. By no means so silently as my guide, yet with little more noise than a prowling tomcat in search of birds' nests.

Up we went and up. From below the distance had seemed a bare forty or less feet. But now I adjudged it little less than a mile. I had ludicrous memories of the tale of Jack and the bean-stalk as I crept upward in the wake of the Indian whom I could no longer see or hear.

It was no pleasant occupation, hanging twixt earth and heaven at dead of night against the rotting wall of a house that was full of men who would ask nothing better than to kill at sight such an interloper as I.

And during that interminable climb I had full scope to reason out

the probable results of my foolhardy act. Even should we by chance manage to reach the roof and from thence the window of Bonaparte's cell, we were not like to be much better off than now.

For in all probability there were one or more guards in the room with him. And in that case what possible chance would we two—one of us totally unarmed and the other with only a knife for weapon—have against such odds.

From the vantage point of the room, while we were hanging helpless outside the bars, they could shoot or stab us like rats.

I had acted on rash impulse. I had thereby risked Aniwaya's life and my own. For the bravos who had staked all on the audacious act of abducting the foremost man on earth would most assuredly not hesitate one whit in slitting the throats of two outsiders who had blundered in upon them to the imperiling of their great secret.

And now, reaching up for a new hold on the vine, my open hand came in contact with a bare ankle. Aniwaya had paused. I looked up.

Just above my head jutted a coping of stone, perhaps ten inches wide. It ran evidently along a goodly portion of that side of the house.

And now I understood why Aniwaya had ceased climbing. The coping just above me went to the right as well as to the left—to the right, where scarce two yards away the semicircle of the turret abutted beyond the flat surface of the rest of the house-wall.

And around the turret, scarce a yard below the lighted windows, the coping was continued.

An inquiring grunt from Aniwaya, an answering whisper from me, and the Indian stepped out on the coping, testing its strength with his great weight and sustaining his balance by flattening himself against the wall in front of him.

But at his action I rebelled. I had brought him into this, and now that the moment for action seemed near I was resolved to take the lead.

"Back!" I whispered.

Stolidly he obeyed me, returning to his hold on the vine-stalk and gazing down to note the reason for so odd a command.

I wriggled higher through the foliage and in my turn stepped upon the coping. Then, flattening myself to the wall, as had he, I started to the right. Aniwaya, with a growl of disgust at having thus been hood-

winked out of his position of foremost in danger, followed me onto the coping.

But where he, in his moccasined feet and with his far greater grace, found easy footing, my own position was worse than precarious.

I was in smooth-soled walking-shoes that slipped right perilously on the slimy stone, and when I stood in ordinary fashion my heels projected a good two inches over the edge. I was unaccustomed to balancing myself thus. The vine was not here to sustain me. My fingers met only the age-worn side of the house.

Something seemed to hang heavy from my shoulders, drawing me outward—out to the forty-foot fall to the earth below. It was not a happy moment.

I set my teeth and edged my way along. After a century or more my right hand reached the nearest window-bar. I gripped it. It sagged perceptibly under the strain, and flakes of rust came off in my palm.

The bars were evidently well-nigh as old as the house; and they had rusted in their sockets; rusted and loosened, as the mortar that held them had crumbled away under the gnawing tooth of time.

I took warning and threw my weight less heavily on the tottering support. Yet the contact served to balance me and to restore my sense of security. That same sense of security, by the way, is an odd thing. Get up now and walk along a ten-inch-wide board of your floor. You can–do it a thousand times without once stepping off or losing your balance. But suppose that solitary ten-inch board were stretched across a bottomless chasm. Could you walk along it without falling? Why not? The conditions would be the same. All but the sense of security.

I leaned over to the right, my hand on the bar, my feet firmer set on the coping. And I looked into the room from one corner of the window. On a cot, his pacing done, his head bent, his hands bound, and his lips bandaged, sat the man of destiny.

Save for him the cell was empty. At the far end was a stout oaken door, fast shut, presumably barred from without. On a small table stood a candle in a pewter stick. The room, save for cot and table, was bare of furniture. There was not so much as a rug on the floor.

And here, awaiting death, was the idol of France, the man whose smile was courted by monarchs, whose frown could unmake empires.

I stepped along the coping a little farther. Attracted perhaps by the slight sound, perhaps from the corner of his downcast eyes seeing my white face against the bars, Napoleon looked quickly up.

Never have I admired him as at that moment. His cold eyes showed no surprise at so weird an apparition forty feet in air. He, whose lightning thought could divine an enemy's plans were they fully made, knew at once why I was there and that I was a friend.

To him my grimed, pallid visage and disordered hair must have seemed the most exquisite and welcome sight under heaven, for I was lifting from him the shadow of death.

Quietly and with no emotion on his marble face he came to the window.

The room being old and not designed for the comfort of its inmates, there was no glass nor even sash in the window opening. In those days glass was still a luxury. And many a house in warm climates or in summer was destitute of a single pane of it.

Napoleon Bonaparte reached the window and stood looking at me, his face not six inches from mine. Supporting myself against the bars by one hand I reached in and unbound the handkerchief from about his mouth.

As I did so a leathern gag fell from between his teeth. Truly the Bourbons had done this part of their work with rare completeness.

"Go at once to the Tuileries," were Bonaparte's first words. "Tell the minister of police and General Lefebvre where I am. How far is it to Paris?"

And I saw he, too, had been fooled by that long detour of the coach. I was not minded to undeceive him.

"You must put yourself for the time in my hands," I answered. "Were the soldiers or the police to attack this château your captors would kill you before the first rescuer could cross the threshold."

"True," he muttered; "you are less of a dunce than I thought, M. Alwyn. What is your plan?"

"Wait a moment," I answered.

I slipped back to the left, out of his range of vision, to where Aniwaya crouched waiting.

CHAPTER XVI.
A Rough Rascal.

"THESE bars are rotten," I whispered to the Indian. "I believe you can bend or break away enough of them to get him out. In case of a surprise, or if we should lose sight of each other in the dark, here are your orders—and obey them as you value my life. For more than my life may hang on your obedience. I want you to carry the man down to the ground the way we came. You are strong enough?"

A disdainful nod from Aniwaya gave assent and I went on.

"You will have to strap him to your back like a papoose, for I do not want him unbound. And when you get him into the garden, if I am not there, tie and gag and blindfold him. Carry him to the road—you can easily open the gate from the inside—and wait till M. Launay comes up with the carriage.

"Tell M. Launay—but where General Bonaparte cannot hear you—to make a drive of at least an hour before reaching the embassy."

"The embassy?"

"Yes, not the Tuileries—the embassy. Take the consul secretly to my rooms there. No one will be astir so early. Answer none of his questions—and keep him there until I come."

"I do not go without you."

"Yes, you do. This is one time where you can serve me best by leaving me, in case I am caught or miss you. I see no reason why I should be captured or become separated from you. But I want to make certain in event of accident that my plans do not miscarry. You promise?"

A grunt of reluctant assent.

"One thing more. Do not let General Bonaparte see M. Launay or know M. Launay is with you. Tell M. Launay that if an attaché of the American legation carries the first consul forcibly to my rooms there may be diplomatic complication. But if my Indian servant does it, General Bonaparte can be made to believe it was through zeal of service to me or through ignorance. Now, come!"

A moment later we were at the grated window. Bonaparte still stood close to the casement. I gave Aniwaya a word of instruction,

and he seized one of the rusted bars in both hands.

Under that fearful grip the age-weakened, rusty iron bent and shook. From the rotted sockets dropped a tiny shower of mortar.

One fierce shake and the bar had come from its place like a wrenched tooth in the forceps of a dentist.

Strong was Aniwaya—but he had not need of half his strength to remove these pastworthy old bars from their decaying fastenings. As a place for safekeeping the cell was a joke.

It reminded me of the famed Spanish prison where Don Ferdinando, after eighteen years of dreary incarceration, suddenly bethought him one day to open the door and walk out.

Three bars were removed.

Then Bonaparte hissed sharply between his teeth. "Some one is coming," he whispered.

"Quick!" I urged. "Come out!"

"My body cannot pass through such a narrow space," he objected stubbornly.

And now even I could hear the approaching steps. Another instant and we should all three be caught like rats in a blind drain.

"Aniwaya!" I exclaimed.

The giant needed no second word. He reached one huge red hand through the opening, caught Bonaparte by an epauletted shoulder and, with a single movement, drew that struggling, highly offended dignitary through the opening and out onto the coping beside us. A stroke of his knife severed the bonds that tied the consul's hands.

"Your arms around my neck. From behind," commanded the Indian as though Napoleon Bonaparte were an ill-treated papoose.

The consul drew back. Aniwaya swung him outward over the gulf. By instinct of self-preservation Bonaparte threw out both arms to keep himself from falling and clasped the savage around the neck.

Without a moment's pause Aniwaya began to retrace his steps along the coping toward the vine ladder. Bonaparte, struggling and cursing, held on like grim death. There was nothing else for him to do unless he relished a forty-foot fall.

"Keep him safe until I join you," I called; for Bonaparte's benefit rather than for that of the already instructed Indian.

Then I darted through the opening into the room, just as a hand

fumbled at the outer bolt of the door.

The exigent had arrived that I had feared, and against which I had provided by my orders to Aniwaya. There had been grave danger that we might be surprised in the act of escaping. And I intended to give the fugitives time to get away clear before their flight should be known.

Were the escape discovered while Aniwaya was carrying the consul down the vines or even before they should be free of the grounds, recapture would be certain. Recapture for Bonaparte and death for all three of us!

My straining ears had just caught the sound of carriage wheels. And I knew that Launay was coming back as I had bidden him. Could Aniwaya but have five minutes wherein to get his prisoner to the gate, into the carriage and away, all would be well.

And I, and I alone, could procure them those five minutes. Were I to seek to follow them now the person who was about to enter the room would find the bird flown. The broken bars would tell him the mode of flight. And in a minute the grounds would be swarming with searching Bourbons.

I bounded into the room, blew out the candle; then, throwing myself upon the cot, wrapped the bedclothes about me—body, head, and all.

I was not one second too soon. The bolt yielded and I heard the door open. I heard a man step into the room and then halt, as if surprised to find the place in total darkness.

Once more had luck been with me, for, by his pause and the fact that he did not exclaim at sight of the gap in the bars, I knew he carried no light.

He had no doubt thought to find the candle still burning. And the darkness prevented him from noting the wrecked casement.

Through a chink in the tumbled bedclothes around my head I peered. I could see the booted legs of a man, and beyond I could see a dim-lit corridor. There was barely enough light admitted by the newly opened door to make visible to any newcomer the faint outlines of the room and its contents.

CHAPTER XVII.
I Hold a "Bed Of Justice."

BUT there was apparently enough light to show my visitor that I was in bed with the covers bunched about me, for he stepped over to the cot and said half roughly, half timidly:

"Bonaparte, you are summoned to your trial. Come!"

I made no reply. He waited for an instant.

"Come!" he repeated.

Still I did not reply, but fell to wondering how far down the vines Aniwaya and the consul might have gone by this time.

"Bonaparte," he repeated, "your judges wait to give you fair trial for your life. Come!"

This time I ventured to snore very gently.

"You are not asleep!" he reproved. "I heard you jump into bed as I unbolted the door."

By way of confuting this statement I snored a little more loudly. But I softly tightened my hold on the bedclothes around my head, lest in exasperation he drag them off of me as do irate parents whose children are slow in getting up.

However, it was evident that he had no such thought. The name of Napoleon Bonaparte seemed still to be a charm, even with his captors. At least this particular captor showed behind his assumption of jailerlike roughness a very wholesome respect for his prisoner.

I bethought me how the glare of the helpless Marius turned to water the brutal strength of the slaves sent to slay him. And I realized what a fillip it would have been to Bonaparte's gigantic vanity could he have known how in this dire hour of his supposed ruin his very jailers shrank from casting indignity upon him.

At the same time I turned cold at thought of how pitiably near we had been to arriving too late for his rescue. Three minutes later and we should have found him already gone to the classical farce that his captors chose to miscall a "trial."

Well did I know what that trial would have been. One after another the conspirator chiefs would solemnly have enumerated his crimes against royalty and against France. His defense would have been

smothered in oratory. And the "execution" would have proceeded as according to the carefully prearranged schedule.

"Bonaparte!" exclaimed my visitor in desperation, "will you go to your trial or must I call help to drag you there like a common felon?"

Still I snored softly and happily. Every minute of time was worth a million francs. And fully two minutes—or two lifetimes—must already have passed.

The man walked to the doorway loudly, ostentatiously, as though to fulfil his threat of summoning others to his aid. I did not seek to detain him.

I am a fair judge of my fellow men. And, from his hesitancy and his unwillingness to precipitate a scene by laying violent hands on me, I inferred the sort of man he was likely to be.

Assuredly not the sort who would care to brave the scoffs of his fellows by appearing before them with the confession that he had not the ability to persuade or coerce the prisoner to leave his cell. I was quite certain he would come back for further pleading ere he abandoned his rôle of summoner.

This, decidedly, was not one of the clever and desperate men who had made the capture. Such a one would have had me out of bed and down the corridor in a twinkling. Rather, probably, was he a noble of old lineage, wealth, and high influence who (for the value of that lineage, wealth, and influence to the cause) must be given a part in the drama.

And he had therefore been chosen to haul me before my judges.

A historic and noble feat to be boasted of by his grandchildren!

Again, in the interim, I reflected on my error in having thought the "judges" would not assemble until morning. They must have gathered at the house, in preparation, even before the consul's arrival. And I understood why De la Roche had bidden Lorraine not to sit up for him.

My caller, after standing for a moment at the door and clearing his throat loudly, as though about to summon aid, turned back into the room. At the same time I heard the stamp of impatient horses and the clink of harness metal at the distant gate. And I knew the carriage was waiting.

"Bonaparte," said my jailor in a monstrous, stern voice. "You will

rise at once and come with me."

He crossed to the bed and laid a none too firm hand on my shoulder. I shook off his touch as might a peevish child.

"Maledetto!" I mumbled through the layers of bedclothes. "Let me sleep."

"Soon enough you will sleep long and dreamlessly," he answered right dramatically. "Follow me."

"Who are you?" I quavered still through the voice-disguising folds of bedding.

"I am the Vicomte de Presle," he replied loftily, "whose father died under the guillotine of your cursed republic."

"De Presle?" I muttered indistinctly. "I do not know you."

"That is an honor to me," he returned. "I have never set foot in your bourgeois court, nor would any man of breeding. You and your sort are not likely to have heard of me, for never until now have I had the misfortune to set eye on you. But history shall hear of me for this night's work."

"M. le Vicomte," I replied, unwinding the bedclothes from around me and sitting up in the dim light, "you seem a man of rare discernment and courage. Such a man as I love to have near me. Such a man as might well rise to the topmost pinnacle of greatness. I say it—*I*, whose judgment of men is never at fault."

"If you are seeking to wheedle me—" he began gruffly; albeit he was vastly flattered by so gross a compliment from the arch foe of his class.

"Wheedle you?" I echoed in pained surprise. "Wheedle *you?* My dear M. de Presle, I have just told you my judgment of men never errs. How should I dare to essay the impossible task of wheedling you? You misjudge me cruelly."

My tense ears caught the sound of a very brief and not overstrenuous scuffle in the garden below.

"Good!" I thought jubilantly. "Aniwaya has trussed him up again and blindfolded and gagged him, as I ordered. And Bonaparte has objected very futilely."

"Napoleon Bonaparte," said the vicomte, almost reluctantly, "we waste time. And my comrades will wax impatient. Come!"

"In one minute, M. le Vicomte," I assented. "Yet it irks me to meet

a man of your caliber at a time when I can make no use of him for his own merited advancement. Under my guidance such an one as yourself might readily hope to grasp the marshal's baton within a year. Think of that! 'Vicomte de Presle, marshal of France!' Nay, even—"

"If you hope to bribe me—" he ejaculated rather shakily.

"What an unconscionable time Aniwaya takes in getting to the carriage and transmitting my message to Launay!" I groaned inwardly, saying aloud: "M. le Vicomte, you have no right to impute bribery to me. And I believe you to be as incorruptible as was Robespierre himself. Yet fame and power and a marshalship of France—"

I ceased. For to my ears came the most welcome sound on earth— the grinding of far-off carriage-wheels, the crack of a whip, and the hoofbeats of horses settling into a steady trot. The vicomte, seemingly bewildered by the vision of splendor I conjured up, muttered dazedly:

"Fame—power—a marshalship of France—"

"All three of them excellent things, my worthy chuckle-head!" I assented briskly, rising to my feet. "And you are as likely to obtain one of them as all. And comfortably certain of gaining none. For a more weak-kneed, addle-pated, spineless travesty on a bold conspirator than your asinine self I have yet to meet. Now, then, if you please, we will go and have a look at your fellow desperadoes. If they are all like you, I shall simply shout 'Boo!' and watch them scatter. Lead the way, M. le Vicomte—I mean M. le Marechal!"

CHAPTER XVIII.
I Play at Toss-Penny with Fate.

DE PRESLE gasped, gurgled wordlessly, and stamped out of the room, motioning me to follow. I doubt not he would right eagerly have volunteered just then to play executioner for me.

Along the short passage he led me, then down a flight of spiral steps and through a longer passage, at whose end was the doorway of a brightly lighted room.

Over his shoulder, as we neared this doorway, I could see perhaps twenty men grouped in formal fashion around a dais on which sat a

richly dressed man of about forty-five.

My eye, trained to take in details at a glance, swept the group. Prominent in it was the Seigneur de la Roche, who was resplendent in a court suit. Few of the others did I know, even by sight. For the *ancien régime* kept to itself in its dull, stately mansions of the Faubourg St. Germain and seldom mingled with the workaday world.

Yet, from seeing him often in my boyhood, I recognized at once the man seated in a gilded chair upon the dais. He was the exiled Comte de Provence, latest of the Bourbon princes, younger brother of the dead Louis XVI, and himself the hope and mainstay of the Royalist party which already hailed him as Louis XVIII (a title he was not to possess until eleven more years of exile should pass).

Evidently this plot had emboldened him to return secretly from banishment in order to be upon the ground when the Royalist *coup* should occur.

De Presle entered the room ahead of me. Standing aside for me to pass in, he announced loudly:

"Your majesty, I have brought the prisoner before you. Napoleon Bonaparte, self-styled First Consul of France, stand forth before the monarch you have so vilely wronged!"

It was really quite prettily done; melodramatic withal, and well worthy the Vicomte de Presle and the Bourbon party at large.

I stepped into the room and into the cleared space before the dais.

"Good evening, *messieurs*," I said pleasantly, glancing about the semicircle of royalists. "M. le Comte de Provence—*ci–devant*—I have the honor." And I bowed low before him.

There was dead and fearsome silence for the very briefest space imaginable—the silence that comes from loss of power to speak or move.

Then arose a clamor, the like of which has never before assailed my ears. It took the form of a wordless cry of amazement—horror—wrath—what you will; in a dozen different keys. Through it I heard De la Roche's gasp of "Alwyn!"

I smiled around me happily, though, faith, I had little enough to be happy about just then, so far as I myself was concerned. But it was the time to smile. And I smiled—a happy, self-complacent smile, I like to believe.

"You dolt!" roared De la Roche, his rough voice cutting through the clamor as he seized the wondering De Presle roughly by the arm. "Where is Napoleon Bonaparte?"

"M. de la Roche," I put in, as De Presle pointed dumbly toward me, "I can answer that question for you, and for all these other worthy conspirators—including the Comte de Provence, who, by the way, would best waste no time in scurrying back across the frontier."

I hesitated, to give my words due effect. And stupidly they glowered at me, awaiting the rest of the speech, Bourbon fashion, ere they should fall upon and slay me.

"*Messieurs,*" I proceeded calmly, "Napoleon Bonaparte—or, perhaps, it were more decorous to say the First Consul—is safe and sound in his loyal city of Paris. I am but forestalling a bit of news which will shortly be brought to you by a regiment of hussars."

"You have bungled and taken the wrong man!" cried the Comte de Provence, scowling at De la Roche.

"Not I, your majesty," stoutly denied the old *siegneur.* "I will take oath it was Bonaparte we captured at the Tuileries and brought here. I sat next him in the carriage. We were all masked. But we had torn off his own mask as we lifted him into the coach. It was Bonaparte. And—"

A man who had rushed from the room at my first words now came running back.

"Your majesty," he shouted, "the turret room is empty! The bars are wrenched from the window."

"Of course they are!" I laughed amid the babel evoked by this announcement. "I helped to set him free. And for the jest of seeing your long faces, I took his place."

"Our 'long faces,'" retorted a dark youth, with mud-spattered boots, "are the last sights you will see on earth."

Whipping out a horse-pistol he leveled it at me.

"My friend," I jeered, looking straight into the pistol's black mouth, "pull the trigger by all means, if you seek to sign your own death-warrant and those of your friends here. If one hair of my head is injured, not a man of you will leave Paris alive. You will be hunted down like rabbits. You and your families. And those who died under the guillotine during the Revolution will have perished more mercifully and

more peacefully than shall you. Yes, from the Comte de Provence down to the man who drove your coach to-night."

"Braggart!" snarled the dark than.

But he did not pull trigger. And I continued; for I was talking for my life—a life that was the more precious to me as I seemed the nearer to losing it.

"Braggart?" I queried jocosely. "Perhaps. Yet I notice you do not shoot. If you did not believe me you would have loosed trigger ere now, and there would be a half-score swords in my body, besides. Do any of you fancy I should have been fool enough to strut, unarmed and alone, into the lion's den—or donkey paddock—if I were not as safe there as in mine own home?"

"Who are you?" sputtered the Comte de Provence.

"Just an American," I replied carelessly. "My name is Alwyn. M. de la Roche knows me. But that is beside the question. Will you gentlemen hear what I have to say? Will you listen to me for two minutes in patience, or do your desperadoes still insist on slitting my throat or blowing out my brains, and thereby sending you all to the guillotine?"

There was a mumble, a mutter, a curse or two, a voice of protest. And, cutting in on the noise, I began:

"In the first place, your poor, silly little plot is discovered. It has failed, as have others, and as others will. For my own part, if I do not arrive at the American embassy safe and well, at a certain very early hour, you will meet the fate, one and all, that I have so generously promised you. If you do not believe that statement—as I see some of you do not—you have but to kill me, or hold me here as captive for a brief time, to have the proof abundantly brought home to you. So much for myself.

"I merely ventured this egotistic statement lest some misguided Bourbon patriot should seek glory by trying to murder me before I have finished what I have to say. Now, for you others:

"Your plot has failed. Your fate lies in the hollow of my hand. And because of the feeling I have toward just one of your number—I am going to let you go."

I beamed around on them like an indulgent school dame who announces a holiday to her little pupils.

Either stunned by my audacity, or because there seemed noth-

ing better to do now that their cherished conspiracy had melted into nothingness, they listened.

"Whether at some future time you catch or kill Bonaparte, or overthrow him, I do not know or care. Personally, I doubt it. But 'tis no affair of mine. For the present, you will realize your game is lost. Soon the cavalry will break in here. Unless I make a certain signal it may be even sooner. By brisk use of the legs God gave you, there is barely time for all of you to escape. Do not let me detain you."

There was a moment's pause. And I knew my life hung in a mighty shifty balance. Indeed, but for the fact that their prey had escaped, and that they knew his capacity for vengeance, I had not lived so long.

But Bonaparte was free. Every one of them knew how direfully the Corsican would punish the attempt on his life. And not one of them could be certain I was not telling the truth. I think the bulk of them did not care to risk even more stark penalties by killing a man who seemed to stand so close to the consul.

Had I been a Frenchman, had I shouted: "I have rescued your victim! Do with me what you will! I die for France!" or some equally dramatic speech, my life would not have been worth a minute's purchase.

But clearly I had puzzled them. Unacquainted with American ways "bluff" was a novelty to them. Nor, I think, could they imagine it possible for me to make fun of them and treat them like a pack of dull schoolboys were it not that I had Bonaparte's power near at hand to bear me out.

At the hint of a chance to escape I saw several men edge near to the door. One or two actually slipped out of the room. The conspiracy was breaking up as an ice-jam in spring.

The Comte de Provence rose and stalked majestically to the edge of the dais. His face was pale.

"*Messieurs,*" said he, "we have failed. Not, I am sure, through lack of zeal on the part of any of my loyal friends, whom I herewith thank with all my heart. There is no longer need for us to remain. M. de la Roche, I bid you good night, and I thank you once more for your gallant service in behalf of the right."

At their leader's words there was a general bolt toward the door. The plotters scarce retained sufficient presence of mind to grant precedence to the comte. But the dark man cried once more:

"This renegade Yankee must die before we go. He has seen too much!"

Again he drew his pistol. And one or two daring spirits close around him laid hand to sword. But De la Roche knocked the pistol aside.

"Do you want to send us all to the guillotine?" he cried.

"I have seen too much, eh?" I jeered. "Have I seen more than yourselves? And at this moment is not a full list of your names on Napoleon Bonaparte's desk? Yes, shoot if you choose. I have told you the consequences. Not a threat, but as a warning."

"What difference can it make in our chances of escape," urged the dark man furiously, "if we kill this Yankee before we go? None! We—"

Messieurs!" called the Comte de Provence from the doorway. "You will put up your weapons and leave this house at once. This American gentleman goes free. It is my command."

With an ill grace the malcontents obeyed and, scowling and muttering, trooped from the room after him.

"Faith," I muttered to myself, "since it seems that only one of the two could be frightened by my bluff, I am right glad it was de Provence and not our dark friend. Otherwise I should have been slain by 'royal' command a good ten minutes since!"

Now that the stress was over I felt a sick reaction pringle my whole body. I wanted to sit down by myself somewhere and let my overwrought nerves rest.

But my work was barely half done. And at thought of what was yet to be accomplished, I hurried from the room and down the stairs in the wake of the fleeing Bourbons.

CHAPTER XIX.
The Land of Heart's Desire.

I REACHED the front door as the Sieur de la Roche was bowing out the last of his hastily departing guests. No servant was in sight, all having been sent out of the way; and the host was acting as his own footman.

As the door closed behind his fellow conspirators, De la Roche turned back into the house. By the light of the guttering sconces, his face showed haggard and very old. He had the look of a stricken man.

At sight of me he straightened and sought to regain his habitual calm of manner. But the effort was pitiful. I could read his thought in that dreary old face of his.

Not so much was he mourning for a mere political chance lost, as for the fact that in his old age he and his daughter must wander, penniless, into exile, hunted fugitives from the wrath of Napoleon Bonaparte. He was over-old and she was over-young for such a dog's life as that.

"M. de la Roche," I said, "will you spare me a few minutes?"

He hesitated.

"My daughter must be awakened and told to make haste in her preparations to go with me," he said. "We must be on our journey within the hour if we are to escape before—"

"You need take no journey, M. de la Roche," I interrupted. "It was on your account that I warned the rest. Your name is not known to the first consul as a mover in this night's work. And it shall not be known. I pledge you this on my honor."

Long and doubtfully he looked at me, seeking to believe the wondrous good news, yet scarce daring to.

"You—you can keep Bonaparte from knowing?" he gasped at last.

"I can."

"But—but why do you do this—for me?"

"For several reasons. For one, above all: M. de la Roche, I love your daughter."

I had not meant to speak so soon. But I knew that reason alone would convince him of my truth and of his own safety. Now that I had made the plunge there was nothing for it save to go on.

"M. de la Roche," I said formally, after the custom of the day and of his class, "I have the undeserved honor to beg your permission to pay my addresses to Mlle. Lorraine de la Roche."

For a full minute he did not speak. His high-bred old face was blank. Then, with a deep bow, he made reply in equal formality.

"M. Alwyn, as head of the De la Roche family, I have the pleas— the honor to consent to your paying your addresses to *mademoiselle,*

my daughter."

"From my heart I thank you," I returned gratefully. "If you desire knowledge of myself or my affairs, I can refer you to—"

"It is quite unnecessary," he broke in coldly. "And—of course you know my daughter will be dowerless, unless we can recover our French estates. And after the affair of to-night—"

"Pardon," I interposed. "But have you chanced to see your daughter since I called here early in the evening?"

"No, I sent word to her by her maid on my return, that I had brought home a number of friends for a night at cards. I requested that she keep to her own rooms, whatever sounds might disturb her; as my guests might become boisterous. 'Twas a flimsy excuse. But I knew it would serve. Lorraine is ever obedient to me. A rare and excellent trait in a wife, *m'sieu'*, as you will find."

"I asked," said I, "because I wished to know if she had told you of her good fortune."

"Good fortune?" he echoed.

Briefly I related to him the version I had given to Lorraine concerning the winning of their case.

Before he could reply there came a crashing series of blows on the front door, as from the pounding of saber hilts, and a voice cried:

"Open! In the name of the Republic of France!"

De la Roche's face went green-gray. And he glared at me as though I had trapped him by a lie. In spirit, no doubt, he saw a regiment of cavalry closing in upon him and his daughter; due to my delaying his departure.

I myself was aghast. Bonaparte must have escaped from Aniwaya after all—must have gained, somehow, the knowledge that it was here he had been imprisoned—and had sent to arrest the household.

For an instant the old aristocrat blanched. Then the blood of countless hero-ancestors came to his aid. His shoulders squared and he threw back his head. With firm steps he strode to the door, unbarred, and threw it open. I was at his side, resolved to stand by him to the last, now that my golden plans for him and for myself had gone awry.

Open flew the door. On the threshold, with three cavalrymen behind him, stood Colonel du Fresne. One arm was in a sling, and he was pallid and thin from his sojourn in the hospital. In his free hand

was a drawn saber.

"I have authority to search, this house," he declared.

"By all means," said the old aristocrat, without the flicker of an eyelid. "For what purpose?"

Without deigning to reply the *aide de-camp* thrust his way in. I barred the passage.

"What is your business here?" I demanded, "and by what right do you search M. de la Roche's home?"

I had been standing in the shadow. At sight of me, Du Fresne started as though he had been stung by a wasp.

"What are *you* doing here?" he demanded vociferously, to cover his surprise.

"Taking leave of my friend and fellow countryman, M. de la Roche," I returned. "Mine was a personal visit. But, since his house is invaded, I shall proceed to make it an official one. I am a member of the United States embassy, as you know. And when the rights of a fellow American in Paris are outraged in this way—"

"No rights are outraged," he growled. "My regiment is making a house-to-house search of this quarter, even as every private house in Paris is undergoing search to-night. I cannot give you my reasons. They are no concern of yours."

He had no need to. Well I realized now the gigantic scale of the secret efforts afoot to find the missing First Consul. Nevertheless, I stood my ground.

"I give you my word," said I, "that there is no one in this house to warrant such a search. And I will be answerable to your government for refusing to allow you to disturb and frighten sleeping women in ransacking the building."

"Your word—" he began angrily.

"Quite so," I assented pleasantly. "And I will call my Indian servant, if you like, to indorse it. He will be glad to meet you once more. This time I shall not interfere with the scalping."

I stepped back as though to summon the Indian. Du Fresne, with a growl of wordless rage, turned and strode away, his men with him.

"You see," I exclaimed to the still frightened De la Roche, "it really would not have done to let him search here."

"Of course not," he acquiesced. "'Twas most thoughtful of you to

spare Lorraine such annoyance and fright."

"Also," I observed dryly, "I chanced to recall, on meeting him just now, that ere I put out the candle in the cell-room upstairs I noticed on the floor a snuff-box and handkerchief that had fallen from the first consul's pocket when he was dragged out through the bars. His monogram was on them both. It might have been just a bit difficult to explain away those trifles."

"It would have meant the guillotine for me!" babbled De la Roche.

"And for Lorraine," I added. "Good night, *monsieur.* I still have much to do before dawn. Half of my heart's desire has come to me this night. And I mean to win the other half by sunrise."

CHAPTER XX.
I Receive the Surprise of My Life.

GRAY dawn was paling the black of the sky as I ran lightly up the stairs to my own suite of rooms in the embassy. Forgotten was my fatigue. And I was nerved for the battle of my whole career.

I let myself in, locking the door behind me, and entered the little drawing-room of the suite. There a right merry spectacle met me. On the sofa, disheveled, his clothes in dire disorder, sprawled Napoleon Bonaparte.

The wontedly marble, fathomless visage of the Man of Destiny was creased into a grin of genuine amusement, as at the antics of some well-loved but naughty child.

Between him and the door—in fact almost blocking the door-way—sat the giant form of Aniwaya, stolid, moveless as a statue, his long, keen knife laid bare across his lap.

He had followed out my instructions to the letter. A glance told me that. But, instead of a raging, fuming, mortified master of men, cooped up in a little room by a murderous savage, I was amazed to see Bonaparte's evident relish of the scene. I had been prepared for a storm, assuredly not for the laugh wherewith the captive greeted my arrival.

"M. Alwyn!" he exclaimed, "you must sell me this fellow. He is worth his great hulking weight in gold. I thought Rustum, my Mameluke, was the perfect servant. But your savage is a hundredfold better."

I probably looked my astonishment. And Bonaparte luckily misread the look—he who so seldom misread.

"I heard you call to him to 'keep me safe until you should join us.' And he followed his master's orders literally. What think you he did? He bound me and blindfolded me—to keep me safe—hailed a passing fiacre and brought me here. For the past ten minutes he has sat guard over me. Had you never come back he was like to have kept me here till doomsday morn."

"A thousand pardons—" I stammered.

He checked me with uplifted hand, and a touch of the dramatic in his voice as he said:

"Never apologize for orders too well obeyed. Had I one army corps who would obey me as this savage obeys you, I should bivouac in Westminster Abbey within a month. He is a born soldier, the perfect soldier, the man who wrecks all to obey his master."

And now I began to understand.

The Corsican's one god was military duty. He deemed that Aniwaya had performed such duty in a way that few men would have dared to. Whereat the natural pettiness of Bonaparte the *man* was quite eclipsed in the insane love of discipline that marked Bonaparte the *soldier.*

"And now," went on the first consul, "before I relieve the worry of Fouché and the rest I want something to eat. Also I wish to talk with you. If your savage can prepare food as he obeys orders, I will give him a cordon blue and make him chef of the Tuileries."

At an order from me Aniwaya swiftly and silently set about the preparation of breakfast. As he left the room on this errand Bonaparte turned to me.

"M. Alwyn," he said gravely, "you have done a great service this night. Not to me, who value my life but as a fleck of dust; but to France, to whom my life means salvation."

I murmured some commonplace; my mind nimbly, yet vainly, seeking the best way to make profit for my mission from what I had achieved.

"You have made the future of France a great one this night," he went on in the same artificial tone of majesty wherewith he ever deceived himself far more completely than he deceived others. "You have changed the map of Europe. If Napoleon Bonaparte had died France must have sunk back into the slough. As it is she shall rise to heights undreamed of. Her eagles shall soar from one end of this earth to the other by my aid. This, indirectly, *you* have done for the world. No small achievement for an obscure American, M. Alwyn."

He fell silent, hands behind his back, head on breast, his hard eyes moodily fixed on nothingness.

"In all my life's battles, whether on the field or elsewhere," he mused half to himself, "it has been as to-night: when all seemed lost, destiny has ever intervened for me."

"Providence, perhaps, rather that destiny," I suggested.

"Providence?" he laughed harshly. "Providence is always on the side of the heaviest battalions."

"We found it otherwise in our American struggle for liberty," said I.

"Perhaps so!" he muttered absently, his mind already on another tack. "Perhaps so. M. Alwyn, if I should ask you how you chanced to come to my rescue to-night—if I should ask you where I was confined and who my Bourbon assailants were—if I should ask you any or all of these questions, you would lie to me, would you not?

"Perhaps so," I quoted.

"Undoubtedly so," he snapped. "So I shall not ask you. I care little for causes. It is effects that count. But one thing I do not need to ask. For any child could see it. Your object in rescuing me was not patriotism. For you are not a Frenchman. It was not friendship. For you hate me."

"M. le General!"

"You do. Or you should, after the way I treated you in the Tuileries gardens when you came to me with your silly little lesson in diplomacy all learned pat. You did not rescue me for patriotism, nor for love; nor, I take it, from mere humanity. You risked your life for mine in the hope that out of gratitude I would grant your request and sign the Louisiana treaty. Confess."

"I confess," I laughed.

"Good. Then remember one thing, M. Alwyn: I do nothing from gratitude. Next to a sense of humor, no quality so militates against success in life as does gratitude. It is a vice I never indulge.

"By the way, know you a shockheaded compatriot named Fulton? A crazy dreamer who believes boats can be pushed by steam? He wishes me to—ah, *breakfast!*"

Aniwaya entered with a tray laden, which he set upon the table. Bonaparte, with no word of appreciation, nor so much as asking me to join him, fell upon the meal.

I had heard tales of his food-bolting prowess, and how he was wont to devour an eight-course state dinner in eleven minutes. But until this instant I had never realized what true gluttony was.

Using fingers as freely as knife and fork, the Man of Destiny attacked the abundant breakfast with the zest of a wild dog. Within three minutes he had swallowed the last morsel. I watched him in a horrified fascination. I do not believe he chewed a single mouthful.

"Your savage is a good cook," he remarked calmly, as he brushed the crumbs with careless hand from his tumbled uniform coat. "And now give him to me as escort back to the Tuileries. I have wasted too much time. I shall be able to spare only two hours for sleep to-night (or, rather, this morning) instead of five.

"By the way, M. Alwyn, I did not like you. As perhaps you guessed. So I planned to reserve my signature to the Louisiana treaty until after you should have gone back to America a failure. I have changed my mind. Be at the Tuileries at ten. And ask M. Livingston to do me the honor to be there at the same time."

"M. le General!" I cried, astounded. "You mean that you—"

"I mean that I have found reason to dislike you less during the past few hours. You will never make a diplomat. And between ourselves, M. Alwyn, you are something of a fool. But you have courage— courage and resource. And a man who can command such wondrous obedience in a servant cannot be wholly without worth.

"Therefore, I shall sign the treaty this morning. And thereby give England a maritime rival that may one day sweep her from the seas. I had planned from the first to sign it. I have had a rough draft of it drawn up for months before ever you left America.

"It is for France's best good that we sell you our American posses-

sions, which are no longer profitable or of prestige to us. And—there is no need for you to tell the world that my consent is not due to your own wondrous diplomacy. By the way," he asked abruptly, "will you sell me your savage?"

"Aniwaya," said I, turning to the Indian, who stood in the doorway, "do you wish to accept service under the first consul? He can make you rich, and you will be admired by great folk and be famous throughout Europe."

The big Indian made no reply. Stolidly he came to where I stood and, dropping stonily on one knee, he laid my hand on his head.

"Master," he grunted.

"Yes," sighed Bonaparte, "he has given the answer. Take him back to America with you, M. Alwyn. One of you is about as fit for court fortunes as the other. Yet—I would give much to win such loyalty. Any man can win a nation. But—loyalty cannot be won. It can only be given. And generally it is given to fools. Good-by, M. Alwyn."

CHAPTER XXI.
THE REWARD I REAPED.

I WENT into my bedroom, my head awhirl. My mission was accomplished! My work was done! The vast Louisiana region was ours. Half a continent was added to the United States. It seemed too marvelous to be true. It was Victory rising unheralded from the very heart of Defeat.

Was there ever another man so wondrously blessed as I? Fame would be mine. My country's future would be assured. And—without which all the rest would have been as dust and ashes—I loved and had every reason to believe I was loved in return.

Staggering, through utter fatigue no more than through semi-delirium of happiness, I threw myself full-dressed upon my bed. And in a minute I was dead asleep.

For hours I slept—the sweet, dreamless, heavy slumber of a tired animal. Then something woke me. I lay for a moment, blinking at the morning sun and wondering drowsily what it was that had awakened

me.

Then a sound near me gave the reply to my sleepy conjecture. Somewhere close by a woman was sobbing very softly, very heartbrokenly, like a frightened little child.

I opened my eyes wide. I was alone in the room. But all at once I understood the odd phenomenon. My bedroom, after the flimsy fashion of the new French architecture, was separated from the embassy's inner reception-room by a partition so thin that the faintest sound was audible from one room to the other.

Manifestly, some one in the reception-room was weeping. And I reflected sleepily that it was probably some compatriot who had come to tell her many troubles to the minister and to beg transportation home.

I even wondered vaguely who had been detailed to talk with her. But at once that question was answered. For I heard Launay saying miserably:

"I never meant that you should know. For he is my friend. And I did not mean to be disloyal to him. But—but when you tell me you don't love him and that your father commands you to marry him because of gratitude to him for saving you both from some political penalty—or in order to protect both of you from Bonaparte's vengeance in future—"

What on earth was the fellow talking about. And to whom? What sort of language was this to use to a weeping compatriot? Was Launay making love to her?

"When I found out all that just now," he went on, "I lost hold of myself. I should not have spoken. It was dastardly. For he trusts me."

It dawned on my sleep-befogged brain that I had unconsciously been playing the eavesdropper. And I rose on one elbow to move out of earshot. But the next words held me spellbound. It was the woman who spoke. And her sob-choked voice went through me like a white-hot iron.

"I didn't know it either till you spoke. At least—didn't *know* I knew it. Then, all in a flash, it came to me that I'd known it always. Ever since the night I met you at that horrible Tuileries salon. Ever since then I've cared—and *cared*. I know it now. I knew it the moment you said you loved me. Oh, *what* shall we do? "

"There is only one honorable thing to do," replied Launay sadly. "He loves you and he is my friend. You love me and I love you. I will go to him and tell him everything. How you came here this morning to see about the transfer of the securities and how all at once you found yourself telling me of your father's command, and then how I lost my senses and said I loved you."

"No, no!" she sobbed. "You must *not*. My father says I must marry him. I have never disobeyed my father. With us French girls such disobedience is looked on as a crime. And I am fond of M. Alwyn. *Very* fond. Why, only last night, when he told me he was in love, I was so glad for him, and I advised him to let the girl know he loved her. Oh, if I'd guessed—"

I waited to hear no more. I rose and crossed to the far end of the room and stood looking out into the pitiless sunlight. My heart was dead. So for the moment was my mind.

Somewhere a clock chimed half past nine. I had but half an hour to reach the Tuileries for the signing of the treaty. Mechanically and with practised haste I began to change my clothes.

The treaty? Of what interest was that to me? The warm sunshine had all at once grown hateful to me. There had been but one thing in all life. I knew that, now it was gone.

When I was ready for the street I walked out into the embassy rooms.

"Aniwaya!" I called. "Is M. Launay in?"

Launay heard my voice and came to the door of the inner reception-room. Behind him I saw Lorraine de la Roche. I nodded good morning to him. Then I entered the room. The girl held out her hand timidly to me. I noticed her fingers trembled and that they were as cold as ice. And a great wave of pity swept over me.

"*Mademoiselle*," said I, "I wonder if I may trouble you to carry a message to your father for me? Will you tell him that the Louisiana Treaty is to be signed to-day and that—"

"The treaty?" cried Launay. "You don't mean—"

"And," I continued without heeding his interruption, "that I am to start for America with a copy of it to-night?"

"To-night!" she exclaimed. "But—"

"Will you also tell him," I went on, "that the work which the car-

rying out of the treaty must entail will keep me so busy for the next few years that I must forego the honor which I requested of him last night? He will understand."

They looked at each other by sudden impulse. And into Lorraine de la Roche's great eyes sprang a light that glorified her. Neither of the two could speak.

But I saw their hands go furtively out toward one another and meet in a long, silent clasp that seemed to me more potent than any embrace.

"I shall not see you again, *mademoiselle*," I added. "But you will permit me to wish you all the happiness that the world can give—and far more than it can take away."

I bent over her hand for the last time and touched it to my lips. Then I went out and left them alone.

"Aniwaya," I said as the Indian and I reached the street, "most people think Napoleon Bonaparte is the greatest man on earth. He is not. The greatest man on earth is back there in the embassy. For he is *loved*."

"Ugh!" grunted Aniwaya noncommittally.

The End.

Appendix
Original source publication

This story appeared, complete, in the April 1914 issue of *Argosy*. The title page illustration is from the original publication.

The title page illustration is from the original publication.

Editorial changes:

Original spelling	Changed to
colluquy	colloquy
asinity	asininity
cocher	coacher

Several other obvious misspellings were corrected.